If
Tomorrow
Could Sing

If Tomorrow Could Sing

ROSEMARY RYAN IMREGI

ARCHWAY PUBLISHING

Archway Publishing books may be ordered through booksellers or by contacting:

Archway Publishing
1663 Liberty Drive
Bloomington, IN 47403
www.archwaypublishing.com
844-669-3957

Because of the dynamic nature of the Internet, any web addresses or links contained in this book may have changed since publication and may no longer be valid. The views expressed in this work are solely those of the author and do not necessarily reflect the views of the publisher, and the publisher hereby disclaims any responsibility for them.

Any people depicted in stock imagery provided by Getty Images are models, and such images are being used for illustrative purposes only.
Certain stock imagery © Getty Images.

ISBN: 978-1-6657-4858-2 (sc)
ISBN: 978-1-6657-4861-2 (e)

Library of Congress Control Number: 2023915305

Print information available on the last page.

Archway Publishing rev. date: 08/14/2023

Contents

Dedicated to the memory of Joanne Linke.
I'll love you forever.

Acknowledgments

Thank-You to Wayne Nicholas
For his contributions to this story.

Chapter 1

1863

*What a cruel thing war is… to fill
our hearts with hatred instead of love
for our neighbors*
—Robert E. Lee

In the early morning hour, Sally Preston stood on her Aunt Gertrude's dual front staircase, a home feature popular in Savannah Georgia. Observing the sight of her adopted city, she marveled at the impact the Civil War had on this once-beautiful city while sipping her morning cup of tea. She would have preferred coffee, a luxury few could afford, or find anywhere in the south.

Although the city had not been plundered by the Union Army, still the war created a pall that settled over Savannah affecting every living creature in this city. From the insects, plants, trees, and humans, nothing had been untouched by this war, and every southerner knew that even though the war was not officially over, they lost. The grey cloud seemed to hover over the city, emphasizing the gloom that every citizen felt. Hearts were heavy and Sally's ached for this place she called home.

She didn't always live here. When she was thirteen years old her Aunt took her in after her parents died from a fever that claimed many lives in eighteen forty-four, including Gertrude's husband Graham.

Sally and her parents had come from their plantation Picadilly to visit Gertrude and Graham when the fever took their lives. At that time Gertrude lived with Graham on a small farm on the outskirts of Savannah.

After the death of Graham and Sally's parents, Gertrude was distraught, not only had she lost her husband, but also her sister as well. Not wanting Sally to be alone on the farm, with her, Gertrude felt that the farm miles from Savannah, and any other neighbors was no place for a young pretty girl like Sally to live. So she abandoned the farm and moved her and Sally to the city where she felt alive again surrounded by people, shops, and opportunities to meet new people. She saw a difference in Sally too once they settled in.

Gertrude adored Sally, she was the daughter she and Graham never had. Sharing their grief, Sally and Gertrude formed a bond so strong that each was able to endure the malicious attacks on the cities of the south. The realities of the war, the sacrifices, and the endurance to cope, only served to make them stronger.

Union armies deprived the south of precious goods by way of stockades to the boats that never reached their destination in the south. It was also good for Sally to make friends. The farm was no place for a young girl approaching womanhood. Gertrude's hunch was correct, Because of that move, Sally met and fell in love with Frank.

Sally took a deep breath smelling the aroma of the sweet magnolia trees, a scent that didn't seem as prominent as it had been before the war. Nothing was the same as before the war. Worse than the killings, and the destruction of the south, the war had taken away the very soul of every southern citizen. Most of all the war had taken away her husband Frank Preston. She often wondered what this land would tell the next generation if it could talk.

She clutched her shawl tighter around her shoulders. It was late December, and Savannah, Georgia, was a city immersed in preparations for Christmas. In recent days, Sally saw the metropolis' citizens hauling Christmas trees while every child anxiously anticipated finding the tree adorned in their homes.

Until Christmas morning, the tree would remain bare except for maybe some stringed popcorn that Mom made. Then to the delight of the children, on Christmas morning, they would find their presents hanging from the tree with some lighted candles which added a realm of magic to the season.

But in this time of war, all the children wanted for Christmas was the same thing they had wanted each year since the conflict between the states began three years before—to have their father and brothers' home.

As she sipped, she thought again of how wonderful life was before the war, when her husband, Frank, was still at home. Her heart ached for him and all the South. Frank was all she wanted or needed, she thought. Yet, for so many days, she could hear the distant sounds of canons and firearms. *What if these battlefields could speak?* Sally thought., *What story would they tell? What if tomorrow could sing so that all generations could know what happened here?*

Pondering these thoughts, Sally took another sip of her tea. Because she hadn't heard from Frank in almost three months, she was in the habit of taking her daily walk to the shabby building that housed the general store, post office, and telegraph. It was in desperate need of some paint and repair to the sagging porch. She checked daily, hoping to finally hold in her hand the precious words she longed to hear from her husband, he was her whole world. From the first day she met him, she was totally in love with this soft-spoken gentleman. He would talk to her about his love of gardening and how he dreamed of owning a farm where he could grow vegetables and fruits.

She would go to the general store in a few minutes and check at the main counter, hoping, as she had every day for the past three months, that Frank's letter had arrived. She stood in this line daily, praying that *today* would bring a letter from her husband, a Confederate soldier, fighting *God knows where.*

On this cold winter day, the wind blew in from the northwest when Mr. Hurly ran into the store. He was Savannah's town crier, always ready to deliver any news he heard. It didn't matter if the citizens had already heard the information, he was giving them; he just liked to think that he was their best source of knowledge—that is when he wasn't playing poker with the other men who were too old to be drafted. This time, Gus Hurly shook as he bellowed his critical announcement. "General Sherman is coming here. He's only a day away!" When someone tried to calm him, he further declared, "He'll burn Savannah just like he did Atlanta!"

Not everyone believed everything he proclaimed; some felt his "news" was just tall tales embellished with his imagination.

"Gus Hurley, you stop scaring these fine people with your ramblings," Martha Baker, a voice of reason, scolded Gus. "Where did you hear such nonsense?"

Many of the patrons were heard doubting Gus's story.

Turning around to face all the doubters, Gus raised his voice, "I heard it from a friend of mine who just came back from Macon. He heard Sherman say, "Next is Savannah."

Panic gripped the patrons in the building as they grabbed whatever they could for survival without stopping to pay. Sally looked around for her brother-in-law, Kent, the proprietor of the establishment, but where was he?

All Christmas commotion ceased on this crisp cold winter day once the citizens realized that General Sherman and his army were, indeed, only a day away from their city. The news slapped Sally in the face as no other had ever done

Tears glistened in Sally's large, bright hazel eyes as she rushed down Main Street her long blonde hair fell out of its clips as she was running toward her aunt's home. No woman of the day would choose to wear her hair in such a free-flowing manner. Never-the-less curls flew behind her as she ran breathless, panic piercing her lungs, or was that sharp sensation the result of her stays, which women wore to accentuate a tiny waist, according to the fashion of the day, forcing her diaphragm to revolt?

Sally didn't care how short of breath she became. Since leaving the small building that contained the general store, post office, and telegraph, she had only one thought on her mind. She had to warn her Aunt Gertrude about what she had heard.

As she hurried along the street, she saw people running past, their faces gaunt and filled with fear. The wind caught her hoop skirt, almost knocking her off her feet. Instead, she wrapped her shawl over her shoulders, pulling it tight with her right fist. People were packing wagons and carriages, removing valued possessions from their homes, and trying to take away as much as possible before the assault of Sherman's army.

She witnessed slaves loading furniture, carefully piling the items into wagons as their masters directed their every move, striking them if they weren't moving quickly enough for their satisfaction. Sally had always opposed the institution of slavery, which allowed the Negroes to be abused as though they had no more worth than a horse. At the same time, she saw slavery as a necessary evil. To her, this was an abomination. full support of slavery was in opposition to her beliefs. But more importantly, in the South at this time, opposing the institution of slavery was not a position one took in public; to do so was an invitation to be called an abolitionist—a term associated with abuse and scorn.

She continued to move toward home along the cobblestone road, her heeled boots tapping out her hurried pace. Suddenly near her, a horse bolted, overturning the light carriage, and dumping the belongings of its owner on the ground behind it. Sally jumped out of the way before any possessions could fall on her. The furious owner ran after the horse while his distraught wife held her hand over her mouth; horrified that her precious belongings were destroyed. A brave man in ragged clothes stepped out to bring the horse to a stop; he held his hand out with a grin, hoping for some form of payment. A scowl was all the well-dressed man offered in return. The Union army was coming. To the agitated gentleman, *this is hardly the time to negotiate pay.*

The street was more congested with people than was usual at this time of day. Sally maneuvered in and around the swelling number of citizens. She raced as fast as she could to her aunt's home; she had to warn her. In her way were two men trading blows, but what they were arguing over Sally couldn't guess, nor cared to find out. She hurried around as others came to pull them apart. The city was on edge, its people in fear.

Nobody was standing still, enjoying conversation like people would do any other Sunday morning. Everyone was in perpetual motion. They were not stopping to savor the winter breeze or enjoy the anticipation of Christmas coming. In these times, the South knew they were losing the war, so looking forward to Christmas was an exercise in futility. People hoped only to distract children from the trauma of war and the loss of food because of the North's tactics to deprive the South of vital commodities by blocking shipments of goods via boat and railroad.

Nobody in the South of 1863 had felt the thrill of Christmas since the war began almost four years before. Fear, lack of food, and money had replaced any semblance of celebration; most people did the best they could for the children's sake.

Sally heard another voice on the street repeat the dire warning. "Sherman's army is on their way here!" Each voice sounded more strained than the next. Panic had now captured their throats. Looking at the faces of those she passed, she saw their fear and shared their terror. It seemed everyone had a single purpose. They were getting out.

Still feeling her lungs complain as she reached her house, she climbed the half dozen steps to her front door. Gasping for air, she slammed the door shut with her back while fighting to regain her regular breathing pattern so she could speak.

Hearing the slam of the door, Sally's Aunt Gertrude came into the staid parlor, which was aglow with a generous supply of natural light from the morning sun. "What is the matter, dear? You look flushed. Are you all right?" Gertrude asked her niece.

She was still breathing heavily, but not enough to impair her ability to speak; she gulped, then blurted out the devastating news. "General Sherman and his army are on their way here to Savannah. We've got to leave now!" Sally's fear was so great that she was crying as she voiced the dire warning.

Aunt Gertrude was a plump woman, though still attractive at her age. Anyone could tell that she must have had many suitors vying for her hand in marriage in her youth. "Are you certain?" she asked calmly. "Where did you hear such news?"

"It's all over the streets. People are running to secure their homes and pack. After what Sherman's army did to Atlanta, can you blame them? Therefore, we must go, too, before Sherman arrives."

At seventy-two, Gertrude had her fill with troubles in her family and the world around her. The worst was when Sally's parents and her beloved husband, Graham, died on their farm just outside Savannah almost eight years ago. Gertrude had been living on a small farm just outside Savannah's city limits. Yellow fever had claimed their lives, despite Gertrude's and Sally's attempts to nurse them back to health. Unfortunately, getting a doctor at that time was impossible; the fever had taken hold of a considerable number of its citizens, leaving access to medical attention extremely rare.

Sally and her parents came to visit her aunt and Uncle's small farm from their plantation in Georgia. The home was her grandfather's plantation in Georgetown, Georgia, which he named "Piccadilly" in homage to their homeland, England. When he died, ownership of the plantation passed to his sons, Melford, who was Sally's father, and Temple. Melford's ambitions never included farming life; his motivation was in law practice. He was also against the practice of owning slaves. But as he got older, he realized that he and his brother needed to make the plantation a functioning income source to maintain the eight hundred acres of land. Melford would have preferred to free his slaves and pay them a living wage, but he knew his law office would suffer. He wouldn't get the clients to justify his practice.

Sally's father had willed his half of the plantation to his brother, Temple Scanlon, and Sally when she married. Temple was in control of Sally's half until she married. An uncle Sally had never liked, Temple was a harsh overseer of the slaves.

Being an only child, Sally found her playmates among the slave children. Her parents had no objection to their daughter's choice of friends. However, Temple vehemently hated the slaves. The arrangement with Temple was that he would oversee the slaves. While her father tended to his law practice, Sally's parents usually left Temple alone to control the slaves, unaware of his cruelty to them. Raping and whipping were part of his usual routine. He chased Sally away from the only friends she had. Then he would stop Sally from running away from him by tightly holding her hand with his left arm, while he whipped the slaves who had allowed their children to play with Sally.

Then Temple would take Sally to her parents, demanding that she get her due punishment for the "crime" of associating with those who were not her kind. But unknown to Temple, her parents never did punish Sally. Instead, they encouraged her to find a place where she could play in some secret area where Temple could not see them. But when Sally tell her parents what Uncle Temple was doing to the slaves, her parents would explain to her that he knew what was best in "these matters." But as far as Temple forcing a young Sally to witness brutal punishments, Melford let Temple know in the most ferocious language he could muster that if he ever forced his daughter again, or touched her in a less than loving manner, he would kill him with no regrets.

Sally loved her parents, but sometimes she also secretly despised them for choosing to ignore the cruelty that Temple inflicted on the slaves so that her parents could live in an imagined utopia.

When the Scanlon family visited Aunt Gertrude in 1853, Sally's life ended as she had known it. Gertrude felt it unwise to send Sally, who was then eleven years old, back to a life she knew would not be in Sally's best interest, and Sally would never return to her childhood home again. Since then, she'd had ten happy years with her aunt and didn't want it to stop now. Not because of General Sherman.

Neither aunt Gertrude, nor either of her parents your typical slave owners. If they could, they would have paid their slaves for their hard work and dedicated service.

Temple could have the plantation as far as Sally and her aunt were concerned. Sally didn't want the memories, and Gertrude didn't want to leave Savannah.

The years since her husband's death had taught Gertrude that life must go on no matter what. That's what Graham would have wanted her to do; she knew he was a man who wouldn't have wasted the rest of his life on tears or self-pity. Because of this, she now stood tall in front of Sally with her head held high, although she was barely five feet tall, her stubborn attitude reinforced her words.

"No, I will not run; no man will chase me from my home. You can go if you choose, but not me. I'd rather fight than run. Your parents would do the same thing if they were here. We would agree that you, a young woman with her whole life still ahead of her, should escape."

"No, Aunt Gertrude, I don't believe that my parents would want to forfeit our lives over some unjust cause; they would want all of us, including you, my mother's sister, to be safe."

"You'll not convince me; I'll not leave. If Sherman destroys Savannah as he did Atlanta, I'll kill him myself."

Then bowing her head and softening her voice, she gave Sally another reason for leaving, one Sally could not welcome.

"I've received word that your Uncle Temple is looking for you," her aunt explained.

"Why I don't know, but you are aware that nothing good will come of his presence in your life. So, yes, you see, you do have to get out of Savannah."

Sally knew her aunt well enough to realize that there would be no convincing her to change her mind when she got in this mood. She admired her aunt's iron will. But for those she dealt with, her aunt's stubbornness was frustrating.

"Aunt Gertrude, you're talking nonsense. You can't fight an army! Come with me; let me now save you."

"It's no use, Sally. I'm an old woman; I would slow you down. Besides, where are you going, and how will you get there?"

Sally didn't know; she hadn't thought that far ahead yet. All she knew was that she was terrified of being in Savannah when Sherman's army arrived. Newspapers told of Yankees across the South looting homes of food and livestock and raping women in towns where only old men were left to give any form of protection, resulting in the Samaritan becoming the fatal victim.

⚜

When the war had started almost four years ago a draft was ordered, stipulating that all men between the ages of eighteen and thirty-five were to report for duty in their state. Those who did not comply would be shot as deserters. Most Southern men didn't need orders to fight; they believed in their hearts that theirs was a just cause. Seceding from the Union was a noble endeavor; they were fed up with the North trying to dictate how they should live their lives and run their businesses. *What do those Northerners know about growing crops?* they thought. *Of course, they opposed slavery. They have their factories for other goods, but they wouldn't be able to eat without our farms.* Fighting to retain their way of life became a noble cause in the South. Many Southerners opposed this way of thinking and instead signed up with the Northern army.

After Graham's passing, Gertrude confessed to Sally that she had never liked farming; it was all for Graham, and, would have done anything for him. But now, in her loneliness with no children, she longed for the city, to be surrounded by people where she would feel safer. So, she sold off fifty acres of land, leaving twenty-five for Sally and Frank, who were newlyweds at eighteen and twenty-two years of age when the war began. The small acreage Gertrude felt was adequate for Sally and Frank who were young and inexperienced farmers. She promised to give them more land once they became skilled landowners.

At first, even Sally didn't want the farm because of the memories it would bring.

But Frank, a tall, slim man with light brown hair and bushy eyebrows, convinced her that this was what her parents would have wanted. Since he was a farmer, or at least he considered himself one, he assured Sally that they could make something of this land, thereby honoring her parents with the prosperity he was certain he could accomplish.

But within months of setting up the house to Sally's liking, Frank was off to war. Frank adored Sally: to him, she was the prettiest girl in all of Savannah. Her blond hair and beautiful bright hazel eyes, which seemed to sparkle each time she smiled, endeared her to all she met.

Because of his love for Sally, he ensured she would be protected and taken care of before he left. He arranged with Aunt Gertrude to take Sally in so that she wasn't on the farm alone. They owned no slaves, as Frank preferred working in the fields on his own. He also spoke to his older brother, Kent, who had no love of farming and was more content to be the city's telegraph operator, which made him eligible to avoid the draft. He was also manager of the general store his father had willed to him and Frank. Although at the age of thirty-six, making him not obliged to join the Confederate army, telegraph operators were exempt from the draft. Unfortunately, Frank was obliged and more than willing to join the war "to teach those Yankees not to mess with our southern way of life," as he said.

Two brothers couldn't be more contradictory than Kent and Frank were. While Frank loved farming and watching things grow, Kent was content to run the business and hoped to expand the store after the war. Kent, who was even taller than Frank, was also more muscular than his brother, with darker hair. In addition, he had a mustache, unlike Frank, who preferred to be clean-shaven.

When the war had begun, and before Frank went to join the Southern cause, as brothers go, Frank made Kent promise that if any trouble came, he would protect Sally and get her to safety. Frank knew his brother was asking a great deal of him; relations between him and his wife were not the best. They stayed polite in social gatherings, but Frank knew they barely tolerated each other. She was too stubborn for Kent's liking, and she loathed his womanizing ways.

The small farm that Gertrude gave them for a wedding present was now left vacant. Sally didn't want to sell it; she knew the sale would break Frank's heart. So, Sally packed her belongings and moved to Gertrude's home in the city, completely unaware of the care a farm needed to remain functional. More than that, in her innocence, Sally had convinced herself that she had done all she could to preserve Frank's livelihood. Having never checked back on the condition of the farm since she moved. Never caring to live alone, she happily accepted her aunt's invitation, and Franks' insistence that she live out the war with Gertrude, suited her just fine. She was oblivious to the squatters who had moved into the small, abandoned farmhouse.

Sally had cried when Frank left. He was her whole world; she needed nothing else. To her, the war seemed no more than an inconvenience at the beginning. She didn't care about politics, and she opposed owning slaves. She mostly blamed the disgusting war for taking away her husband, along with a piece of her heart.

She and Frank never wanted or believed in forcing another human to work for them without pay. Abolitionist beliefs were not spoken in public for fear of violent retaliation from those who favored the institution of slavery.

At the beginning of the war, most people in the South were confident the war would last only a few months. As far as Sally was concerned, the reason for this war was weak. She thought men were just trying to impress women by exerting their masculine muscles or facing what they believed was a noble death. All Sally wanted was for life to be as it should be—living with Frank, having his babies, and working alongside Frank tending his gardens. But she knew that dream was fading with every passing day without Frank. She had not heard from him in three months and had no way of knowing if he was alive or dead. Frank had to come home soon, she thought. Sally and Aunt Gertrude agreed that Lee had to surrender before the war sacrificed any more lives. As sad as it was, Sally knew there was little she could do to stem the rising loss of the maimed and dead.

Frank couldn't come home to her and start the family they had always dreamed of having until then. Little did they know at the time that there would be three more bloody years of war to face.

While Sally paced on the colorful hooked rug that her aunt took loving care of, she tried to come up with another tactic to convince Gertrude to leave Savannah. *At least until Sherman's army leaves the city, she thought.* But there was no changing her aunt's mind. Sally knew where her streak of stubbornness came from; her mother had often told her when she was growing up, "You're just like my sister, Gertrude."

"Please, Aunt Gertrude, you're the only family I have left; we have to stay together."

Gertrude retaliated, "Besides, what about the farm? If I leave, who will take care of it? How will Frank find you when he comes home?"

"Don't you worry none about that. I'll leave a note on the door telling Frank where to find us."

"You're the one who is being foolish. You have no plan about where you will go or a means to get there," Gertrude argued, her arms firmly folded across her chest. She then crossed the room to come closer to Sally.

Putting her hands on Sally's arm, she said, "I love you very much. You're the daughter I never had but always wanted. You're young, beautiful, and talented. But what do you know of the perils that await you out there? Indeed, you cannot travel alone. If you insist on leaving, then take Eric Winters with you. He was a trapper in his younger days, so he knows the land and how to live off it."

"That dirty old geezer? I'd feel safer with the town drunk."

"But Sally, you need an overseer; Gus could be that for you."

Now it was Sally's turn to be the stubborn one. "Never! But I won't stay here, and you shouldn't either."

Before either of them could continue the debate, there was a pounding on the door. Hard pounding, like someone, was desperate for help or it was an invasion of Yankees. Sally quickly grabbed the rifle Aunt Gertrude kept propped next to the large fireplace.

Gertrude gasped, "No, Sally, don't shoot! You don't know who it is."

As Sally neared the door with the rifle held in firing position, she released one hand from the weapon to open the door.

Kent Preston merely seized the rifle from Sally's arms and then lectured her about the responsibilities of holding a gun at someone.

"What kind of fool thing are you trying to do? You could have killed me before you even knew why I was here."

Sally's temperament soared with excitement, forgetting for the moment the threat of General Sherman on their beautiful city.

"You've heard from Frank, haven't you?" Her smile was beautiful but premature.

"No, I've come to get you and your aunt out of the city. I'll be your overseer, so I can make sure you stay safe.

Sally recoiled from Kent. Disappointed at no news about Frank, her smile vanished, and her aversion to Kent returned. The possibility that Kent may have information about her husband had distracted her.

Sarcastically she asked Kent, "And where do we go, to the ends of the earth maybe?"

"I'm not sure, but we can get far enough out of the city to be safe and then return when the war is over, which, I wonder if you know, is but a sure loss for us."

Putting her hands on her hips for emphasis, she countered, "Of course, I know we're losing; the damn Yankees have made sure of that. But I'll still not go with you.

I'll stay here with my aunt. She doesn't want to leave; we've already discussed this. And further—"

"But you have insisted that I go with you," Gertrude interrupted.

Sally turned quickly around to face her aunt. With her wide-open eyes, she saw the wink and looked at her aunt's now confusing face. "I know what I said before, but now I've changed my mind." It was a game her aunt was playing, trying to convince her niece to leave the city without her.

Looking at her niece, Gertrude realized what was going on. Then she had a thought that she had forgotten to mention earlier.

"Go with Kent," she said. Then, looking past Sally, she directed her question to him. "Do you know how to get to Saint Augustine?"

Surprised at Gertrude's inquiry, he hesitated, not sure why she would mention Florida. Then he said, "I, um, yes, I was there once, but it was before the war. I bought some goods for the store there. Why do you ask?"

Sally was equally stunned by Gertrude's mention of Saint Augustine. But though she said nothing, she stood up from the red settee, waiting to hear what Gertrude's motives were.

"I have a cousin, Claire, who lives there. In letters, she tells me that, although the Northern army now controls the city, it is quite a pleasant place to live. The Union has no reason to terrorize the city now that they own it. I know she will take you in. I've told her all about you and Frank. Kent, you'll be welcome as Frank's brother."

Sally was horrified, "But what about Frank when he comes home from the war? He won't know where we are. How will he find us?"

Kent spoke up then, "You forget your aunt wants to stay. She'll tell Frank where we are."

"Yes, my dear, I'll write to you and tell you when it's safe for you to come back."

Tears were beginning to fill Sally's eyes at the thought she may never see her aunt again. "But what if something happens to you? Then I won't know, and if Frank has come back, he won't know where to find me."

Kent couldn't listen to any more of her negative talk. But unfortunately, he wasn't immune to his fears, and her dire scenarios only magnified the situation. It was time for him to take charge, "Ladies, please, stay calm. Mrs. Marrot, I appreciate your offer of a place for us in Saint Augustine. It seems like it may be a solution—

Pouting like a child, Sally stamped her foot and stated with rage, "I'm still not going anywhere with you!"

But Kent was just as adamant, "Look, I promised my brother I'd take care of you, and that's exactly what I'm going to do, even if I have to tie you to the wagon."

Sally felt caught up in a dilemma, not to her liking. It was a question of the lesser of two evils. Either stay and face the wrath of Sherman's army or go with Kent to a city she had never seen or meet Cousin Claire for the first time. A relative she only knew about through family talk but had never laid eyes on her.

Covering her mouth with her hand, Gertrude giggled. She liked Kent. She thought he had more grit than Frank and appreciated his comment about tying her to the wagon. During the years Gertrude had raised Sally, she had found Sally to be a loving child, full of life to its fullest. But Gertrude learned that she was equally stubborn and opinionated. As much as Gertrude loved Sally, she wasn't able to tame the demons that came out to play in the most inappropriate times.

"Go. Get out of here, you two. I have my rifle, and I know how to use it. So don't worry about me." She then went to Sally. Wrapping her niece in her arms, she hugged her. Then she whispered in her ear, "Remember, your parents and I will always be with you. I love you. Oh, and one other thing. It has come to my knowledge that your Uncle Temple is looking for you. Here in Savannah.

"What does he want?"

"I don't know, I've not seen nor spoken to him, but this is what I've heard from my neighbors. They promised they hadn't told him anything."

Hating her Uncle gave Sally another urgent need to leave Savannah as quickly as possible. Temple was the last person she wanted to confront.

Moments later as she struggled to drag the large trunk to the door, she looked to Kent for help. But he was busy conferring with Gertrude on the best route to take to Saint Augustine. She had packed months ago, just in case of a scenario like this. Then, out of patience and unsure how to handle two crying females, Kent picked up Sally with one arm and dragged the trunk with the other arm out the door without saying a word.

Chapter 2

Sally's kicking and her screaming pleas to "Put me down!" didn't distract Kent from his promise to his brother. He unceremoniously deposited Sally on the sidewalk in front of Aunt Gertrude's home. Then, raising his right hand with his palm facing her, he ordered her to "*Wait.*" Immediately he turned to the street and looked around for his lost wagon. People were still in perpetual motion. Some were panicked; others were unsure what to do. He could tell by the looks on their faces that confusion and fear dictated their actions.

Some seemed calm in the face of danger. Kent wondered how some could go on after all the death and carnage the Yankees had executed in the South. How could they still believe the war could be their victory?

Seeing Kent frowning while looking up and down the street, Sally couldn't resist some sarcasm of her own. "Lose something, Mr. Smartie?"

"Yeah, where the blazes did my wagon go?" As soon as the words left his lips, he saw somebody across the street waving his arms. Taking his hat off, a shabby rendition of what used to be his father's brown hat with a large brim, which now was weighted down by age, and over-use. He strained to see who was trying to attract his attention.

Sally realized that his concentration was no longer on her. She thought this would be the time to seek an alternate route out of the city. Anything was preferable to being with Kent Preston.

Underestimating Kent's ability to be aware of his surroundings, Sally suddenly felt him grab her wrist before she could take two steps. If anyone had asked Sally why she was with Kent, her response would have been to declare that he was *kidnapping* her. It would have been a lie, but preferable to telling the truth. Still scared of remaining in Savannah, Sally suggested a very dumb suggestion. It was so foolish she didn't even know why she made such a statement. Desperation brought the ridiculous out of most people, or courage that we don't know to exist until we are tested. "What about the train? I have money to pay for our tickets." Fear had taken hold of her senses.

Kent turned around to look at her with amazement, "You have lived a sheltered life, haven't you?" He responded, returning her sarcasm.

"Pardon me, sir, and what do you mean by that?"

"I mean that the first thing the Yanks do is destroy the railroads so that we Southerners are at their mercy for food and other supplies. Why do you think the shelves in my store are so empty? I saw you in the store earlier today, but you couldn't find anything, could you? Well, thank the Yanks for that."

Sally suddenly felt the fool. He was right; she hadn't made the connection. But she wasn't going to tell him that. She wouldn't dare give him any indication that she was intellectually inferior to him. Naively, she had merely assumed that business was brisk. She knew, of course, that times were hard, and people were suffering, but she'd thought that people were bartering for goods.

Without answering Sally, Kent instead pulled her across the street to the person waving at them. "Henry Kelly, what are you doing with my wagon?" Kent inquired as he shook Henry's hand. Then turning to Sally, he introduced them to each other.

"I know this pretty lady. I've seen her around town quite a few times, but we've never formally met." Taking Sally's hand from Kent, he gently kissed it.

Enjoying Henry's attention, Sally cooed, "My, you are the bold gentlemen."

Kent rolled his eyes as he stood nearby observing this display of flirting.

"Never passed up the opportunity to make acquaintance with a lady such as you," Henry answered.

Feeling the need to interject, Kent brought them back to the reality that the Northern army was about to disrupt this ill-timed flirtation. "Henry, you still haven't told me why you're in my wagon and why you moved it."

"I moved it because someone was about to steal it, which is why I'm sitting in it, waiting' for you. I can see you've got all kinds of supplies here, ones that a lot of people could use, so I figured you must be leaving the city too. So, I want to come with you wherever you're going."

"We're heading for Saint Augustine, Florida. It's a long ride; are you sure you're up to it?"

At seventy-six years old, Henry was still in good health. He walked a little slower with hunched shoulders, but his eyes and mind were as acute as they had ever been. He produced a distinguished look with his full head of white hair and a clean-shaven face. If he were wearing a crisply tailored suit instead of the faded coveralls on his lean body, Sally could imagine he must have been quite the catch in his day.

"Sure, I can handle the ride, and you young'uns need me. I've been to Saint Augustine many times in the past, and with me, you'll have another gun for protection."

Kent knew there was no time to argue with Henry or Sally. When he had deciphered the telegraph that had come into his store earlier, it stated that General Sherman was coming with an army of up to six thousand soldiers. Reading the wire, he knew he would have to deliver the message to the mayor, his job dictated that he report any telegrams that affected the city. When he did, he warned the mayor that Sherman might leave Savannah in ruins as he did Atlanta, two hundred and fifty to the northwest. He then handed the mayor his resignation, refusing to work under Union control. Kent was certain that with Sherman there could be no other outcome entering his hometown, where he, his brother, and his parents had lived an entire life in the city that had deep roots in his soul. He was sure this would be the beginning of the end of Savannah if not the war itself, and the South would never regain its former glory.

He thought about his brother then, fighting for a lost cause, a war he violently opposed. Kent fought Frank about it before he departed, leaving Sally's fate in his hands. "You're a fool just like all the rest of them. War is not some noble cause. You could be killed or maimed, and how would that make life any better for your wife or the rest of this country should we win? I guarantee you we won't, not with the army the North has."

Kent thought he had given Frank compelling reasons not to join the Confederate army. Still, his brother's mind was convinced that they needed to show the Federals that Southerners were willing to die for their virtuous way of life. No amount of Kent's antiwar talk made a difference to Frank.

In a way, he sympathized with Sally as she hated Frank for promising to protect her Like her, he was leaving what they loved behind. Deserting the store his father had built for Sherman's invading army felt like another curse generated by politicians who wouldn't let the South secede or own slaves. However, he had never approved of owning slaves or seceding from the rest of the country. The war was costing the South too much—families divided, homes destroyed, and children starving. *It must end soon, or none of us will survive,* he thought.

Staying behind to protect the vital war connection would be futile. Once the North took over the city, he would be shot or thrown in prison as a spy, simply because he would still be the rare male in town, whom the Northern army considered a likely spy. Sally, Henry, and he had to leave. There was no choice.

From Henry's vantage point in the back of the wagon, he pointed to the approaching army of what seemed like thousands of soldiers. He saw General Sherman sitting straight on his horse with his army trailing behind him. They were marching victoriously down the center of Bay Street past the Customs House, where they seemed to have stopped. Henry wasn't sure; his vision wasn't as good as it used to be. As they continued to move farther out of the city, the sight faded as Kent taunted the horses to run at full speed.

Galloping into the terrain of green meadows magnolia and pecan trees, a stark contrast to the imagery behind them. Yet, even with gray skies threatening their travel, they were still grateful to have escaped Savannah.

Kent was also fortunate enough to have a large, covered wagon, although it was not covered now; *There will be time for that later,* Kent had thought, as he quickly packed making sure the canvas was there.

The distant sound of pounding hoofs coming from the northern part of the city alerted them all. People were now running to gather whatever they could in the short time it would take the soldiers to come into view. Panic became the city's theme. The citizens had waited too long, hoping that Sherman's invasion was a false alarm. Sally noticed flocks of birds flying from the limbs of the majestic oak trees that lined the street. A mass flutter of birds' wings, though loud, didn't drown out the sound of the approaching horses or the vibration of the ground under their feet.

Glancing at Kent, Henry declared, "That's it, we have to get out of here now!" Kent agreed and hustled Sally into the wagon, sitting her next to him. Henry nestled himself in the back among the blankets and the baskets of fruit and vegetables. Kent had gathered all the food that he could from the garden that Frank used to tend. Besides beets, lettuce, carrots, onions, potatoes, and corn, an apple tree, and a peach tree grow in a small garden behind the store. Kent wasn't the gardener that Frank was. He loved digging in the earth and watching his land sprout vegetables and flowers too. Which was why he was so happy when Gertrude had given him and Sally the farm that she and Graham had owned. When he'd passed away four years ago, Gertrude had no desire to hold onto the farm that Graham loved so much. So, she buried him on that farmland and handed the deed to Sally and Frank on their wedding day. Frank was thrilled; he would now have ten acres to plant and grow the way he had always dreamed of owning. He vowed to Sally that someday he would more than double the size of the farm.

Kent was sure of one thing: he wouldn't leave any food for the bummers, scavengers, and looters who victimized every farm and plantation all over the South. So, he packed every vegetable and fruit he could. Even the ones that weren't quite ripe went into the wagon. The way, Kent figured, the food that wasn't ripe yet would be so in a few days, which would keep them from starving. His supplies may not have been abundant, but it was all he could accumulate.

Kent cracked the whip to get his horses, Betsy, and Tango moving, plus two others he had bought from a desperate farmer Who was moving them out of the crowded streets of Savannah? As he passed, some folks called out to him, "Take us with you." But he dared not stop; Henry directed him to "Go faster, my boy." Sally clung to the rail on the right side of the seat while she hung onto her white bonnet in her lap with her left hand.

Chapter 3

My religious belief teaches me to
feel as safe in battle as in bed. God has
fixed the time of my death.
—Stonewall Jackson

They had driven for about an hour when the rain began. At first, it was more like a mist. Sally complained about getting wet, but Kent admonished her, "Quit your complainin'. It ain't that bad, just a few drops."

Sally, annoyed by Kent's lack of empathy, scolded him back. "Oh, what would you know? You're a man who doesn't care about decency and good appearances."

Kent couldn't believe what nonsense Sally was spewing. "Appearances!? For what? We're in the middle of a war, with no civilization for as far as the eye can see."

With a flick of her hand, she let her hair fall behind her right shoulder as she placed her bonnet over her now damp hair, explaining, "Well, a lady should always 'be prepared,' as they say, for whatever may come." Though Sally was no pampered Southern belle, she believed that women should always look their best whenever possible.

"It looks like a lot more rain is gonna come," Henry injected. "I think it's time to get that canvas on the wagon."

Kent agreed, mostly because he figured it would shut Sally up. Then she could bend Henry's ear instead of his own.

Henry insisted on helping Kent to secure the canvas to the wagon. By now, the skies had completely opened. Rain was coming down in sheets, almost blinding them to the task they needed to perform as quickly as possible, which wasn't comfortable with Sally getting in the way. She was desperate to find refuge from the downpour.

But unfortunately, she couldn't get under the canvas fast enough for the men to finish the job.

Their wet clothes magnified the cold December air, sending chills to their exhausted bodies, and still, the rains came. Hours now since they had departed Savannah, the fading gray skies would morph into an evening, and the trio began to search for a dry place under a tree. Next, they needed to find a place to make a fire; a warm meal of roasted vegetables would help warm their bodies against the cold, wet air. Then Kent announced, "We will all sleep inside the wagon for tonight."

Of course, Sally had her objections. "I beg your pardon. I'm a married lady, as you well know. I sleep with no man other than my husband."

"Oh, get off your high horse. We have no intention of touching you, and besides, we men will sleep as far away from you as we can. If you like, I'll take out the fruit and vegetables to make more room for us. It doesn't matter if they get wet; they get rained on in the garden, after all. I'll put them under the wagon anyway."

Henry looked around the inside of the wagon thinking about how they could set up sleeping arrangements. "What about that large trunk? That could go under the wagon too."

Sally gasped, stamping her foot on the floor of the wagon; she declared, "That's my belongings! Including all the letters from your brother," she added as she turned to face Kent. But before he could respond, Henry persisted.

"Your clothes, letters, and anything else you have in there will stay dry under the wagon."

This time it was Kent who interrupted. While Henry and Sally discussed her trunk's fate, Kent noticed that the unyielding rainfall produced puddles everywhere, even under the wagon. Tapping Henry on the shoulder, he stated the obvious. "That's no longer true; Sally's valuables won't be safe under the wagon. Look; ponds are forming already."

Sally felt triumphant sitting on top of her trunk; she didn't want her belongings outside even if it was not raining. "Well, that settles it; my trunk stays here." But, in her logic, she wasn't comfortable putting her belongings out of sight. *What if someone stole it?* she thought, ignoring the fact that there wasn't a living soul for miles around. Since leaving Savannah, nothing had made sense to Sally. Her world had turned upside down, including her sense of logic.

Kent ran a hand through his hair, puzzled about how all of them would sleep in the wagon. He hadn't equipped it for such sleeping arrangements. He knew of a few families who, before the war, had stocked their covered wagons from his store before they set out for gold they heard could be found in California. Some of these families had several children. He vividly recalled one family with seven children and wondered how they all fit into that wagon at night. Right at that moment, he knew some of that knowledge would come in handy.

They were unable to build a fire, not only because they couldn't find a dry spot, but because any wood in the surrounding area was soaked, unfit in no condition to burn. So, they forfeited the idea of a cooked meal. Instead, they stayed in the wagon by lantern light, eating raw fruit and vegetables.

Sally rummaged through her trunk for another shawl to ward off the chill. She dug deep in among her clothes for that elusive garment and felt something odd, almost square, soft, but also a little challenging. Pulling the small parcel out, she unwrapped it from its cocoon among her undergarments as the men watched her, wondering what she was doing. "What are you looking for?" Kent asked. But before she answered, she had unwrapped the mysterious parcel from her trunk.

"Lordy be, it's a loaf of bread. Aunt Gertrude must have put it in here when I was talking to you. Remember when she left the parlor for a few minutes, then returned, asking you and me, Henry, to help her bring in the trunk?"

"Yeah, Yeah, I remember," Henry announced.

Kent was puzzled, "Great, but how did she get the flour to make the bread? I haven't had flour in my store for months."

"She didn't use flour; there was none. So, like everybody else, she used corn meal," Sally explained

Henry was beside himself at the sight of the sweet bread. "Been dreaming of good bread for many a night. God bless Aunt Gertrude. Please hand over some of that; we'll have a proper meal now."

"She must have bought the meal some time ago because I haven't had a shipment of that stuff in my store for some time."

"Well, I don't care," Henry said before taking a generous bite of the closest they could get to an actual loaf of bread. "This is good enough for me."

Repeating his previous warning, he reminded them, "We shouldn't eat it all right now. We're going to be traveling a long way, it may take us weeks. So, make it last." He looked at his portion, trying hard to resist the temptation to take one more bite from his share, which was about the size of his fist. Then he admonished himself, *I was never very good at practicing what I preach.* Finally, he tucked the bread back into the sack it came in. This bit of bread would be his breakfast the following day.

Sally chewed on a juicy apple while her mind consisted only of worry for her aunt. At first, she imagined what her aunt and her companion, as Gertrude liked to call her, were eating right now. But then the prospect of them enjoying a hot meal of maybe pork, beans, and potatoes just made her mad.

Then to neither Henry nor Kent, she said out loud, "Those awful Yankees robbing our food we need. I bet they're living on home-baked bread, while we beg for whatever we can get from those who are more fortunate."

Kent frowned as he looked at Sally's forlorn face. He suspected there was a tear in her eye, but he couldn't be sure in the glow of the single lantern. Her hair was hanging loose around her face with a stray curl or two touching her hazel eyes. Kent was suddenly aware of how beautiful she was. *Why haven't I seen her before this?* Not wanting to admit his attraction to her, even to himself, he ignored the sensation.

Returning to the issue she was expressing, Kent asked, "You mean the wealthy plantation owners? I ain't never begged from them or anybody else. Did you?"

Sally was embarrassed. She didn't mean to start a discussion of how hungry the South was. But she answered Kent anyway, "No, I never begged from anyone, but if I had to choose, those would be the people I would go to."

From the corner of her eye, she could see Kent sitting in judgment of her. "Do you think my brother would approve? I mean of you begging," Kent said as he took a bite of a peach.

"What does it matter? Frank isn't here, and I know he would want me to do anything I can to survive. Just as I want him to do all that he can return home to me." She was near tears now. Henry wrapped his arm around her trembling shoulders.

Sally reminded Henry of his daughter. They were about the same age. He felt protective of her, as he would Grace if she were near.

Kent, in his way, apologized to Sally. "I'm sorry. This conversation is pointless. I should never have asked such questions." He was about to add, *you're right, Sally, we all must do what we can to survive.* But he wasn't about to let her know that she could be right about something.

Sally just wanted to change the subject. Choosing to ignore Kent, she asked Henry, "So what is your story? I mean, how did you come to Savannah?"

Henry was delighted that Sally was interested in him. He rubbed the top of his head, almost as though the gesture would ignite a fire, making him feel young again. But, instead, she was allowing him to enjoy the attention. For her, Henry was a father figure. She frequently dreamed of her papa and the days he would sit her on his lap and tell her stories of princesses in ivory towers.

As the evening sky displayed its rich presents of sparkling stars the splattering of raindrops on the wagon's canvas made a noise like the heels of a women's shoes across a cobblestone road. Loud, but not enough to discourage a cordial conversation.

Henry put his hands in his lap as he sat perched on a box—of what he wasn't sure. That was for Kent to know. "I've been living in Savannah for most of my life—"

"Henry was the town barber for many years, I've been going to his shop for as long as I can remember. He—"

"Don't interrupt Henry, Kent. I'm talking to him, not you!" Sally scolded.

She turned back to face Henry, who had concealed a smile, feeling flattered that Sally would defend him when she spoke to Kent. "Now, you go on with what you were going to say before you were rudely interrupted."

"Well, yes, tis true that I was a barber. I took care of your husband's hair too. He was a great talker. Told me all about your courtship and how much he loved you. So, you see, even though I'd never met you before this, I've known quite a bit about you. I guess I pretty much know most of the men in Savannah. I cut their hair and give them shaves when they want. But like Kent here, I ain't seen much business since the war started. Maybe when this war ends, I'll be able to start up again. But I got nothing to hold me in Savannah now."

"Were you ever married? Don't you have any family?"

"I was married to my dear wife, Agnes, for sixteen years, but she died giving birth to our third child. They're all gone now—my children, that is. Nathan, Robbie, and Grace. I got a letter from Grace after the war started that both her brothers joined the Confederate army. Dang fools. Haven't heard from either of them. Then my daughter married a Northerner, so it doesn't look like I'll be seeing her anytime soon either."

Sally could see that his face was a mix of scorn and anguish. She sympathized, knowing what it was like to have a family ripped apart like that. She had heard of more than a few families in Savannah similar to Henry's.

She put her arm around Henry's shoulders, giving him a squeeze for comfort. Then, resting her blond head of hair against the side of Henry's forehead, she whispered, "I'll be your family." She was sure she saw a tear roll down his cheek.

Kent was sitting nearby on a crate filled with ropes and tools, which would be needed for any wagon repairs. He could hear Sally and Henry's conversation,

He knew Henry's story, but he thought Henry had gotten over the losses and put the past behind him. Seeing the pain on his face confirmed the truth he never admitted to anyone. *There are some things that you can never forget, nor would you want to.*

Chapter 4

Sally awoke with a jolt, not the gradual awakening when you stretch and yawn, playing with the covers while snuggling under the soft warmth of your favorite quilt, striving to squeeze an additional episode of sleep. Then ponder if or when you will greet the dawn of a new day.

Instead, she felt disorientated, and confused about where she was. A ray of orange-fused-with-pink light peeked into the wagon from the front and back in that early morning.

Opening her eyes wider, she focused on what was her sleeping chamber. She lay on the floor of the wagon, a blanket under her and another over her. A bag of uncooked rice became her pillow. Her neck and shoulders ached, no doubt from sleeping in the cold, damp wagon.

The discomfort was not all that was keeping her awake. The croaking of frogs blended into a chorus that harmonized with the falling rain, her forehead was wet and so were her feet. Then, observing her surroundings more accurately, she acknowledged that the relentless rain was again enacting havoc through the openings at either end of the wagon.

She took notice of Henry, curled up in a sitting position against her trunk. His left arm was on top of her belongings in an upside-down V position with his head resting on his boney elbow. *How can he sleep like that?* she wondered. *He's going to hurt a lot more than I do.*

Above him and Sally lay Kent. He had a blanket under him and another on top as well. He slept on top of the crates containing their meager food supply.

Sally was hungry, cold, and tired. *Damn, this war! It's just not fair that we suffer so. Life's not fair; nothing is,* she moaned to herself. What she wanted was to be back home in her brass bed with clean sheets and lace curtains on the window in Aunt Gertrude's house. *No, even that; I want to return home to the farm with Frank.* Tears stung her eyes as she thought about her husband and the pack of children, they prayed God would bless them someday. *How can life be so cruel? It just isn't fair.*

Sally wept quietly, not wanting to wake either of the men. She blew her nose into the only available handkerchief, a torn piece of her shift. Despite her efforts, the sound of her sniffles woke both men.

Henry spoke first. "Good morning," he said. Then taking a second look at Sally, he asked, "Are you crying?"

Not wanting to appear weak, she waved her 'handkerchief' in the air toward Henry, hoping to assure him that she had merely caught a cold from sleeping in a wagon devoid of any source of warmth besides the damp blanket.

"Yeah, well, women are more delicate like that," Henry admitted. "I guess we men don't feel such things as you do. At least, that's what my daughter used to say."

Kent jumped down from his perch above them. The rain still vibrated on the wagon's canvas. "Well, one thing is for sure, we can't just sit here any longer, we wouldn't want Sherman's army to catch up with us, so somehow, we're going to have to move this wagon through the mud until this rain stops. Are you ready for this, Henry?"

"I'm ready for whatever we have to do, my boy. I just wish the rain would stop long enough for us to get some hot food into our bellies."

Raising her eyes to the heavens above, Sally echoed Henry's thought, "A cup of *real* coffee would be so good right now."

"Yeah, well, the sooner we can get moving, the sooner we might find some civilization that has food and shelter," Kent responded.

Handing a pair of gloves to Henry, Kent put on his own set. "Here, Henry, you help me push the wagon, Sally, you sit in front and make these horses move, you hear me?"

Sally was about to object to being subjected to the relentless downpour, but she stopped herself, realizing that fighting with the men would not accomplish anything. *Besides,* she thought, *if Henry can do his part, I'm not going to let him imagine any less of me if I can help it. This is what my papa would want me to do.*

As Kent and Henry went behind the wagon, they could see that the wheels were sunk into the mud by about twelve inches, which was better than Kent had expected. In the daylight sun, Kent could now see that towards their left, green grass was visible. That meant that dry land was possible. "Sally! Steer the horses to your left while we push." Kent instructed her. Following his instructions, the men gave a mighty shove to the wagon. Their boots sunk to their tops into the muck. As their forces ignited, the wagon began to move. It was slow progress. More than thirty minutes later, they reached the green grass only eight hundred yards away. With the current weather conditions, Kent's hope to make Saint Augustine in about a week by traveling thirty miles a day would be a definite challenge for all of them.

Finally, when they reached what they had hoped would be dryland, instead turned out to be marshland.

They were surrounded by water, mud, and marsh, with only small patches of dry land. Fortunately for them, the rain was slowly decreasing. They would have intervals of bright sunshine for a few hours, then the rain would begin again, but not as ferociously as it had poured down the previous day.

The rain was relentless. The three of them had time to build a fire during the dry periods and stew some apples, which took some of the December chills off their bodies. At one stop, Kent had gone off hunting for some meat to fill their complaining stomachs. Henry and Sally enjoyed the restful opportunity to relish the sun that peeked through the clouds, some of the clouds looked like bales of cotton, while others in the distance were gray and menacing on an otherwise tranquil day.

"So, tell me, Sally, when did you last hear from Frank?"

"Henry, I haven't heard from him in months, and neither has Kent. I'm so worried. Do you think the Yankees are stealing our mail, just like they're taking our food?"

Patting Sally's hand, Henry wanted to reassure her, not add to her worries, but he couldn't find the words. Maybe she knew it already in her heart but didn't want to say it aloud. The North wasn't stopping the mail. It was more likely that Frank was no longer alive or was a prisoner of war.

Henry now took both her hands in his. "My dear, I'm sure he's too busy fighting and too tired to write. Maybe he doesn't have paper or pen to write with." It was the best lie Henry had ever told.

"Henry, you always know the right things to say, you're probably—

Suddenly they heard a rustle of branches coming from the east, a short distance away from where grand magnolia trees swayed in the winter breeze. Henry grabbed his gun immediately. Sally reached inside the wagon for her rifle and started loading it while keeping an eye on the trees' movement.

Both hid behind the wagon, on the opposite side of where the noise was coming from. Then, with their eyes, they peeked around the corner of the wagon and waited nervously for the intruder to reveal itself.

Two men emerged from the dense brush forest. They looked like they could be soldiers, unshaven and wearing clothes that were filthy and ragged, with bony legs extending from torn pants. Both had rifles slung over their backs. Worse was how they walked. Or rather how they shuffled their feet in front of themselves, as though each step would be their last. They pointed no gun at Henry or Sally; their faces were vacant, devoid of human emotion. Sally frowned as she looked at Henry. Still pointing her gun at the intruders, she discerned how they look like they were walking dead. Their complexions looked a blueish-grey color. She wasn't sure if she should take pity on them or fear their presence. A look of conformity passed between them. One thing was for sure: both Henry and Sally would not let down their guard until they knew what these men's objective was, even though they recognized that these men were probably no threat to them. As they came closer, Henry and Sally could see their mud-crusted faces, their beards dripping with moisture, from either sweat or rain. It didn't matter; they were in dire need of some salvation.

"We need food," whispered one of the men as he fell to a sitting position in front of the fire. The other man, leaning on his musket, confessed, "We're deserters from the Confederate army. "Then he collapsed unconscious, where he had been standing.

Sally let out an audible gasp, "You dare to desert our cause? How could you?! No wonder we are losing the war; men like you are causing our downfall."

Despite her words, Sally's sense of humanity took over her contempt for any anti-southern- mentality. She immediately began cleaning the face of the fallen soldier. "He's still breathing," she informed Henry, who handed the one sitting a peach.

"It's not much, but it's all we have right now. Hopefully, Kent will be back soon with some meat for us." Henry inquired with his booming voice, "So what's your name, and where have you come from?"

Devouring the peach while he spoke, the soldier told Henry his name was Damian Aarons and his friend was Joshua Brunt. "We came from the Andersonville prison; we ain't never going back. It's a hellhole, all of it, this whole fucking war!" Henry patted Damian on his back, assuring him he was safe now.

Sally was still tending to Joshua. She couldn't find any physical wounds on his body, but she did overhear Damian mentioning Andersonville Prison. "You were prisoners of war and walked all this way from the prison? It must be about a hundred miles from here. No wonder you two are in such bad shape."

"No, we were guards at the prison."

Chapter 5

*I destroy my enemies when I make
them my friends.*"
—Abraham Lincoln

Even though finding dry branches was problematic, they had enough to make a decent fire. In addition, they could now add warm rice to their meal, making the dry-kindling hunt worth it. Rice was the only food source that anyone could find in abundance in the South. "I guess the Yankees think we'll be satisfied with a diet of rice and nothing else," Sally commented as she boiled the meal they had most nights.

While Sally tended to Joshua, who was moaning and shivering terribly, she called to Henry, "Can you get me a blanket for this poor man; he's feverish and unconscious."

Damian, savoring the taste of the peach, commented. "Oh, he'll be all right. He needs sleep, lots of it. I mean, compared to where we came from, you wouldn't believe the filth and horror of that prison. Men are sleeping, peeing on each other, or puking all over because there is no place to sit. The stench was sickening, and the food, well, I couldn't tell you what we ate. But when you're starving, you'll eat anything."

Sally sat on the ground next to Joshua. Damian's words explained the putrid odor that her patient emitted. Sally questioned out loud, to no one in particular, "Maybe he has cholera. Can we get it from him?"

"No, you can't catch it from him. If it is cholera, you get it from infected water, which could be the case if you consider where we came from. So, if we keep drinking the water collected in those buckets, we'll be fine. But Josh, I don't know about."

Henry asked, turning to face Damian, "So how did you get out of that hellhole?"

"I'm not sure; other guards herded a bunch of us to the gate and shoved us out with no given reason. Do you think we cared why? They just told us to run. I was sure they were going to shoot us in the back, so Josh and me ran as fast as we could until we looked back and didn't see anything."

"Then you weren't deserters," Henry stated.

"How long ago was that?" Sally asked.

"I don't rightly know; it seems like a few weeks. We only survived this long because, along the way, we were finding signs that said, "For Andersonville Prisoners," with baskets of food, blankets, socks, and all kinds of stuff. God bless those people who put that stuff on the road for us. I mean, I don't know where they got the things they left for us, most of the South is starving and their homes destroyed. But as I said, that was days ago." Sally remained sitting next to Josh as she listened to what Damian had to say.

"So, how did you escape such a horrid place?"

"I don't know; they just let a bunch of us go with no reason given. Do you think we cared why? They just told us to run. I was sure they were going to shoot us, so Josh and me ran as fast as we could until we looked back and didn't see anything."

Suddenly Sally had a thought. Without leaving Josh's side, she asked Damian, "you said you're a Confederate soldier, right?"

"Yes"

"Well, then, maybe you know where my husband Frank Preston, is. He's with the Fourth Georgia Battalion Infantry.

"Sorry, ma'am, I ain't never heard that name, and besides, I come from a different regiment."

Sally's disappointment was obvious to Damian and Henry, who were still sitting by the small fire. Upon hearing the negative response, Sally bowed her head into the palms of her hands, not wanting either of them to see her tears. It was her problem to deal with alone. Damian, for one, already had enough grief. She had to be tough.

Wiping her face with her hands, Sally composed herself thinking, *nothing to fret about. His words are no proof that Frank is in any danger.* Then to change her thoughts, she stomped her foot, asking out loud to no one in particular, "Oh, where is that lazy Kent Preston with our food? He's probably found some shelter somewhere and is taking a rest without a care for us back here waiting for his return."

Henry stood up, pulling on his faded suspenders. As he walked to Sally's side, he assured her, "He's not that kind of man. He wouldn't desert us. But if he says he's gonna do something, you can be sure he will."

Sally groaned, not wanting to accept Henry's portrayal of Kent. She had formed her opinion of the man a long time ago when his brother was courting her. She still remembered that day when she first met Frank in the General Store. He had been bringing baskets of fruit in from the back door. He'd smiled at her, a smile so tender to look at, she knew immediately that this was a man who could understand a women's heart and learn how to take care of it.

"Can I help you with anything, ma'am?" he had asked. She had been surprised since she often came into the store but had never encountered him before.

"I don't recall ever seeing you working here. Are you new to Savannah?" Sally inquired.

"No, actually, I've lived here all my life; this here is my family's store." Then, pointing a finger behind him, he further explained, "We live up above. He said pointing to the ceiling. I guess you haven't seen me because I tend the gardens out in the back, so you and everyone else can get fresh food. I love to watch things grow."

That was how their friendship began before blossoming into love. Sally would visit the store as frequently as she could, just to see Frank. Sometimes they would sneak out to the garden in the back and steal a kiss, even though etiquette of the day said it was improper for a woman to be alone with a man before marriage., they, giggled in the face of a society that would trounce a union of two people so devoted to each other.

Then one day, Aunt Gertrude announced they had received an invitation for dinner at her good friend Emma's home. Emma had been one of the reasons why Gertrude had moved into the city after losing Graham. Her friend had been a great comfort, as she, too, was a widow. So, accepting a dinner invitation from Emma Preston changed Sally's life forever.

When Sally walked into the warm parlor with its stuffed chairs and brightly colored cotton curtains, she was shocked to see Frank standing there, ready to greet her. They hugged each other. Amazed, Emma looked to Gertrude with an approving smile.

Frank had told her about his older brother, Kent; he had even pointed him out to her on occasion when she was in the store, but she had never spoken to him, nor were they ever introduced. This dinner invitation would change all that.

She came into the shop all those times, checking if Frank had written or any news about him. Funny thing, though, she didn't realize that the man behind the counter was Kent each time she was there.

Looking around, Sally expected to see the mysterious Kent; when she didn't, she asked Frank if Kent would be joining them for dinner. "Yes, of course. He must be busy with some mail or a telegraph. He'll be here as soon as he can."

They'd already had their tea and dessert when Kent slammed the door as he entered the parlor. Sally was stunned not only by Frank's explosive entrance but by the fact that she had been waited on by him in the store numerous times without ever knowing that he was Frank's brother. His mother admonished him as though he were a child. "Kent! We have guests. Don't be so rude!"

"I'm sorry, Ma, but sometimes I feel like strangling some people!"

"Well, certainly not now. Come sit down with us and have a calming cup of tea."

Without moving, Kent fidgeted with the keys in his hand.

He made a slight bow to Sally and Gertrude, "So sorry, ladies, but I'm not in the mood for idle chitchat." Sally felt he said it with discernable sarcasm. Then he left the room with no further comment. Sally thought he was the rudest man she had ever encountered, and over the years, her opinion had not changed.

Sally's memories were interrupted by the sound of Josh moaning. Though still delirious, he became more agile. He called out, "Clara, help me!" Sally bent ever closer to him, running her hand over his cheek to soothe his agony.

Speaking softly in his ear, she assured him, "It's going to be all right; you're safe now. Nobody will harm you again." "

Then he suddenly grabbed her around the neck with such force that Sally fell to one side. His face was so close to hers, she could smell his breath, which was more putrid than his body odors. She tried pulling away from him, but all she could manage was to get one hand free to pound his chest, while his filthy hands probed her under things with his spider-like fingers. His grip on her was too muscular for her. "Please, Clara, it's been so long since I had a woman." His tongue probed the inside of her mouth as she gagged, unable to scream. Panic set in as Sally realized what in his dazed mind he was trying to do. Not seeing where Henry or Damian was, she wondered why they weren't coming to her rescue. *Oh, dear God, don't let this happen.* Despite Josh's weakened condition and unconscious state, he was powerful and fast with his hands and mouth.

As her brief prayer ended, she heard a loud gunshot; Josh immediately rolled away from her, then she heard Kent's voice as she fought to stand up. "Get your filthy hands off that woman, or I'll shoot you dead where you lie."

Sally couldn't believe that Kent was defending her honor. She stared at Kent, unable to say anything. Then emerging from the forest surrounding their campsite, Henry and Damian appeared, seeing Kent pointing his gun at Damian's friend and Sally arising beside Josh. She steadied herself and smoothed out her dress, which was covered in dirt and leaves.

"What's going on!" Henry demanded.

"You tell me," Kent reciprocated

Sally was pointing to Josh, still lying on the ground. Then, on the verge of tears, Sally made her demands known. "Where were you when this man was trying to violate me?"

Henry gasped, "What!"

Damian was astonished as everyone else. "I'm so sorry, miss, but we thought he was still unconscious. You were tending to him. That's why you didn't know we were gone, so we went to relieve ourselves. We had no idea he would wake up in that state of mind."

Kent still had his gun pointed at Josh, who hadn't moved a muscle since Kent's return.

"Now that you're awake, here, chew on this apple to give you the strength so you can get out of my sight!" Sally smacked Josh's face, then ran into the wagon and closed the canvas at one end.

"How the hell could you leave her alone like that?" Kent was devastated

Henry knew that Kent was directing his anger at him. He felt awful. indeed, he was guilty. Henry thought, *Thank God she's all right. How am I ever going to make things right with her?*

Kent put the gun away once Sally had gone to the safety of the wagon, but he was still furious. He kicked the side of the wagon wheel. He was infuriated, not only at Henry but himself too. *I promised Frank I would take care of Sally. I shouldn't have been away so long.* Then he remembered his reward for a pathetic hunting expedition—two gray rabbits, tied together flung over his left shoulder.

They may be enough for the three of us, but not for two more, whoever they are, he thought.

"So, who the hell are these two strangers, and why are they here?" Kent asked Henry, gesturing toward Damian, who was hovering a few yards away. Damian remained a short distance from Henry and took a drink from the rainwater bucket. Damian was confident of one thing; staying out of Kent's way was an intelligent decision.

"They wandered in here while you were gone. They're Reb soldiers. They walked all the way here from Andersonville prison. Half-dead when they got here too. This one here," Henry explained, pointing to Damian, "he's better now 'cause I gave him some peaches and water. The other one, Josh, collapsed when he arrived." Then noticing what was hanging over Kent's shoulder, Henry commented, "I see you got us a couple of rabbits."

More interested in these two invaders and what one of them was doing to Sally than food, Kent asked Damian, "So is the Army after you two? I don't want any trouble. Otherwise, you can find your way home, or where ever your heading."

"Don't you worry we don't want any trouble either, I promise."

Kent looked down at Josh who was still laying on the ground where he had assaulted Sally. She was hiding in the wagon with Henry, no doubt comforting her.

Damian's face contorted thinking about his captivity in Andersonville prison. His face morphed into a look of disgust; he lowered and shook his head. Turning to Kent, he answered the question he knew Kent was thinking. "It's worse than any hell you can imagine. Please don't be so hard on Josh. I'll admit he's a cantankerous soul, but it was the fever and missing his wife that made him go after Miss Sally like that."

Not wanting to communicate any further with Damian, Kent returned to the subject of his hunt. "Sorry, Henry, but this is all I could get. Two rabbits. All the animals must have run for the hills with all the canons and shooting goin' on. It's going to be slim pickings to spread these rabbits to five bellies instead of three."

Henry was delighted, "Don't matter; it's sure better than no meat at all."

❦

Sally sat in the wagon, shaking from the trauma of what had almost happened. She felt dirty in her mind and her skin. Crawling with hate, she felt repulsed by the checkered blue dress that came so close to his filthy clothes and face.

She tore off her dress, not wanting to see it ever again. She knew it would be a reminder of an ugly memory.

As she undressed, she felt the cold December air more acutely. Sally desperately wanted to bathe, to wash the stench from her body. but where? How? It was too hard to go in the water.

She stuck her head out of the wagon. Josh was still lying on the ground where she had left him; Kent was standing over him with his back to her. "Maybe you're out of your head with a fever right now, but I think you'll understand this: if I ever see you even look at Sally again, I'll cut your privates off."

Sally couldn't believe what she was hearing. Kent was defending her. Why she couldn't fathom. Then she saw Damian run to Kent's side, "Don't you worry. I'll keep an eye on him from now on. You or Miss Sally won't have anything to worry about; just let us stay with you until I have him back on his feet."

Kent took a hard look at Damian, wondering what he was all about, "Where do you and that piece of trash call home? Don't you want to be heading there?"

"Me, I'm from Arkansas, so is Josh, but a long way from me in the northern territory. We heard there's not much left; they say that pretty much every farm and home is in ruins. The damn Yankees left us with nothing to go home for. So, we may as well start new somewhere. Florida sounds as good as any place to put down new roots.

"But what about family? his wife? Don't you want to find them?"

"My brothers are dead; I got a letter from my ma that they died at Gettysburg. That was a year ago, and I haven't heard from my ma since, so I guess she's dead too. So, as I said, there's nothing to go home for.

"Josh was allowed to check on his wife when our regiment was in his part of Arkansas. When he came back, he was extremely distraught. His wife and child were nowhere. Instead, settlers were living in his home, swearing they never saw a woman and child. It's enough to make you cry. All he's ever talked about is his "lovely" Clara. I guess you'll have to speak to him about that. If he makes it, that is."

Kent nodded his head in acceptance. He may not have been in combat, but he knew enough about the suffering of soldiers and families through the telegraphs and newspapers that passed through the store daily. "Yup, you can come, as long as you behave and help when needed. Especially stay clear of Sally."

Damian eagerly accepted Kent's conditions, thankful that maybe they would find safety in numbers.

Chapter 6

Sally squirmed into a clean cotton dress; it was one of her work dresses. She decided that there was no need to ruin her superior dresses until they came to some civilization. They still had a long way to go. Sally didn't care how she looked. As long as the two intruders rode with the men, she had no desire to look attractive. She let her hair hang loose and barely brushed it.

What was Kent thinking, letting them come with us after one of them attacked me? I thought he cared about me; at least, that's what I felt when he defended my honor, she thought. But now the possibility that he cared just felt like a fantasy that she threw away. *We'll get to Saint Augustine* and *find safety. Aunt Gertrude can tell Frank where we are, and all will be as it should.* Sally was an optimist and had been one all her life. No matter how dire a situation became, Sally would find the bright side and stick to it.

They continued to trudge through wet mud under marsh grass, which slowed them down considerably.

Even though it had been days since Josh had attacked her, Sally still looked around for a place to bathe. A place where no frogs or other fish resided. She wanted clean freshwater. She frequently had dreams full of images of herself under a beautiful waterfall, surrounded by the sweet fragrance of flowers. Sally cherished the goal, but the reality hit her that even if she did find that elusive waterfall, she would probably freeze to death before she could enjoy it.

The two intruders rode in the back of the wagon; Damian sat poised with his rifle, ready if any threat was coming their way. Sally sat up front, sandwiched between Kent and Henry. Even though Josh had apologized profusely when Damian told him what he had done to Sally, there was no way she was going to share any amount of space with them.

Josh recovered, with Damian and Henry feeding him whatever game they were able to slay. Returning from one of their hunts, Henry commented, "Seems the critters are smarter than we are; they got out of here long before we ever thought of fleeing. But, then again, they weren't watching a whole army march into their territory."

"Maybe they did; that's why we can't find many of them," Damian joked as they trudged through the high brown grass surrounding them.

They had traveled for days now, sitting in silence, each person caught in their thoughts, trying to ignore the ruins of war surrounding them. They felt numbed by the miles of wreckage that lay along the road. Not one fence they passed was intact, nor did they see a house that hadn't been pillaged or burned. Carcasses of dead horses, cattle, and hogs littered the land of scorched grass. The stench was awful, forcing them to cover their noses. the odors that assaulted their senses were nauseating. "Why is the Union army so cruel to us? I mean, if they would only leave us alone to live as we want, then we could all stop fighting," Sally gasped. Trying to imagine what this land used to look like made Sally wonder, *What if this land could sing its praises of this once beautiful South, what if this earth could talk?*

"They're just a bunch of animals, those Northerners, no morals, no caring for anybody but themselves." So, Damian pronounced while he held a part of his shirt over his nose and mouth.

Kent voiced his observations about the wreckage they viewed. "It may not have been the Northern army that created this carnage. I've heard that people will destroy their property when they know the enemy is coming. Those who fled felt it was better not to leave anything that would benefit the North. Let's face it, the explicit goal of the Northern army is clear—starve the South to surrender." Not one of them debated Kent's point, each remaining silent, pondering Kent's words.

The weather was becoming more pleasant as they drew closer to Florida, and the rain was cooperating enough to bring about a more pleasant atmosphere. Sally was finally able to pull out her knitting from inside the wagon, for it was preferable to speaking to Kent. However, she suspected that Kent felt no urgency to talk to her either.

Looking around in every direction, Sally's fear of Indians ambushing them at some point gave the idea of another peril possibly awaiting them. It wasn't like she had seen any Indians, that's what peaked her question to Kent. She needed to break the silence anyway, it was the only logical thing to

With five mouths to feed, Kent realized his supply of food was running low. While their stomachs cried out in self-pity, Henry commented on how he wished the abundance of pecan trees they passed was edible. Now January, the pecans would not be ripe for picking until September. Their hunger mocked the sight of rotted pecans that created an even more massive void in their stomachs. They needed to find a town, a fort, someplace to replenish their supplies, feed their horses, and fill the void their bellies cried to be filled. Hunger and rest were their top priority.

After they finally found a road out of the marshland was a relief, making the driving and the horses less stressful. They had been on the road for seven days now. But it was abundantly clear that they had lost a few days of travel while trudging through all the mud.

They had been riding for miles when Henry broke the solitude with his usual exuberance, startling Kent. "Look to your right; there's a sign. It's pointing east to a place called Brunswick. Let's get there, quick, my boy."

"I don't know Henry; I heard that the town was deserted back in '62. So, I don't know if there is any point in going there." Kent said as he rubbed his chin with his hand for no apparent reason but to help him think.

Sally turned her head toward Henry. "Wish I could remember who spoke about that. Was it Frank?" Then, with a shrug of her shoulders, she concluded, "Oh, it doesn't matter," with a wave of her hand. "It'll just be nice to see, to sleep in a real bed tonight if nothing else."

It was going to be dark in a couple of hours. Not knowing how much longer they would have to travel to the town, Kent whipped the reins, urging the horses to move faster.

Damian and Josh, who were still in the back of the wagon, let out a triumphant sound of achievement. "Woo-hoo! Here we come, Brunswick!" They had kept their word to behave and be another set of eyes to spot any sign of potential danger co. They felt it was the least they could do for these people who took them into their trio.

Chapter 7

*It is only those who have
neither fired a shot nor heard
the shrieks and groans of the
wounded who cry aloud for blood, for
vengeance, for desolation. War is hell.*
—General William T. Sherman

At first, Kent encouraged the horses to run as fast as they could. However, each of the passengers had already set their mind on what they wanted from the town. Sally longed to have a warm bath, while Josh and Damian dreamed of a cold beer from the saloon. Kent and Henry wanted real beds to sleep in, no blankets on top of crates, next to a crackling fire to soothe their aching bones.

But as they drew closer to the town, it became noticeable that something was wrong. Henry looked past Sally, sitting next to him, and focusing on Kent, "Do you hear anything?"

Sally first looked at Henry, then Kent, "Wh-what's wrong?"

"Stay calm," Kent told Sally. "It may be nothing."

He slowed the animals' pace, moving more quietly so they could distinguish any threatening noises.

The closer they got to the town, the more mysterious the absence of any sounds became. Something wasn't right. Damian and Josh stuck their heads out of the canvas behind Sally, Kent, and Henry.

"What's going on? I thought we were heading into town?"

"We are."

Josh retorted, "But it doesn't sound like it."

Kent turned his face to Josh, "That's just what we were thinking. Have you got any ammo for those guns of yours? Now would be a good time to check, in case. Sally, you get in the back; you guys get up front here."

"Wait," Damian told Kent. "We don't have any ammo; We stole these rifles from somebody's barn before we found you. We held on to these figuring we could either scare a Federalist by letting them think we would shoot them or at best use the rifle as a club to beat them to death."

"Why didn't you mention this earlier?" Kent asked, "Well then, I guess that's how you'll have to keep it until we can get some ammo. Henry, Sally, are you loaded?"

They both acknowledged that they were prepared with ammo when they left Savannah.

Slowly they moved forward. They were inching toward a mystery that baffled them. Gone was the exhilaration of expecting to find some small comforts they had sacrificed in the ten days since they left Savannah.

Hoping their fears of the silence were ill-conceived, they realized that their imaginations had not deceived them once the town came into view.

They moved forward on the main road like a mirage in some fantasy, passing buildings frozen in time. The only sign of life was themselves. There were no sounds of children at play, music from the saloon, horses clopping down the street, or anything that resembled what this town used to be. A bank built of brick with two white columns on either side of the entrance was in Brunswick's center. In the small park next to the bank, a neglected flower garden displayed limp, lifeless petals of lavender, yellow, and white.

A white-painted church stood across the street from the bank. The town also included a hotel, a saloon, a sawmill, a printer, a stable, and what looked like a doctor's office,

Kent guided the wagon to the stable. The horses could rest there while they checked out the town.

"Henry, why don't you and Sally see what's doing at the hotel? Damian check the saloon; Josh see if you can get into the bank. I'll unhitch the horses and scour the stables. Oh, and grab anything you think we'll be needing or could use. Then we'll all meet up here in the street when we're finished.

Kent was in the vacant stable when he heard a woman scream. Dropping the yoke from the horses, he ran to the hotel. He knew the cry came from Sally; it had to be her. There was no other female in the town. Or was there?

As he entered the dust-filled lobby, he saw Sally rushing down the stairs, with Henry close behind her.

Sally ran right into Kent, then without thinking, she wrapped her arms around him for protection, motivated by fear. He was the last person she would seek for comfort if she were more lucid.

"It's horrible, absolutely horrible," Sally spoke, her eyes closed, her face buried in Kent's broad chest. Kent tenderly pulled Sally away from his chest, and with his right hand, he gently raised her chin, so her hazel eyes filled with tears met his. "What's so horrible? What's happened?"

Henry caught up with them as he descended the hotel stairs, "There's nobody alive here; we checked every room. Except in one, a decaying man's body was on the floor, magots and rats crawling all over it." Feeling terrible about Sally being a witness to such a horrific sight, he confessed his regret. "I should have checked the places myself so she wouldn't have to see anything like that."

"Was there any clue how he died?" Kent asked.

"I wasn't goi0ng to look that close; the smell alone made me gag." He shook his head in a gesture of disgust. Then he chose to change the subject. "Oh, we got a few things out of the rooms like blankets, pillows, and a washbasin, and we even found some money in a drawer. Whatever happened here, it must have been in a hurry for people to leave their money."

Once she'd stepped away from Kent and composed herself, Sally suggested they see if there was anything in the hotel's kitchen.

The men agreed it was a good idea, but Kent had another idea. "While you two do that, I'll go see what's at the general store and if Damian and Josh have discovered anything useful."

It was getting dark outside, which meant their time to explore the town and discover any clues about the inhabitants were limited. However, Kent noticed a few things in the hotel lobby: a massive fireplace, plenty of overstuffed chairs, and two couches. He planned to sleep in front of that fire that night if only he could find matches, lots of them, to keep the light going. He had a few matches left, but they could use more to last until they got to Saint Augustine.

The general store here was not like the one Kent had left in Savannah. This one was smaller and more compact. The shelves, for the most part, were stripped bare. A minimum of goods remained. Either the residents had taken whatever they could, or the Union army had, and if it wasn't them, then the only other explanation was bushwhackers. Those criminal deviants terrorized the South, mainly in Missouri and rural areas where they looted and murdered anyone, they suspected of supporting the Union.

There was no sign of any food in the store. Whatever edibles had been there were gone now. But Kent did find a box of matches to his relief; now, he was sure he would have a comfortable night's sleep. Then he had a thought. If this store were like his, there would be a meat cellar. That's where he'd kept all his meats for his customers. Although he didn't have much use for the basement in the past year, he did the best he could since ammo and traps became scarce due to the blockade. His dad was the hunter who had always provided meat for the family. He had always promised Kent that he would take him hunting with him one day to show him how to do "a man's job." But that one day never seemed to come.

After checking the barren basement, Kent walked out to the street to wait for Damian and Josh to report back.

As he waited, Kent became consumed with his thoughts. The irony of his current situation reminded him of his life without his father. Suddenly he couldn't eject the thoughts of his father from his mind. Strange, he hadn't thought of the man in years.

When Kent last saw him, his father was getting ready to go on his semiannual hunting trip. As he did before every previous hunt, his father promised Kent that he would bring his son with him next time. Then he would disappear for a month to three months, and each time he left, Kent asked to go with him, but his mother, Emma, always objected. "No, I need you here to look after your little brother." What she meant was that she needed Kent to look after *her* and Frank.

The year Kent was seventeen and Frank was eight; his father had not returned at his usual time from hunting in the hills of Georgia. Four months had gone by when Emma sent Frank to summon their neighbor Edwin Nelson. He was her friend, as well as Sam's, and Emma had relied on him for help when she and Kent could not handle a chore by themselves, or when he had too much to drink. Ed, was a good man, scolding Sam when he drank too much and bringing him home to Emma many times.

Emma was in a panic when Ed arrived at their home. She had convinced herself that something terrible had happened to her husband. She needed Sam home, and she begged Ed to form a search for him.

Ed returned in only five days, and Sam's body was wrapped in a blanket draped over his horse. Ed bowed his head as he explained, "I'm sorry, Emma, I found him not far from here. It looks like a bear, or some other animal got him." She immediately started to run to his horse. Ed stopped her, "No, you don't want to see him, all torn apart like he is. I had to leave parts of him where I found him. It's best if we bury him just as he is in this blanket."

Ed then motioned to Kent to come. "Help me with your pa. Emma, where's a good resting place for him?" Emma chose a spot next to her flower garden near the store.

Kent smiled to himself. Here he was, now in his thirties, still taking care of people. Maybe he should have married Joan, he wondered how his life would be now if he had.

Chapter 8

It's a matter of taking the side of
the weak against the strong,
something the best people have
always done.
—Harriet Beecher Stowe-

The four of them stood in the middle of the road alongside Kent. Nobody was saying anything, each lost in the web of their disappointments. Coming into Brunswick, they had anticipations of food, a warm bed, beer, and real coffee, which were now evaporated dreams.

Josh broke the silence. "It's getting dark; maybe we should take one last look around before we call it a night."

"Yeah, that's a good idea." Kent stated, "I'm sure we haven't checked every building, and don't forget the homes too."

Henry nodded his head. "Sure thing, Kent," he said as he put an arm on Josh's shoulder, "You and I will take the left side of town."

Though Kent had already known Brunswick, Georgia, was abandoned, he was still in awe of how the citizens must have fled.

With the day morphing into the night, the hazy purple sky created a ghost-like atmosphere, sending a wave of foreboding into each of them.

They wrapped rags around branches, dipped them into an abandoned bucket of tar, and lit them to help guide their way through the deserted streets.

In some buildings doors were splintered; other windows were demolished w. It was clear that someone had selected which homes or businesses to burn. A few had only minor damage, which made the mystery even more bizarre as it was just a select few that bore any destruction. For the most part, the town looked as though the residents had walked away.

❦

When they had not turned up any evidence of the town's fate, or any other food, the group headed back to the hotel.

Sally volunteered to cook whatever she could from their meager supply of vittles. The kitchen was large, compared to any kitchen she had ever seen. Looking around, she determined, as Kent had done in the lobby, that this establishment was a first-class destination for the rich and powerful. The stove was gleaming white with two ovens with shiny silver knobs. There were four receptacles for pots on the top, with a place in the middle to warm biscuits. Silently she wished that when Frank came home, they would own a stove like this.

As Sally prepared biscuits, she emptied a can of beans into a sauce she made out of some tomatoes, found in an old garden, and the last of their other vegetables. But she couldn't get the thought of how or why these people had vanished out of her mind. It had to be because the Yankees were coming, Sally thought.

Thinking about the tour of the town she took earlier while searching for food haunted her memory. She recalled the sight of the barren town ransacked more than pulverized which only amplified her curiosity. The vision just wouldn't go away.

Then while passing a home with fresh white paint on its exterior, There on the side of a home with fresh white paint on its exterior, Sally bent down to pick what she hoped was a carrot. After pulling the plant out of the ground and getting a closer look at it, she realized that it wasn't what she had hoped, but instead, a lone dandelion growing out of the destruction of an oppressed land. *How did this one flower survive when nothing else did?* The thought brought tears to her eyes. Then, it occurred to her that a moment ago, that flower stood erect, proud to be alive among the ruins. But now, holding the flower in her hand, she realized that she had killed this once-proud living plant by picking it. As though it was a tiny, helpless puppy, she gently replanted it. *Maybe if there is a God, he will find new roots for this flower to rebloom. After all, anything is possible with God.*

Sally's thoughts were interrupted by Henry coming into the kitchen, "Oh, whatever you're making sure smells good."

"I'm doing the best I can with what we've got. I found tomatoes. I was keeping them as a surprise for everyone. I hope you like them."

"I'm sure I'll try, li—

"Hey, what's taking so long? We're starving out here," Josh stated.

Sally tolerated Josh. Kent and Henry had assured her that they would make sure she was never alone with him. However, she insisted on keeping her distance from Josh. Not only was the trauma of his violation to her lingering in her head, but Sally also didn't like him. He was too coarse and a complete waste of any woman's attention, as far as she was concerned.

❦

The glow of the enormous stone fireplace in the hotel lobby cast an orange radiance on the faces of its audience as they devoured Sally's vegetable stew.

Kent sat on a blue stuffed chair facing Sally, with Henry, Jason, and Damian in between them. Nobody was saying much while they filled their empty stomachs.

Looking at Sally in the firelight, Kent saw something he hadn't noticed before. Maybe it was the fire or his loneliness, or merely the subtle way he watched her slowly change since they left Savannah.

Am I falling in love with her? No. He immediately brushed the thought aside. Instead, he admonished himself that all of them were changing during this journey. Sally was just the most obvious. On occasion, he had witnessed a softer and tougher woman, not the spoiled brat she was when Kent had thrown her over his shoulder in Savannah. He wondered if he should tell her how he admired her resilience. Was he starting to see what his brother, Frank, saw in this woman? The more Kent thought about Sally, the more he became convinced that he should keep his thoughts to himself, and that Sally wouldn't want to hear what he thought, anyway.

Chapter 9

*The Northern onslaught upon slavery
is no more than a piece of
specious humbug disguised to
conceal its desire for economic
control of the United States.*
—Charles Dickens, 1862

Kent slept on the couch in the hotel lobby that night, electing himself to be the guardian if any intruders entered. He slept with his rifle propped beside him. He wanted it to be nearby if any danger was imminent.

The rest of the group found beds in the vacant rooms. Sally had talked the men into providing her with warm water to take a much-desired bath. She banished the men from where the tub resided in the kitchen. Disrobing and stepping into the luxurious water felt like heaven for her parched skin. There was no comparing this to the inferior feel of creek water for Sally.

For the first time since leaving Savannah, Sally slept the entire night dreaming it was the end of the war, and she joyously ran into Frank's loving arms.

The morning delivered a bright sunny day, with a blue sky like they hadn't seen since beginning this journey. Sally stretched as she awoke, feeling refreshed and ready to face whatever challenges may come their way. Sally was dressed in the same gray dress that she had worn the previous day; the only difference was that she had washed it the night before in her bathwater, making it smell of the same sweet fragrance of the toilet water she had added to the bath.

Coming downstairs, she saw that she was the last to get up. More surprising was the smell of bread and coffee emanating from the kitchen. "Where did you get the flour and coffee?" She asked all of them. "And who made the bread?"

Henry smiled, "After all these years of living alone, I had to learn my way around a kitchen."

"But where did the food come from? I thought I had used up all the flour last night when I made the biscuits."

"It ain't flour. Josh and I found a barrel we had overlooked last night, figuring it was just a negative thing since everything else was gone. But Josh here got curious and opened the lid. It's full of cornmeal!" Damian explained.

Henry held up one of the golden-brown biscuits, "So that's how baking these delicious biscuits come to be. Who would have thought cornmeal could be this good?"

Kent frowned, questioning their judgment. "But is it still good? I mean, we have no idea how long that stuff has been sitting there."

Sally was quick to respond, with a smile, due to their good luck finding a source of nourishment. "Oh, don't you know that cornmeal can last for up to two years if stored properly, and that sealed barrel was surely the right way to store it. Didn't you ever sell cornmeal in your store?"

"No, I can't say that I have; people usually make their cornmeal. No need for me to carry it."

After they had satisfied their stomachs, Kent was anxious to get moving on to Florida. But, again, nobody protested, each eager to leave this ghost town for someplace among the living in Jacksonville.

Despite the sunny weather, it wasn't easy leaving Brunswick. It was surrounded by water, on a peninsula east of Spring Bluff. They either had to figure a way to cross the Saint Simmons Sound or backtrack for miles on the same road that got them into Brunswick, which would get them farther away from their destination than if they had crossed the sound.

Kent sent Damian and Josh to search the water's edge for any sign of a barge or a bridge that could take them across. They saw only one barge, with Union soldiers surrounding their wagons getting on and off. "We can't go that way, Josh, they'll know we're Southerners, and I'm not taking any chances. We know what a prisoner of war camp is like while we were at Andersonville. I sure don't want to know what Union prison camps are.

Josh agreed; they would tell Kent that there was no way to go other than the same road they'd come in on. But Damian pondered, *why are all those Yankees here?* He wondered if they were traveling to Jacksonville like them. *I hope not,* he prayed.

Damian and Josh didn't know that northern Florida had become a place of refuge for displaced slaves and Southerners who lived under Union laws even before the war was officially over.

"We're going to have to backtrack over the same road we took into this town; there's just no way to cross the water near here," Josh explained to Kent when they returned to where Sally and Henry were waiting.

Kent rubbed his chin with the palm of his hand, then slightly shaking his head, he pondered out loud, "Damn, that route will add at least another day until we can get to Jacksonville."

"Oh no, I'm not sleeping another night on the hard ground, if I can help it. My aching bones can't take much more." Henry protested.

"Sorry, Henry, but if taking the long way back is the only way, then that's what we'll do."

Sally wasn't happy either, but she was sure that her objections would fall on deaf ears if she complained. In her mind, She reasoned Kent had not listened to anything she'd offered on the whole trip. So why would he start now?

Though the sun was shining, and the warmth felt good on their backs, unfortunately, the dry road created a dust storm under the wagon wheels. Sally couldn't decide what was worse, the mud from the rains or the bare soil infiltrating every part of her face and clothing. Riding under the wagon's tarp offered some relief from the dusty road, only to feel the suffocating heat from the breeze that the wagon's interior couldn't control.

They were on their way for about an hour when they saw a brick two-story home up ahead with smoke floating out from the brick chimney.

"How did we miss this house on the way into Brunswick? Let's stop and ask those people if they know what happened in Brunswick," Sally suggested.

Kent turned to look at Sally, sitting behind him in the wagon. "Don't you read a newspaper? Everyone who does knows that Brunswick was deserted in sixty-two when the Union army was approaching. Besides, I thought you didn't want to spend another night on the road. If we stop to ask questions, I can guarantee you will be sleeping under the stars tonight."

Sally didn't know what prompted her overwhelming sense of curiosity; all she knew was that something was propelling her to enter that house.

"I just got to see if we can find out where those people went. I mean, are they safe now? You know it could have been us who disappeared."

With a wave of his hand and turning his head away from Sally, Kent dismissed her theory. "Sally, you've got quite an imagination, but if it's that important to you, we'll inquire when we get to Jacksonville." Then seeing her pleading eyes, he relented. "Okay, okay, we'll stop at this house. Who knows, maybe you're right; somebody here might tell us something."

Sally felt much better; she couldn't shake this nagging feeling that they must check out this house. She had no explanation for this compelling need to know. All Sally was sure of was that her conscience would not let her forget this house.

For Kent, it was more critical for them to concentrate on getting to Jacksonville. There was nothing in or near Brunswick that would warrant them losing more time on the road. They were all bone-weary from being on the road for two weeks now. But despite their exhaustion, Kent, Harry, and Sally had planned a route toward St. Augustine a few days ago. Jacksonville was a planned stop; it was in direct contact with St. Augustine. *Then again, there was smoke coming out of **this** chimney, indicating that life existed inside.*

They approached the house slowly; just as they had entered Brunswick, there was that same aura of mystery surrounding the home that seemed to beckon them to come into a realm that none of them were sure they wanted to go.

Chapter 10

"I prefer to be true to myself
Even at the hazard of incurring
The ridicule of others,
rather than to be false, and to
incur my abhorrence."
—Frederick Douglass

Not a sound could be heard, except a dog barking in the distance and the sounds of cannons and gunfire.

"Jumping Josephat!" Henry shouted in surprise. "We're walking right into a battle!"

Sally sat frozen in her seat. Terrified, she screamed, afraid they might be killed at any moment. The horses were getting jittery too. It became difficult to control the animals.

Their heightened wild imaginings exasperated Kent. "Calm down, you two; we are not that close to the battlefield."

Sally jumped again, "What was that? It sounded like a man in pain, and you say we're not close to the battle?"

"Well, it's too close for me; I say let's get out of here." Henry declared. When that was said, he whipped the horses into running."

Looking at the home as they came closer sparked a recollection in Sally.

After the burning of Atlanta, she had read in the Savannah newspaper why the Union army seemed to take so much pleasure in destroying the properties of well-to-do and elite homes where only a woman lived with her children and any slaves she owned. Because of that article, Sally was sure she knew what had happened there.

The Union soldiers obeyed their commanders' orders to shame and demoralize the women they believed were sustaining the rebel efforts. But it was the Union armies' efforts that were of no use. Not on the fiercely devoted Southern women. Instead, they faced a force that wouldn't give in to the enemy. In its place, the Southern women continued to do whatever they could for their men, their homes, and themselves.

This two-story house fit the class of a home well taken care of, with its spacious porch, a wood front door with floral carvings in the center, and a brass doorknob. There was a barn on the property, but it was devoid of any animals.

Sally related to Kent and Henry what she had read. They knew about this type of warfare the North was using. It was not a surprise to either of them.

Otherwise, there was no sign of life. Kent and Sally were the first to reach the door. Henry followed behind, while Josh and Damian stayed behind all of them with their guns pointed, ready for any threats that may accompany them.

"Hello, is anybody home?" Kent asked as he pressed his ear and cheek to the ominous door. Sally knocked, receiving the same response as Kent—nothing. Then they heard what sounded like a chair or some kind of furniture moving. Whatever they heard, they were sure it was scraping on the floor. Sally and Kent looked at each other, then slowly opened the door.

What they faced when entering was nothing even close to what they guessed would be there.

Sitting on the floor, staring at them, were three pairs of terrified eyes belonging to three children. One of them, a boy who looked about nine, was holding a rifle that was pointed at them. Kent, Sally, and Henry weren't quite sure how to react. The boy looked traumatized; his arms were shaking as the rifle bounced in its position on his shoulder. He was sweating; the beads of moisture dampened his forehead, as well as his hairline. He had a purplish-blue welt on his cheek right under his left eye. It was evident to Kent that one quick move from any of them would propel the boy's finger to engage the trigger.

Without speaking, Kent raised his hand, a signal for the others not to come any closer.

The other two children were girls. One looked a bit older, maybe twelve, and in her lap sat another child, with the saddest eyes Sally had ever seen. She guessed the child to be about four or five. But it was what was behind the children that had them puzzled. A woman's body lay next to the fireplace, a puddle of blood encompassed under the woman's head. Sally took one step forward toward the children. "My name is Sally. We came here to help you, and maybe you could help us. Would that be, okay?"

"But first," Kent interjected, interrupting Sally, "put down the rifle."

"No!" The boy said, in a commanding voice. "You get out of here, or I'll shoot you!"

"You don't want to do that. What will your parents think when you go to jail?"

"I ain't got no parents."

"Is your dad a soldier? Is that why he's not here?"

"He's a doctor," Then, looking at his sister, he asked her, "How long has Dad been gone?" Again, Kent and Sally were not surprised; this home looked like one a doctor could own.

Annoyed that her brother would ask such a question in front of these strangers, she responded with an edge in her voice, "I don't know, a long time. Mama said he might never come home."

While the children were speaking to Kent and Sally, Henry moved unnoticed to see if the person behind them was still alive. He started to bend down to feel for a pulse when suddenly, the boy remained sitting but turned and screamed at Henry, "Don't you touch her!"

Startled, Henry stood up, with a frown on his face, wondering if these children knew their mother was dead. Henry knew without touching the woman. "Is this woman your mother?"

Backing away from the women's body, Henry looked to Kent as he shook his head, to indicate that the woman was dead.

Sally, aware of the silent signals between Kent and Henry, knelt on the floor at the children's level. She smiled and stroked the light brown hair of the youngest child. With gentle hands, she held the little girl's dirty face in her hands. Then she turned her attention to the older girl, squeezing her hand that remained wrapped around the youngest. At the same time, she could see from the corner of her eye that the boy had laid down his rifle.

Kent and Henry strolled around the room; furniture everywhere was in shattered pieces. Shards of broken glass littered the kitchen. A vacant pan revealed evidence that somebody had devoured a loaf of bread. But who? The children, or soldiers who would leave three innocent children with no living adult to protect them?

Damian and Josh remained outside, guarding them all.

"We have to bury the mother before we leave," Henry stated with trembling lips, not comprehending how any human could justify doing this. During his life in Savannah, he had witnessed the cruel treatment of slaves, convincing him that the practice of owning slaves was an evil institution created by men who would inflict torture on another human for the sole purpose of money and prosperity. This scenario was just as horrifying as anything he had seen while witnessing the treatment of black slaves.

As he and Kent walked back to the children, still sitting on the floor in dirty, torn clothes, Henry bowed his head and covered his eyes as he shed tears at the loss of innocence in these children's lives. Quickly though, he wiped his eyes with the back of his hand, not wanting the children to see the shame and fear in his eyes. Right now, what these children needed was not signs of defeat, but instead, hope to go on, a reason to be brave, and a return to some sense of security.

Kent led him back to the once comfortable front parlor. But before they were in front of the children, Kent stopped Henry, telling him that they should give the mother a Christian burial.

"Go tell Damian and Josh to start digging a grave."

When Kent returned to the children, he saw Sally sitting between the boy and the girl with her arms wrapped around their shoulders. The oldest girl was still holding the youngest in her lap. Sally was whispering to them; Kent couldn't understand what she was saying. But he could see the tears rolling down their dirty faces.

Sally looked up when she heard Kent approach them. Nodding her head left toward the boy, she told Kent, "His name is Lukus, but everyone calls him Luke. He's nine. To my right is Margaret. twelve, and on her lap is Amy, who is four. The poor child, so traumatized since the soldiers were here, hasn't spoken a word since."

Kent looked at each of the terrified children. Lukus was trying hard to be the man for his sisters, who had dark brown hair and he had red hair. Amy had tendrils hanging over her beautiful large blue eyes, the same color as her brother's and sister's eyes. Amy's eyes followed Sally as she arose from where she knelt before the children.

Standing, Sally stretched her arm out, with a welcoming hand, willing one of them to take hold of her.

The door opened, and Amy screamed. Josh's was a face she had never seen; he was, in her young eyes, another threat. He had stepped inside to tell Sally it was time to bring the children outside. But, to the terrified little girl, he was another man who would do horrible things to them. Tears streaked her cheeks. She quickly ran behind her sister, wrapping her tiny arms around Margaret's leg, forcing the skirt to shake with Amy's tremors.

At first, Luke objected, suspicious about the need for them to go outside. Then, angry, he grabbed the gun again and pointed it at Josh. He demanded to know why they would go with him and Sally. "I'm not leaving my mother or my sisters to you! Get out!" he screamed.

Sally ignored the gun; he was just a scared, grieving boy. *Why should he trust us after the horrors they've seen?* she asked herself.

Stepping forward, she took Margaret's hand, then whispered in her ear, "We'll bury your ma now. Can you tell Luke that? He'll trust you." Nodding her head yes, Margaret went to her brother. Sally looked down at Amy, who looked back at her with the saddest eyes she had ever seen. She stretched her arms out to Amy, and to Sally's surprise, Amy ran to her, wrapping her tiny arms around Sally's neck as Sally whispered in her ear, "You're all right now. Nobody will harm you; we'll take care of you now."

She looked for Luke and found him still holding the rifle which was almost as big as him. She asked about their father. "He's a doctor off tending the soldiers."

Kent, hearing him, had questions of his own. "What's your pa's name? Do you know where he is or what regiment he's in?"

"His name is Lionel Hicking. In the last letter Ma got, he said he was in Charleston. But that was a long time ago." Then, with his head hung low, looking down at the floor, he added, "I don't know where he's at now."

Kent felt for the kid; he was just as worried about his brother. "I haven't heard from my brother, either. It's rough out there, and I suppose it's hard to write a letter in the middle of a battle." Kent knew it wasn't possible to write while in battle, he said it to help the boy gain a greater sense of security, hoping the kid would feel better about not hearing from his father.

"So, tell me exactly what happened here and when."

Sally was still holding Amy. She and Henry moved closer to Kent, eager to hear how this tragedy came to these children.

"Was it Indians, or soldiers who attacked your town?" Sally asked Margaret.

Henry was astounded by her question. "Don't be silly. You haven't seen no Indians anywhere during this trip."

"I know, that's why I wonder about no Indians. Isn't that strange?

"I read in a paper from back home in Savannah that a lot of the Seminole Indians are helping to fight this war."

Sally couldn't believe what she was hearing from Henry.

"On which side are they fighting?"

"Don't matter much to them Indians. They're on both sides, some for the North, and some for the south. So don't worry, they're not about to attack us."

Kent was rummaging through the rubbish that was once a tastefully decorated home, when he responded to Henry's statement

Luke bowed his head as he shielded his eyes. He didn't want anyone to see him cry.

"We were fixin' to have dinner when the door was busted open. Five or six Yankees came in, pushing us aside." Luke looked at the three adults in the room, confident that he could continue now that he was relating the story like any man of the house would do. "Ma yelled at them to get out. But instead, they started demanding food. Ma gave them a sack full of vittles; I'm not sure exactly what. But they wanted more when Ma tried telling them that we didn't have much food and that she had to keep some for us kids."

When Margaret wanted to share what she witnessed, she looked to Sally, Kent, and Henry. "They started going through all the cabinets, breaking everything they could put their filthy hands on."

Again, Luke spoke, interrupting Margaret. He had venom in his voice as he described the Yankees' next catastrophe. "Those snakes even went down to our meat storage under the house! They even took our three chickens and two cows. So, when Ma was trying to stop them taking and breaking our things—"

"Yeah, they pushed her toward the fireplace where she hit her head," Margret said. When Luke tried to stop them from hurting Ma, they hit her in the face with the back of their rifle.

Sally held the children closer now, wanting to instill a sense of security, something else the soldiers had robbed from these children.

Henry was beside himself with rage; he paced the floor littered with the debris from a once happy home.

Damian had come to the door again, asking Kent, "Where should I dig the grave?"

Sally overheard Damian's question; she was sure the children did too.

Margaret looked to Sally as she still held on to Amy, "There's a family burial site in the back. My grandparents and aunt are buried there. Ma would want to be there too."

Amy and Margaret collected wildflowers to spread on their mother's grave. They all said prayers.

"You'll all come with us; we can't leave you here alone," Kent announced.

"But what about our pa? When he comes home, he won't know where we are." Luke asked Kent.

"I know; we'll leave a note on the front door explaining that you are safe, and he can get you in Saint Augustine."

"Saint Augustine? That's so far away," Margaret worried. She liked these kind people who came to their rescue. Although she didn't know them for very long, something inside of her trusted them. She wanted to trust them completely, but she just didn't feel comfortable going to a new location where she's never been before.

Sally suddenly had a thought, "How long ago were the soldiers here again?"

"Three days ago," Luke stated.

"Land sakes!" Looking to Kent and Henry, she demanded, "We have got to find food for these poor children. You must be starving."

Without saying a word, the three children nodded their heads yes in unison.

Kent immediately arose from the edge of the fireplace where he was sitting. His eyes were distracted by the blood-stained floor left by the mother's death. It was a reminder that the killing those soldiers had executed was likely by orders from sadistic commanders.

"I'll take the wagon and see what I can find for them," Kent asked Josh and Damian to come with him. He wasn't going to leave Josh alone with Sally again. It was the best solution to a delicate situation.

Sally and Henry did all they could to keep the children's minds off the empty stomachs they couldn't ignore much longer.

They sang songs with the children and told stories. Then Henry suddenly remembered he had a pack of cards in his bag.

The children were delighted by the game of solitaire. They were all laughing and giggling as they fought to get their cards on the numerical piles. Henry had the three of them playing the same game at the same time.

They were having so much fun that they almost forgot how long the men had been gone, Luke. growing tired, rubbed his stomach; with a cry in her voice, she said what the others were thinking. "I'm hungry; I want to eat."

Margaret lovingly placed her arm around her sister, "We're all hungry. But we have to wait until Mr. Kent and the others get back from their hunt for food."

It was difficult for Amy to comprehend what was going on around her; she fell silent again. Fear and anxiety wrapped their tentacles around her, crushing her soul and any trust she had in people. Margaret became the only person she would trust; Amy remained Margaret's shadow.

In the few hours that Kent was gone, Amy had fallen asleep with her head in her sister's lap, while Margaret sat on the once beautiful blue sofa, her mother's prized possession, now torn and scratched by the invading soldiers.

Kent finally arrived. Puzzled, Sally wondered why Kent was walking alongside the wagon. Henry saw the dilemma Kent was in; somehow, the rear left wheel was broken.

With his usual slow gait, Henry went to assist Kent in getting the horses unhitched. Then he asked, "Did you run into some Yanks? Is that what happened?"

"No, nothing like that, thank God. I brought the damn wagon figuring or hoping to get us a large deer. I saw one in plain sight; it was on the other side of a pond. So, I got off the wagon to get in a better angle to get the animal. But when I shot my rifle, the horses ran off as if they had never heard a gunshot before. I don't know what got into them. Anyway, they went over some rocks, which broke the wheel. But the good news is I got us deer."

"Good work, Kent," Henry exclaimed as he patted Kent on the back.

By now, Sally had come to join them. "You're going to fix this, right?"

"We're going to try," Kent said as he scratched his head. "If we can find the tools we'll need."

"Maybe we should go back into town; maybe we can find what we need."

"Which reminds me, where are Josh and Damian?"

"They're in the house with the children."

Kent was shocked, "You left those kids alone with those two strangers? How could you," he said as he pushed past them to get back in the house.

"Josh, Damian, come outside. I need your help. Don't worry, kids; I'll send Miss Sally back with you."

Outside Henry was on his hands and knees examining the broken wheel. "What do you think, Henry? Can we fix it?"

Standing up, Henry brushed the dry dirt from his pants and hands. "I don't know; it depends on what we can find to do the job. The wheel is loose from its axle, and the wheel itself has cracked. I think we may need a whole new spin. Even if we fix the axle problem, we won't get very far before the wheel falls apart."

"I still say we should go back into Brunswick to see what we can find," Henry said as he pulled up his sagging pants, which had become even baggier since they began this journey. Lack of regular meals had forced Henry to tie a rope around his waist, which often came loose.

"You're right, Henry," Kent replied, then he asked the men to help get the deer into the house.

Sally was sitting on the floor, surrounded by the children as she played a silly game clapping her hands to their hands. "Patty-cake, patty-cake," he heard her say.

"Sorry to interrupt whatever you're doing, but I got us some deer meat for tonight's supper. Do you know how to cook it?"

"Well, I do love venison, but that's when someone else cooks it."

Kent wasn't aware of Henry being behind him until his booming voice offered the solution.

"I know how to butcher a deer; I've done it many times. We'll cook it together, Sally. Then, Kent, you take Josh and Damian to find whatever tools we need.

"But I don't have spices to add to it," Sally protested.

"It doesn't matter how you cook it; at this point, all we want is to feed our empty bellies, especially the children."

Sally looked to the three wards they would take on for the rest of the journey to Saint Augustine. "Yes, you are correct, Henry."

Kent, Josh, and Damian were gone by now. Simultaneously, the children looked on in disgusted horror at what Sally and were Henry doing to the carcass.

Seeing their faces, Henry asked, "You never saw your pa butcher hunt?"

"No, he always did it in the meat cellar," Luke recalled.

"Yeah, we never wanted to see him do that," Margaret said with her face scrunched in a disgusted look, then she ran out of the room. Henry could see her hand clasped around her mouth, assuming she was about to vomit.

Chapter 11

*No damned man kills me
and lives.*
—Confederate General
Nathan Bedford Forrest's
response after being shot by
subordinate officer

Sally thought that with their bellies now satisfied from the venison and after two days, they were finally ready to get back on the road. It was a beautiful day to be traveling. She, the children, and Henry rode inside the wagon. Sitting anywhere they could among the trunks, boxes, and various supplies. They weren't the most comfortable seats, but they had little choice. The men rode up front, balancing their rifles across their laps just in case they met with any hostile visitors. Kent found this quite amusing; Josh and Damian still believed that the mere sight of their rifles pointed at a foe would deter a crime from being committed against them.

"Why are you even bothering? You still don't have any ammo; what happens if someone calls your bluff? What will you do then?" Kent asked them with a sarcastic smirk on his face.

"You're not a soldier; you don't understand what tactics work against an enemy," Josh retorted.

With a frown and a click of his tongue, Kent urged the horses onward. *I'll feel a whole lot better when I can get some ammunition for these two clowns. We've got to find a town with food and ammo soon.*

Sally had pulled back the wagon tarp's flaps to allow the refreshing breeze to caress their faces. The sky was just like the pale blue gown she had worn to the governor's Fall Gala in Savannah only a few months ago. It felt more like a lifetime ago. Sally's recollection reminded her of how much her world had changed since then. The thought prompted her to think of Aunt Gertrude and wonder how she was. Did she survive Sherman's invasion? Had she lost her home and was now living in a tent somewhere? Sally knew that she shouldn't say anything to anyone about her aunt or Frank. It would only cause anxiety, reminding them all of the loved ones left behind. So instead, she silently prayed that letters would be waiting for her when she arrived in Saint Augustine.

"Look, those clouds look like cotton," Margaret said, pointing skyward, interrupting Sally's thoughts. Then, placing her arm around Margaret's shoulders, Sally assured her that she was in complete agreement, adding, "Don't you wish you could reach up and touch them? They look so soft."

"Aww, you girls are loco, talking about clouds and stuff like that when there's a war going on," Luke said. Then he had another thought. Raising his eyes to the sky, he asked sadly, "Do you think Ma is up there with those clouds?"

Sally smiled at Luke, his comment, was both painful and affectionate. "You just said that us girls are loco for talking about clouds, and now you're doing exactly what you scorned. You boys are loco too." Which made them all laugh.

Sally's eyes filled with compassion for these orphaned children, alone, away from home and family. Reaching past Margaret, she took Luke's hand and squeezed it, "Your mama, I'm sure, is looking down on you and your sisters, so she'll always be here in your heart." She said, patting her chest. While Amy slept with her head on Sally's lap. She still had not spoken a word.

Kent stopped the wagon just outside Saint Mary's, a town on Florida's east coast. He and the horses needed to rest, and this looked like a good enough place to regain their strength.

"Where are we?" Sally asked. "Are we there? Is this Saint Augustine?"

"No, we're in Saint Mary's. According to the map, we're just over the border from Jacksonville."

Kent told Sally to stay in the wagon with the children until he returned. "The men and I are going to see if we can get some ammo in town. We won't be long; it's a small town."

"You're leaving the children and me all alone with no protection?" Sally demanded to know.

"No, Henry will stay with you. He may be getting on in years, but he's healthy and has a good shot. So don't worry."

Returning to Sally and Henry the trio felt lucky to now have some actual ammo,

Kent, Josh, and Damian Kent could see Henry and the children. But looking around, he didn't see Sally.

"Henry, where is Sally?"

"She and Margaret went into the woods to relieve themselves. They have a gun with them."

Kent was livid. "Dang blasted woman! So now I'll have to go looking for them. How is it that you can never keep a hold on Sally?"

"I'm sorry, my boy, but what was I supposed to do? A gentleman never follows a woman when she is taking care of her personal needs."

Still irritated but understanding Henry's logic, Kent picked up his rifle from where he'd thrown it down when he heard Henry explain where Sally had gone.

The woods were thick with trees and other various foliage that Kent had never bothered to learn about. That was Frank's expertise.

Entering the lush woodland, Kent didn't know where to begin looking. But with both hands, he kept his rifle poised on his shoulder, ready to shoot when necessary.

His eyes darted everywhere, making sure that he hadn't missed any clues. Then, finally, he called out their names, hoping that they would respond.

He took a few more steps ahead, going deeper into the woods. That's when he heard a growl. It sounded like a bear or a mountain lion. Whatever it was, it was not far away. Kent moved even more cautiously. Suddenly he felt the sweat rolling down his face. He didn't know who he was more petrified of—him or the girls.

Out of the corner of his eye, he saw movement in a few bushes to his left. Spinning left to face the possible threat with shaking hands, he held tight to the rifle.

Then he moved one step closer, parting the brush slightly so that he could see better.

Shocked but not surprised, Kent saw the girls crying while clinging to each other as a giant bear stood on its hind legs, terrorizing the girls with growls that threatened impending death.

Kent kept his finger on the trigger, took aim, and shot the brute. He didn't kill the animal, but the shot changed everything. While the wounded bear limped away from its prey, the girls ran to the safety of Kent's arms.

"You girls have to be more careful. I know it's not proper, but there are times when a protocol must be adjusted to meet the situation. Like now, having a man with you would be to your advantage. All he has to do is turn his back on you to save your dignity

Sally and Margaret hung their heads in shame, embarrassed that they could be so naïve; of course, they should have thought this situation through more rationally. Besides bears in the woods, other animals or maybe Northern soldiers hid in the thick forestry.

When they had returned to Henry and the others, Sally asked Kent, "I saw you talking to a gentleman before we went into the forest. But I never heard what that was all about. What did he want?"

Kent gave Sally a gracious smile; she was prettiest when she got riled up. *Why has it taken me so long to notice her fair ivory complexion, her crystal hazel eyes, and a waist he would love to get his arms around?*

He shook his head, forcing his return to reality. They were in the middle of a war, hungry, and without a roof over their heads. *There's no time to get mixed up with a woman like Sally or any woman, you fool. Didn't you learn anything after Joan left?"*

"We were discussing how the war had devasted this town. His name is Ray; he invited us to his house for some soup his wife was cooking. He told us to wait here while he went to tell his wife there would be eight more mouths to feed. Then, he'll be back to show us the way to his house."

The children's eyes became alert and danced with anticipation. "What kind of soup is it?" Luke asked.

Margaret, like any big sister, admonished her brother. "Who cares what kind of soup it is? Mama told us always to be grateful for any gift given to us, even if we didn't like it. So be quiet."

Luke lowered his head, ashamed that he would ask such a question. However, the mention of his mother's words reminded him that he was thankful, especially for Miss Sally and Mr. Kent.

Sally patted Margaret's hand. "Now, don't be so hard on your brother; times like this are trying for everyone." Annoyed that Kent would leave her on her own after just rescuing her and Margaret from a bear. She was relieved to see him return with the stranger she had seen him talking to earlier.

"You men look like you've accomplished your goal. Congratulations."

"Yup, we're all set now if any trouble comes our way." Josh said, triumphantly waving a box of ammo over his head."

Ray came up behind them and patted Kent on the back, "My wife is adding more turnips to the soup, so there will be enough for all of us. Come, follow me."

Chapter 12

*I freed a thousand slaves. I
Could have freed a thousand more
If only they knew
They were slaves.*
—Harriet Tubman

"Come in, come in," Anna, Ray's wife, said, greeting them with a big smile. She encouraged them to walk through the small parlor, which expanded into a dining room with a large table, that could seat them all, with little effort.

The soup smelled wonderful. Sally assumed that the enticing aroma was at least partly due to their ravenous hunger, which, at this point, would make anything taste like a virtual feast. The deer was large enough that they each had a generous portion, but that was two days ago. Their stomachs were screaming to be whole again.

As they devoured the hearty soup, all agreed that Anna had to be the most fabulous cook in all of Georgia.

"You have a lovely home, Ray and Anna," Kent observed out loud.

Ray smiled, "Thank you kindly; I made most of the furniture. That's what I do; I make and repair items for the people of this town. He took another sip of the savory soup. "At least that's what I used to do before this blasted war.

"There are plenty of trees for me to get my wood, but with the Union blockades in place, I haven't been able to acquire other things I need for my trade like stains or oils to finish the pieces nicely. Most of it came from Atlanta. Thank God we have our land to grow our food and livestock still. Without them, we'd be destitute."

When they had finished eating, they all remained at the table, as there was no room in the parlor for all of them.

Damian and Josh agreed it would be best if they were the ones to remove themselves from the group for a while. They were giving the others room to have their conversation in private.

They were grateful to ride along with them to Saint Augustine. Though they still felt like intruders, having no connection to the rest of them, like a dog who takes on the care of a kitten whose mother rejected him because he is different from the rest of the litter. But the dog nurtures it as she would if it were one of her pups. The dog metaphor is Kent.

Damian and Josh were content to sit on the front porch enjoying the cold February breeze of Florida. When they settled in the two wicker chairs available, Damian announced, "This is great; I mean, its winter, probably lots of snow up north. I ain't never going back to that bitter cold. What about you, Josh?"

"Yeah, it does feel good, but it ain't home where I grew up." Josh indicated that he didn't care one way or the other with a shrug of his shoulders and then glanced at a jackrabbit running from an unseen prey. "I suppose I'll stay in Florida for a while; then, when I can get me a horse, I'll head back to Arkansas."

Inside, Anna apologized for the lack of room, explaining that they had six children living in this house at one time. "Now they're all grown. We had four girls and two boys. Two of our girls, Christine, and Laura, died when they were two and three years old. Nancy and Louise are married, and living in Tennessee. They married brothers. Isn't that ironic?" She said with an almost sarcastic chuckle. She was smiling weakly, proud, and sad for her daughters. "That's why the table is so big. But of course, Ray made it."

Henry was almost afraid to ask, not wanting to upset the woman who so graciously fed them and welcomed them into her home. But his curiosity got the better of him. Where are your boys?"

Ray responded to Henry's probe "They joined the Confederate army in Jacksonville when the war began. Bill and Gabe came home once last year for just two days, then they had to return or be shot as deserters. I begged them to stay. I mean, what's the difference if they are wounded here or on the battlefield? At least here, I can give them some protection. But no. They said they didn't want to have accusations of being cowards thrown at them. Last we heard; they were in South Carolina." Looking to his wife for confirmation, he asked her, "That was, what, two months ago we got their letters?"

Anna took a handkerchief from her apron pocket, wiped her nose, nodded yes, then turned toward the kitchen.

She then turned her attention to the children. Looking at Kent, she asked, "Are these your children?"

"No," Henry replied before Kent or Sally could speak. But Kent quickly jumped into the conversation.

"We found them alone in their house a way back."

With the back of his hand, Luke wiped his mouth of the soup's residue. Then he interrupted Kent, "Them Yankee soldiers killed our ma and left us with no food." A tear rolled down his cheek, which he quickly wiped as he thought, *that's* what his pa always said.

Anna stood up and walked to the opposite side of the table where the children were sitting. She embraced them, saying, "You poor dears."

Anna attempted to cheer them up, announcing that she had made a peach pie. "How would you kids like to have the first choice of a piece of the pie?" Even Amy, who still had not said a word, nodded her head yes in unison with her brother and sister. The forlorn expressions on their faces had disappeared into smiles of anticipation.

"Our mama used to make the best blueberry pie, that is…," Margaret stated before Anna steered the conversation in a different direction.

"Oh, now let's not think about that. God is taking good care of your mama now, and I'm going to take good care of you." With that said Anna gently led Margaret into the kitchen. "You can help me serve."

Kent asked, "So tell me, Ray, what is the latest news from the war? We've had no access to any news since we left Savannah."

With a furrowed brow, Ray hesitated while he gathered his thoughts. Kent wasn't sure if the man's creased face was due to age or tension. It wouldn't be surprising if it were a combination of both. The war had cost thousands of lives, but it had aged immensely for those who were still alive.

Ray took a long hard look at Kent. He sipped his tea slowly and wondered how much this young man wanted to know.

"There hasn't been a battle here in these parts since Olustee in February, almost a year ago. Thank God."

"Well, we heard cannons and gunfire back a way, not sure what town we were in, but it was mighty scary, feeling like we were walking right into a battle."

"I'm sure what you heard came from Fort Myers unfortunately, it continues to be a 'devil's nest' led by Lieutenant James D. Green. He and his Federalists are terrorizing the Jacksonville area with raids to plantations and large farms. From what I've heard,

Green had orders to capture as many horses, livestock, and food as they could. But, of course, the cowards attacked only those homes where just women and children resided, leaving them to fend for themselves, much like these poor children who were left destitute.

"What's happening in Jacksonville, we feel it here." Waving his arms, he encircled the room, illustrating the expanse of an occupied city. "You can see for yourself the enemy walks everywhere in this town as they pass through to Florida. But not before they remind us by their presence and vulgarity that although we are not behind bars, we are still their prisoners."

Kent was silent for a few moments; Ray had given him a lot to absorb. He had traveled as little as possible during the war since it was common knowledge that traveling was not a wise decision. So, any wisdom he'd acquired was from reading the weekly *Savannah Morning News.*

Ray looked at Kent, waiting patiently at the table for his response, afraid that he had supplied the visitor with more information than he could handle. But Kent surprised him when he asked Ray, "When I go to Jacksonville, will Sally and the children be safe?"

"You still want to go there?" Ray had a look of concern. "You amaze me; I didn't think you would want to take the risk of entering that city. Why don't you just bypass it and go straight on to Saint Augustine? It's only a two-day ride from Jacksonville."

Suddenly feeling uncomfortable, Kent stood up, "Can we move into the other room? I'm tired of days sitting on a hard wagon bench. Your table is so beautiful," Then with a chuckle, he added, but I would prefer a chair with some padding." Stretching and moving toward the fireplace, Kent turned to Ray, who had followed him to the front room.

"I realize the distance between the two cities, but your town has little to offer; even though your wife has graciously taken care of us. We won't take advantage of your kindness any longer. We must move on in the morning. We're anxious to get to our destination."

Ray patted Kent on the back of his shoulder as he rose to retire for the evening. "I understand how you feel. I just wish we could be of more help. Get some sleep now. I'll see you in the morning."

Kent remained sitting in front of the fire and watching the flames dance as they elicited thoughts of Sally and the children. *Do I want to risk putting them in danger? But if we don't go, we won't get to Saint Augustine, Gertrude's cousin Claire, or letters from home. We've come too far to turn back now; besides, we don't even know what condition Savannah will be in when we return.* Ray had pleaded ignorance about Savannah; he hadn't heard any news about that part of Georgia

Kent made up his mind; they would continue to Saint Augustine. As far as he could see, they had no choice.

Chapter 13

*The river was dyed with
the blood of the
slaughtered for two hundred yards.*
—General Nathan Bedford Forrest

Upstairs, Sally and Anna tucked the children into warm, comfortable beds. Anna hugged Luke, wishing that he were one of her boys who had returned home safe. Luke wanted to protest; she held him so fast that it felt suffocating. Even his mother had never hugged him like this. Nevertheless, he welcomed the warmth of another body being close to him once more. Luke hugged her back.

Sally made sure the girls were snug in their beds on the other side of the room. She looked into Amy's pleading brown eyes; there was no smile, just a look of hope. Sally felt her heart break for the child. She wondered how this child would ever survive with the trauma she was carrying deep in her soul. Margaret lay next to her,

Leaning over the girls, Sally adjusted the covers for them, saying softly, "Remember you're safe now. No harm will come to you, not while you're with us."

Reaching under the covers, smiling, Sally gave them a little tickle. To her surprise and delight, Amy giggled. Sally was so thrilled she leaned in to offer the girls another vigorous hug.

When she did, Amy whispered in her ear, "Don't go away."

Startled by Amy's voice and what she said, Sally sat erect, looking at both girls, "I promise that I will stay with you until we can reunite you with your daddy when he comes home."

From behind, she heard another voice as Kent stepped into the room and added his thought. "I'll be with you, too, until we find your father. Will that be all right, children?

The children greeted Kent in a positive response—a chorus of yes.

Overcome with emotion, Anna brushed a tear from her cheek and left the room.

Walking out of the children's room, Kent and Sally stopped in the hallway. "We need to talk, but not here. Let's go back downstairs; we'll have more privacy there," he suggested.

Sally wasn't sure what Kent would want to discuss in private; the man had been distant but polite the entire trip. So, she wasn't afraid to be alone with him, though Sally still felt his agitation toward her each time he looked at her. She didn't like how he seemed to be staring at her so often; the implication made her feel uncomfortable. It never occurred to Sally that his "staring" could be admiration. Her curiosity was piqued, and she agreed to hear what he had to say.

"I had a long talk with Ray this evening. He tells me that the Union army has captured Jacksonville and Saint Augustine. He says the local commanders aren't as hostile as the Union army has been to the rest of the South, but they are good at making life difficult for the residents with excessive rules and unkind behavior. We should be able to get there in about two days. Do you still want to go there?"

She was relieved that his "talk" was only about a trivial matter, as far as Sally was concerned. Kent's interception of her as a damsel in distress, a princess in fairy tales flattered her at the same time as it made her giggle at how naive the male species can be sometimes. But then she thought, *why would a guy like Kent be reading fairy tales? It had to be because of Frank.* She could see Frank as a little boy in her mind, begging his big grouchy brother to read him fairy tales with princesses.

"Oh, I've handled rude men plenty of times; remember how rude you were the first time I met you at your mother's?"

Kent was embarrassed that she would recall that particular day, but he still had to chuckle at the thought.

"Yes, I remember that day. I wish you could forget it."

"Why, Kent Preston, I do believe you're blushing?"

Annoyance gripped his face as he denied her accusation. "No, I'm not; besides, men don't blush," Kent said, while he shifted nervously from one foot to the other as he stood in front of the fire.

"Well, I think it's very becoming when a man can show his emotions; your brother is excellent about that."

"Hmm," was the only response Kent could give. "Which brings me back to the question about how you want to proceed with our journey to Saint Augustine."

"Oh, my, yes, let's see what mischief the Union army is up to in Jacksonville. I'd love to spit in one of their faces."

Infuriated by her obsession to get even somehow, Kent responded, "Jumping Jehoshaphat! Am I going to have to keep you gagged while we're there? Or would you instead prefer to get us killed?"

"Oh, don't be such a fuddy-duddy! I won't spit in their face; I just meant that I would like to."

Kent visibly relaxed, "All right, then, we'll leave first thing in the morning." Kent started to turn toward the stairs next to the room where he would sleep next to Luke; Sally would sleep on the opposite side with Margaret and Amy. But before he left, he had second thoughts. He turned back to Sally, who was smoothing her stray hairs from her face; he hesitated for a moment, admiring her beautiful heart-shaped face.

"I just want to say that I couldn't help seeing and hearing what you told the girls when you tucked them into bed. You're very good with them; I had never thought of you as the motherly type. I hope someday you'll have a child of your own; you'll make a great mother."

"That's just what your brother and I want. I love children, and so does Frank. Oh, and thank you."

Kent nodded "sure" before they each went to their separate beds.

Chapter 14

*I was now taken to
Andersonville, where I remained
about seven months, and
the horrors I met there
it is useless for me to
describe.*
—Henry Hernbaker, Union Soldier
Captured at Gettysburg

Anna made sure that they had a belly full of food before heading to Jacksonville in the morning. She served a generous feast for them of eggs, hotcakes, syrup, biscuits, jam, and coffee. It had been quite some time since any of them had seen a breakfast like this. Which prompted Kent to ask, "How is it that the Northern army did not take your home and chickens while the rest of the town lost everything? Especially the coffee—where did it come from?" Kent inquired, as he sipped the savory treat. Anna, about to pour a cup for Henry, heard hearing Kent's question, she hesitated to reply, wondering how much she could trust them with personal information. paused her action, when deciding how far she could trust these visitors. In her mind, although she liked them, she couldn't forget that they were still strangers. Ray, seeing his wife's struggle to answer the question, answered Kent's question himself. "A friend of ours shared a can of the precious commodity with us he found after a troop of soldiers abandoned a campsite where the union soldiers had carelessly left it deserted for him to embezzle."

They devoured their tasty food with grateful hearts, then thanked Anna and Ray profusely for their home and hospitality before they departed.

Anna shed a few tears while hugging each of the children, wishing they could stay with her. In her mind, she argued that she had a loving home for them, while Sally and Kent had no idea where they would live. They had never met Claire and didn't know what kind of house she owned.

But even arguing with herself, she lost the fight. The defeat came when she understood the children had to wait for their father to return, if he did. She couldn't ignore that part of their lives. If the father was alive, he would know where to find them from the note Kent had nailed to the front door. One thing was for sure, she would never forget any of them, and when this war was over, she promised herself, she would visit them, no matter where they were.

Kent rode in silence at the start of their trek; he was too deep in thought about what Ray had told him

Once they got to Jacksonville, they would need ammo, food, shelter, and horses. The problem was Ray said their paper money was no good anymore. The only currency accepted in a small town like Saint Mary's coined. However, paper money had not been abolished everywhere. When they had left Savannah two weeks ago, paper money still had it's worth. Whether it was still that way back home, he couldn't know for sure. Kent wasn't too surprised at that bit of news. He had been aware of the dwindling Southern economy for some time, which was why he was sure that the war would be over soon. *How much longer can the South hold on to this war?* Kent reasoned to himself.

Fortunately, Kent had thought to bring all the coins he had in the store before he left Savannah.

In his haste to get Sally and flee the city, he never counted the money but just dumped it all into a box. So, he had no idea if they had enough to pay for all their needs. He hoped that Sally or Henry had some coins of their own.

"How far did Ray say we have to go to Jacksonville?" Henry asked while sitting between Kent and Sally.

"Two to three days, he said."

Sally pouted, "That means sleeping in this wagon again." Then, with a sigh, she said dreamily, "It was so nice to sleep in a bed again." Then, her thoughts turned to Saint Augustine, creating a spark in her speech and actions, as though someone had wound her up like a spinning top. "We have to get to my cousin quickly so that we can end our use of this wagon. I'm so sick of it."

"I'll do the best I can…."

"And no more than one night in Jacksonville, promise?"

"Sally, I can't promise you anything. We've been on the road long enough for you to know that lots of things can happen to slow us down."

Henry patted Sally's hand. "That's right, Kent is speaking the truth. He'll get us there as fast as he can."

Sally nodded, feeling a bit ashamed for making demands on Kent. He had taken good care of all of them up until now. She had no reason to doubt he would continue to lead them to safety in Saint Augustine. She leaned forward, looking at Kent, and said in a low voice, "I'm sorry."

Josh and Damian were in the back of the wagon with the children, against Sally's better judgment. She still felt uncomfortable around them, especially Josh. She tried making excuses so the children could sit in the back of the wagon with her, not the men. But feeling defeated when losing an argument, especially with children. She could hardly argue with them, particularly the children, who, for some unknown reason, had wanted to be with them in the back. "They're fun," Luke told Sally when she tried to convince them to have her or Henry in the end with them. Even more surprising was Kent's stamp of approval for such an arrangement. Sally was certain she had heard Kent wrong, "this was the first time Kent ever agreed with her.

Kent's motive was to have Sally next to him.

As they rode, Sally pondered when and how things had changed. Why hadn't she noticed how Josh was always telling them stories about his life back in Arkansas while she was confident those tales were just a bunch of lies? Or when Damian would show them how to make shadow puppets with their hands in front of the evening fires. She would hear them giggle with awe and delight at the magical transformations Damian's fingers became.

Instead, she had considered Josh and Damian's efforts as pure nonsense in her observations, never believing that the children would want more from them.

Even Damian was in awe of the alteration in Josh's personality when he was around the children. It was the only time the man's sour look turned into a smile. He didn't want to ask Josh why his temperament changed when the children played with him; perhaps these children reminded him of the wife and children he lost in Arkansas. But not wanting to antagonize Josh any further, Damian proceeded with his inquiry with discretion for fear of an even more intense, maybe violent reaction in Josh. Damian wasn't sure of what response Josh would take.

Then one day, while they played a game of Pick-up Sticks, he again saw Josh laughing with the children. Luke was picking up the stakes as fast as he could. Finally, however, Margaret won the game once more. Josh always let the children prevail; he'd even helped Amy win a round earlier. Then the children went to see what Sally was doing. Damian's curiosity could wait no longer.

With his furious face showing again, Damian asked Josh, "So why is it that I or anybody else only get to see you smile when one of those kids is near you?"

"That's not true. I smile sometimes; you've just never noticed. Besides, how anybody can smile these days is beyond me."

"Well, what are you going to do when those kids are gone, taken back home with their pa?"

"I haven't thought about it. The thing is those children, especially the little ones, remind me of my lost little girl. I look at Amy's sweet face and see my Edith. She was five years old when I left her. She and my wife were the loves of my life; I reckon they were the only love I ever had in my life. My ma and pa threw me out of the house when I was twelve years old; they said I was no good. So, I ain't got much to smile about, except those kids."

As bad a time as he'd had with Josh at Andersonville, Damian found himself counting his blessings. He might have thought his blessings were few, but his troubles now paled in comparison to what Josh had just told him.

"I'm so sorry, Josh; I had no idea what your life was before the war. Forget I ever asked."

"Yeah, you and all the others with your spoiled lives will never understand someone like me, and that's just dandy as far as I'm concerned."

Sally had to admit, though, that it was beautiful riding up front on this gorgeous day. The sun shone with golden rays, reflected between the white "cotton" clouds surrounded by a lovely pale blue sky.

Palm trees were beginning to become a more frequent sight the more they traveled south toward their destination. The change in the land's topography made them all positive that Jacksonville was closer than they thought.

It was now February 8; they had been on the road since December twenty-second. So nobody could blame them for wanting to settle in one place.

Then to Sally, Kent, and Henry's surprise, Josh, Damian, and the children began singing the southern rendition of "Yankee Doodle," a song from the American Revolutionary War changed to "Dixie Doodle."

The tune was so contagious that the three in the wagon's front seat couldn't resist joining in.

Chapter 15

"Weather claimed remnants
Of clothing, rusty gun-barrels
And bayonets tarnished
Brasses and equipment
With blackening bones and
Grinning skulls marked
The memorable field."
—Union Private Warren Goss reaching Chancellorsville and
the blackened ruins of the old Chancellor House, 1864

When they pulled into Jacksonville the sight was far different than any they had seen since leaving Savannah. Finally, there was a city with life. People walked the wooden sidewalks and horses, and wagons packed the muddy road, filling the air with the stench of manure and mold. Children played "dueling" games with sticks, while women walked arm in arm, looking in store windows on the main road. Mostly, there were lots of blue-uniformed men, just as Ray had described. But to Sally's delight, she could see a mercantile store, a church, a hotel, a print shop, and a dressmaker, among other retailers.

Kent parked the wagon in front of the hotel. Across the street was the sheriff's office, but the sheriff wore a blue uniform like most men in town, from what he could see. Kent shrugged it off; he wasn't surprised that the Union army was now the law of Jacksonville.

As soon as he stopped, Sally jumped down from the wagon, announcing to the children, "Come on, let's do some shopping. We'll get you some clothes and ribbons for your hair, girls, and if they have it, we'll get some candy for you, Luke, to share with your sisters.

Eager to see what Sally could find for them, they rushed to her waiting side.

Damian and Josh had one thought on their mind—the saloon. "Finally, a beer—something I've been dreamin' of since this war began," Josh confessed to Damian as soon as they hit the ground.

Kent was still standing nearby, allowing the horses to drink from the trough. As Josh and Damian began to pass him, Kent grabbed Damian's arm. "Two things. One, do you have money to buy ammo for your guns? I think it would be a good idea to have your guns loaded before you do any drinking. Don't you agree with the number of Union soldiers occupying this town? Second, speaking of money, I hope you have coins cause that's about all that is accepted here."

"Yeah, we got money. Not much, it's our last miserable pay from the prison," Josh explained.

"Yeah, you're right. Who knows what these damn Yankees will do given a chance to raise hell," Damian stated?

Kent decided to stay by the wagon to make sure that Sally and the children returned safely.

Henry had been quiet, "I don't like the look of all this. Too many Federalists for my liking."

"Let's face it, Henry, this is the way life will be for us from now on. The South has lost; if we had won, we wouldn't be seeing all these Federalists. Have you seen the American flag above the courthouse?"

"Yeah, I saw it. Sad. A real sad sight to see." Henry was a devout Southerner; Georgia was where he wanted to be. So, his heart broke at the sight of the American flag flying where a Confederate flag once waved proudly.

The two were quiet while they deliberated their situation. Each man was wondering in his way if they had done the right thing by fleeing Savannah. Henry had pondered the escalating feeling ever since he heard that the Union army occupied Florida. The thought had gnawed at him for days—was this flight from home worth being back in the hands of the enemy?

Kent's thoughts were of Sally; she was holding together much better than he had thought she would. What he knew of her when they had left Savannah was that she was spoiled, rude, and too demanding. But over time on this excursion, she had changed dramatically. *Or,* as Kent thought further, *is it I who has changed so much?*

Henry announced, "I think I'll go see what the rest of them are doing in the mercantile store."

Kent, with his arms crossed across his chest, nodded silently, then spoke, "I'll wait here for all of you to come back. Then I'll see about sleeping arrangements."

"Hey, maybe tonight, when we're settled, I'll give you a shave and haircut. I got my tools with me. Never travel without them."

Kent smiled, "That's an excellent idea, Henry. I'd be obliged."

"Good, I'll see you back here." He yanked up his sagging pants once more before he headed to the mercantile store.

"Henry, do you think we were right to start this war?

Henry stopped in his short trek to the store and turned back to Kent. He didn't have to think before he answered, "In the beginning, it seemed like the only thing we could do to preserve our way of life, but now I'm aware, as I know you are, too, that we should never have started this damn war. It cost too much."

Chapter 16

*My duties…were numerous and often laborious; the family was
on the increase continually, and everyone added increased labor
and responsibility. And this was the case with the typical
Southern woman.*
—Victoria V. Clayton, wife of Confederate General Henry D. Clayton of Alabama

Kent had been waiting by the wagon only a few minutes when two soldiers approached him. He had noticed them when they came into Jacksonville. They seemed bored while leaning against a post in front of the saloon. They carried guns and swords on their belts. Kent thought it was odd since they weren't in battle and the weapons were unnecessary. Instead, it appeared they were looking for trouble. Kent and his entourage looked like the perfect candidates to break the spell of an otherwise lackluster day.

"Is this your wagon?" asked the plump dark-haired soldier, who gave no introduction or welcome to the city.

"Yes, it's my wagon."

The other soldier, taller with fair skin, had scars from measles or smallpox. Quickly he jumped in with his opinionated thoughts. "Where did you get this wagon?"

Kent looked around, wondering why his wagon was such a curiosity to these soldiers. "It was my father's; he had it for all of my life."

"So why isn't your father driving this?"

"What is this? It's none of your business; I'm not in your army or the Confederate army. I'm a civilian. plain and simple."

The plump soldier instructed the taller one to inspect the wagon for military insignia.

As Kent watched the tall soldier stroll down one side of the wagon, another soldier appeared. This one did introduce himself while looking straight at Kent. "I'm Corporal Yates. What seems to be the problem?"

Before Kent could respond, the other soldier saluted, then said, "We suspect, sir, that this man may have stolen a military wagon."

With his hands behind his back, the corporal looked at Kent. "You do know there is punishment in prison for stealing military property?"

"This is not stolen property. I told this other man that my wagon was my father's until he passed away some years ago. Now may I go?"

"No," said the plump soldier, "we're not done with you yet." With that, the soldier took hold of Kent's upper arm. "I have more questions to ask."

The corporal satisfied that these two soldiers could handle the situation, announced to them, "You take care of this while I have other work to do; I'll be in my office."

Getting back to business, the soldier asked, "So why do you need such a large wagon? What are you carrying, supplies for the rebs?"

"No, you can…,'

Just then, he heard Sally's objections, "No, leave me alone. No, no, I'm not interested."

Kent couldn't see what was happening to Sally; her voice was coming from the side of the wagon. He knew for sure, though, that she needed his help. But when he tried to turn and break free of the soldier's grip, the soldier just tightened his grasp on Kent's arm., Not knowing what else to do, with a fit of rage, he took a hard swing at the man's jaw. Fortunately, he landed the punch just where it was most effective, and the soldier fell to the ground. That's when all hell broke loose.

Kent rushed to Sally. He could see that the soldier, who was supposed to be inspecting the wagon, was trying to grab Sally's purse, with the drawstrings wrapped around her wrist. Kent was within steps of being by her side, when Josh appeared, yelling at the would-be thief, "Get away from that woman!" Instead of heeding Josh's warning, the soldier fired at Josh. Kent lunged for the soldier's gun. At the same time, the soldier Kent had punched fired his weapon at Kent, and the bullet hit him in the back above his waist. He fell to the ground bleeding.

Kent heard another gunshot, but he didn't know who fired it.

Sally cried and screamed for help as she knelt beside Kent. He was barely conscious. As she looked around, people were surrounding her, "We'll take care of him, Ma'am, someone said, "We have a small hospital; we'll take him there." She looked at their faces, so kind, so compassionate. She could also see Damian in the distance being escorted away by two soldiers. Asking nobody, in particular, she inquired, "Where are they taking that man?"

"He's the one who killed the soldier who shot your man." There were too many legs and arms surrounding her. Voices were blending into one another, leaving her unable to interpret what they said or impossible to know who said what, until one woman's voice, Sally heard above the others. Still kneeling on the ground next to Kent, she watched as three men picked Kent up and carried him away. Hysterical now, Sally bellowed, "Where are you taking him?"

A woman spoke as she gently raised Sally by her shoulders.

"Come on; I'll show you where the hospital is. Then, I'll have some men take your wagon and the horses to the livery stable."

Once Sally was on her feet, the woman put a welcome hand out to her. "My name is Elinor—"

Sally abruptly interrupted her. "No, no, where are Henry and the children?"

"Children, you have children?"

"Yes, well, no, they aren't...,"

At that moment, Sally saw Henry running toward her. "Oh, my God, I saw them shoot Kent. Is he alive?"

Before Sally could answer Henry's question, she had one for him. "The children, where are they? Are they safe?"

"Yes, yes, I left them in the care of the lady who runs the mercantile store. But I'm afraid they saw it all. I left them crying."

"Oh, dear, what should I do? First, I must see how Kent is, but the children—they need me too."

"I'll go check on Kent's condition. You go to the children, and then when I get a report about Kent, I'll come back and tell you."

Before they parted, Sally placed a gentle hand on Henry's shoulder. "They said that Josh was dead." Then, with tears in her eyes, she questioned Josh's motives. "He died defending me. Why did he do that?"

"We'll never know, my dear," Henry responded as he patted her hand. "I guess he wasn't all bad; besides, he may have been trying to atone for trying to molest you."

With that, Sally turned toward where the frightened children waited.

Rushing into the store, she swooped all three into her outstretched arms, embracing them with reassuring words.

Chapter 17

Sherman's orders were that
Atlanta should be destroyed by
the rearguard of the army and two
regiments were detailed
for that purpose.
—David P. Conyngham, a correspondent
for the *New York Herald*

By nightfall, Sally had found out from Henry that although Kent's wound was severe, the doctor was confident that he would survive the ordeal, although it would take a few days of recovery before they could take him to Saint Augustine. They would have to have him travel on a bed in the back of the wagon. "We're stuck here until Kent recovers enough for him to travel, so we best get settled in."

"We better get a room at the hotel then. I'll gather our stuff from the wagon." Henry offered.

"You'll need help, Henry. You can't get everything out of the wagon yourself. I'll check at the hotel if there is someone who can help you."

Henry shook his head sadly, "I sure didn't realize what a help Josh and Damian were when they were here. I sure feel bad for them both."

"Well, I don't, Josh was fat and ugly, angry all the time, and I'll never forgive him for what he did to me. Damian was a bit better, although he had no manners either."

"This is why we have war. Your young'uns don't know how to forgive or learn to live with others."

"Oh, Henry, your generation wasn't much better. Land sakes, you had the Revolutionary War with General George Washington."

Harry clicked his tongue and nodded. "You surely have a point, Sally." Once said, he strolled toward the livery stable. Sally took the children by their hands and entered the hotel.

As she approached the front desk, she was greeted by a bespectacled gentleman with graying hair and a robust build. "Good afternoon, miss. Are you checking in?"

"Yes, I'll need two rooms with enough space to sleep two in one room and three in the other. Oh, and is there someone who can give my travel mate a hand carrying our belongings?"

Before he could answer, a soldier in blue appeared beside the desk clerk. "I'll take over from here, Jed."

Sally was not too surprised after what had happened out on the street a few hours ago. But she had also hoped that episode was behind them, and this intrusion was an annoyance to her.

"What do you want now, officer? Isn't it enough that you killed one of my travel mates and seriously injured my brother-in-law? Have you no shame? As you can see, I have innocent children with me. Will you harass them too?"

"No, ma'am, we simply want you to sign a voucher or take a pledge."

"What voucher? What pledge?"

"It's merely a pledge that you will obey all rules in this town set by the Union army and never voice allegiance to the South again. If you don't, then you and the children will be exiled to Green Cove Springs across the Saint Johns River."

Lifting her proud head, she replied, "I cannot leave until my brother-in-law recuperates enough to travel to Saint Augustine. Your men shot Kent. So that makes it your fault that we're still here. And I will never pledge my support for the death of the South. I promise you, as soon as Kent is fit to travel, we'll be happy to be gone from this awful town."

Tipping his hat to Sally, he backed away as he said, "I will give you what's given to every person who comes into this town: three days to make up their minds about what they want to do."

Sally ignored his comment; instead, she asked again about the rooms just as Henry walked in carrying her trunk and his travel bag. "Kent's belongings are coming with a boy I found around the stable. The guy there says the boy worked for him. Like these kids, he's got no home anymore. He's eight years old, poor guy."

"What will happen to these orphaned children?"

The desk clerk shrugged his shoulders. "Don't know. There's an orphanage in Tampa, but that's south of us; it's a few days' ride from here. But who is gonna take them?

The clerk then handed them their keys as the soldier left, saying nothing more about the homeless child.

This young boy and his story touched Sally's, compassionate heart. According to the desk clerk, many orphaned children roamed the streets of this town, begging or finding food wherever they could. As did every orphan in the other cities in the South.

Chapter 18

And now, while the nation is
rejoicing…it is suddenly
plunged into the
Deepest sorrow by the most
brutal murder of its
loved Chief"
—Sergeant Lucius Barber, April 1865

Henry and Luke shared the same bed in one room, while Sally and the girls snuggled up to each other in the other room right next to the boys.

Both Sally and Henry would compare how they slept the night before when they all joined together in the hotel dining room for breakfast. Of course, it wasn't as grand as the hotel lobby and dining room in Brunswick, but the aroma of ham, eggs, grits, and real coffee due to the presence of the Federalists, offered a world full of all kinds of possibilities for weary travelers.

As they entered, Amy looked around the dining room, then turned to look up to Sally, asking in her soft sweet voice, "But where is Mr. Kent?"

Sally bent down to Amy's level and explained to her that Kent was still in the hospital. "The doctors are taking real good care of him. Pretty soon, he'll be back with us. But we have to wait until he's well."

Sally had dressed in her blue-and-green-plaid dress with lace and a black ribbon tied in a bow at the neck and with oversized puffed long sleeves. Her hoop skirt swayed slightly to the right and left as they walked.

Sally had bought the girls a dress each in the mercantile store the previous day, which they now wore with pride, and matching colored ribbons in their hair. Yellow for Amy and pink for Margaret.

People stared at them as they crossed the lobby to the dining room; they looked like an average family—father, daughter, and three grandchildren out for a breakfast treat. It would be an acceptable conclusion if it were not for the war that was still going on; people didn't dress in their best clothes, simply because there were no "best" clothes anymore. Things that were taken for granted before the war now became luxuries everyone wished they had, such as a needle and thread to mend the once "good" clothes. Even a bar of soap was hard to come by, making it difficult to keep anything looking clean. If you did possess a bar of soap, you shared it with the rest of the family, but no one else. Soap had become a precious commodity along with salt and a few other staples once easy to obtain.

While in the mercantile store, Sally observed that although the store had an abundance of merchandise, there was still a shortage of many common goods, unlike other towns they had passed through. Even with the blockades instituted, they could recall what stores in Savannah had for sale was far more than Jacksonville offered.

Once the children had their plates of scrambled eggs, biscuits, bacon, and cups of milk, Henry and Sally put their heads together as the children gobbled their food with gusto.

"As soon as we finish breakfast, I want to be with Kent. Will you watch the children for me? We'll take turns. When I'm finished visiting with him, then you can see him."

Just then, a waiter served them their eggs, ham, biscuits, and coffee. Henry had only swallowed one mouthful of his food and was about to speak when they were interrupted by Elinor sitting down at their table without invitation. "I'm sorry to barge in like this, but I wanted to ask about your man. I do hope he'll survive this ordeal."

"Yes, the doctor is confident that he will recuperate, but it will be a few days before he's able to travel again," Sally assured her.

"Thank you for asking," Henry said as he patted her hand.

"Well, since you are staying a few days, I need to warn you about a couple of things going on in this town. First, they'll order you to sign our pledge to the Federalist law, which requires obeying all their rules and never voicing any support for the Southern cause. If you don't, they'll ship you from Jacksonville to Green Cove Springs. From what I hear, it's a pretty dismal place, just gray dirt. They can hardly grow anything there, and it's isolated, so people are unable to acquire many necessities

"Yes, yes, I heard about all of that yesterday when I was checking into the hotel. An officer rudely interrupted the clerk who was serving me, then told me all about this pledge and what would happen if I didn't sign it."

Henry was astonished. He touched Sally's arm and turned to face her, then admonished her, "You didn't tell me about this. Why didn't you?"

"Oh, I gave him a piece of my mind, telling him that I would never forsake the South, my home, or my family."

Elinor was quicker than Henry to ask, "What did the officer say?"

"He said he would give me the customary three days to think it over. Henry? They haven't talked to you yet. That's good since we are together; that will give us four days until we have to get out of here, which will enable Kent time to heal and travel."

"But there is more I need to tell you," Elinor stated. Looking at both Henry and Sally, she placed her dainty lace gloves on the table. "Sally, you have got to be careful with your mouth here. You're lucky you ran into a patient soldier. He's the exception. Believe me; there are women and children in these jails for lesser crimes than you just committed. So be careful what you say and do."

"But how do you live here like this? Why not move away?" Henry inquired.

"Where would I go? Here is my home. I've lived here all my life. I met and married my husband here, and our daughter is buried here next to her father. Elinor explained as she looked around the familiar downtown, she lovingly called home.

Sally took Elinor's hand, "I'm so sorry. When did this happen?

"My daughter, Nora, died when she was four years old. I adored her; she was my greatest joy in life—that is, as was my husband. She died when she caught a fever, which was eight years ago. My husband's body came back here from the battle of Olustee, which was in February, a year ago this month. That's also when the Federalists took this town. One more thing, most people just ignore the soldiers as much as they can. Even if you hate them, as most do, learn to pretend to be cordial and accommodating. Show them Southern hospitality.

"There have been parties in this town, with both the Northern army and Southerners having a good enjoyable time."

"I suppose once you remove the guns and threats, people will forget for a brief time why hostilities even existed," Henry observed.

Elinor nodded in agreement. Her bonnet swayed with her head movement. "Recently, there was a wedding of a Northern officer and a Southern woman."

"Really? My word! That is amazing; maybe there is hope for all of us yet."

"Just don't forget when walking about the town the soldiers feel they own the walkways. So, they will not step aside for you or any other lady. But they will be a gentleman when and if they feel like it."

Chapter 19

Our Federal Union
must be preserved.
—President Andrew Jackson

Sally sat beside Kent's hospital bed. He was conscious now, his fever was gone, and his color was improving.

"You don't have to sit with me. Go to the children; they need you," Kent uttered breathlessly. The doctor, standing nearby, was concerned; he had warned Sally that Kent was still not fit enough to travel.

Although it was an effort to talk, Kent asked how Henry was, if he was well and looking after the children. Kent imagined something was wrapped around his neck, squeezing, preventing his voice from projecting. Kent felt he was shouting, but in reality, Sally could barely understand him.

Sally kept her face and ear close to Kent, not wanting to miss a word he had to say. "You don't have to stay with me."

"Nonsense, this is where I want to be and where I'll stay." Then, hesitating a moment, she added, "Except I wish it weren't here in this boorish town."

Kent gave a weak smile, looking into her beautiful eyes; he was glad she wanted to be with him. That he could not ignore or even wanted to

Sally was delighted to see the smile on Kent's face, as feeble as it was. The smile reassured her that she would not lose him. Not today, not before they got to Saint Augustine, not ever if she could help it.

During the past few days, she had come to realize that she was spending a lot of her time fretting about Kent. As she brushed her hair while looking in the hotel room mirror before visiting Kent, Sally thought about the possibility that she was drawing closer to Kent with each passing day. At the same time, thoughts of Frank were fading with each passing day.

She had agonized about his health all last night, unable to sleep; she prayed as she had never prayed before. Though she had to admit that Kent was uppermost on her mind, it was almost like Frank had become an afterthought. Silently, lying next to the girls in their bed, she had gotten little sleep while admonishing herself for not being a trustworthy wife. As the days and weeks passed and the longer the span from when she last heard from Frank grew longer, his memory began to blur.

"Do you think of your brother these days?"

Kent frowned, his eyes focused on Sally, but his thoughts were on her question. "Of course, I think of Frank; I desperately hope that when we come to Saint Augustine, there will be a letter from him." He coughed, then groaned with the pain the cough brought on.

Sally started to rise to search for doctor she had seen earlier, but it was apparent that he had left the premises or a nurse, most of whom were nuns. She wanted to find someone who could relieve his pain. But Kent grabbed her wrist. "No, don't go. It—"

"You need something to help you, mayb—"

"It's all right It happens now and again. The doctor says it should stop when I'm stronger."

Relieved, Sally sat back down on the hard wooden chair. Kent reached out for her hand again. She took it, noticing that his hand, which had felt cold, had become warm again.

"So, tell me any news about the war?"

"Just the same as before. What I do hear, though, is talk that they may arrest you after you're fit for striking an officer, just like they did with Damian."

"But the officer wouldn't let me assist you. They have to know that."

"I agree, but these Yankees rule this town; Elinor says if they see fit to arrest you, there will be nothing we can do."

"Who's Elinor?" Kent inquired.

It was Sally's turn to smile. "She's a lady who helped me when you got shot." Then leaning even closer to Kent, as though it mattered if someone heard her speak. "I think Henry has a thing for her, and what's more, she seems to have a liking for him too."

"How long have I been here?"

"Two whole days. Kent, you were in a bad way," Sally explained while she felt that knot in her stomach again. The same one had attacked her heart when she first saw

Kent collapse on the ground, bleeding like nothing she had ever seen before. Seeing him smile now put her fears of him dying behind her. Silently she counted her and his blessing that they would make it together to Saint Augustine.

"I'd like to meet this, Elinor; maybe you can bring her here. Have to check out Henry's love interest, you know," he said with the same weak smile he had shown her earlier.

Sally nodded her head in agreement. " will ask her the next time I see her. If I can tear her away from Henry, that is," she said with a giggle.

Sally stayed long enough to help Kent eat his soup and then fall asleep.

It was time to give Henry a rest from having the children all this time. *The poor man must be exhausted,* she thought. So, she first looked in the hotel lobby for them, but there was no sign of them there or in their rooms.

Walking back out of the hotel, she noticed a small crowd to her left. They were gathered under a few orange trees. Former slaves flocked to Florida once they were free. Ex- slaves followed the Federalists, believing the soldiers would protect their rights since they were the ones who had fought for their freedom.

There were other civilians, whites, and some soldiers in the crowd. Sally approached cautiously, wondering if she would find Henry and the children in the group too. Then panic set in when she thought about possible reasons why they could be involved. She started to run, picking up her hoop skirt under her plaid short-sleeve dress. They weren't were not very far away, - but running in her boots and the swaying dress made the distance seem like a mile.

Stopping behind the handful of spectators, she strained to see what the attraction was. Then she saw and heard him. Henry was arguing with one of the soldiers, while Margaret and Luke looked up to Henry and little Amy cried into her sister's gray skirt. Pushing her way through the gathering, Sally demanded that someone tell her what this commotion was about. Then the same officer she had tangled with while checking in to the hotel that first day turned to face her. "Oh, you again. I might have guessed somebody like you would be involved with thieves."

He was an average height, about her age, and a bit overweight with a long brown mustache. Not at all attractive to Sally.

"I beg your pardon, sir. I do not associate with thieves, nor is this gentleman or the children anything of the sort."

Henry explained what had happened to Sally.

"The kids saw the oranges and wanted to have one. Well, when I reached up to get them one, this officer pulled a gun on me, telling me to drop the orange and step away from the tree. He says these fruits are only for the soldiers; civilians are not allowed to touch them. So, if we want any, we'll have to buy it," Henry explained furiously to Sally.

"That's right. It's the law here now. All of you go home." Then looking again at Sally, he commented, "This is the second time I'll let you off the hook since you don't know all the rules here, but you had better learn, because there won't be a third time without punishment." Looking down at Amy, he yelled, "Can't you quiet that brat?"

"She's not the brat. You are!" Sally responded, motioning to Henry and the children, Sally picked up Amy to comfort her, then led them to the hotel.

Chapter 20

Frank attempted to focus his eyes but blurred everything in sight. He blinked a few times, hoping that would help clear his vision, then he wiped his eyes with the back of his hand, dissipating the impaired vision.

He fluttered his eyes open. The first thought in his mind was aching that felt like someone was holding a hot iron to his head. Still, he prayed to his God. "Praise be to God I'm still alive."

Looking around the room now, it was apparent this was no hospital; it looked more like someone's home turned into a hospital. There were four beds in this one small room with just enough area to walk sideways between them. One man had a bloody bandaged arm hanging from the cot; he wasn't moving or making a sound. Had *he bled to death, and nobody noticed yet?*

He then observed curtains on the windows, a floral carpet on the floor, and a crystal candelabra on a dresser in the corner. *No, this isn't a hospital; it's somebody's home. Where* am I?

He couldn't raise his head above his pillow, due to the pain such a movement would precede. So, he lay shouting as loud as his voice would project, which wasn't much above a whisper, speaking to nobody in particular, "Please, I need water."

He spotted a Negro girl standing in the corner, holding a bucket. She now moved quickly toward him.

When she knelt beside him, he eagerly took the water she handed him in a large vessel. She tried to slow him down. "Master, you gon to drink it all and not leave some fa later. Yous got to save some."

"I need the doctor; what happened to me, and where am I?"

"I'll go fetch him for you, but it may take a while; he's powerful and busy."

Before she could leave, he grabbed her arm, stopping her for a moment, "Paper. I need paper and something to write with; I got to tell my wife I'm alive."

"Ain't no paper or writin' stick here; Doctor has the only one for writin' patients' names and medicines."

Annoyed, he gave a slight slap to her leg, "Then just get the doc and hurry."

As he closed his eyes, he could hear laughter. The patient beside him with the bloody arm still hadn't moved, so he knew the voice came from behind him. "You fool, there's no point in writing a letter to the missus. We're prisoners of war. Don't you know that? You may never see her again."

Then he heard another voice from behind. "Yeah, a Yankee soldier came here yesterday, telling us, as soon as we were able to travel, we'll go to Fort Delaware prisoner of war camp. That's where we are now—Delaware."

With his head aching so bad, he was having a hard time thinking. *No, this can't be, I got to get back home. Please, God, don't let me die before I see my Sally again."*

"No, they can't do that to me; I've already been a prisoner of war at Libby camp in Virginia. They sent me back to fight; that's how I got here. I ain't going to no stinking prisoner camp twice. I'd rather die first."

Feeling a tap on his shoulder, he opened his eyes. He was looking at the kindest face he had seen since joining the war. The man had full cheeks and a bushy white beard and mustache. It made him think he was looking at the real Santa Clause, only it wasn't Christmas, and the man looked exhausted. "I'm Dr. Hicking. Let's see how you're doing; I'm glad to see you're awake. What's your name, son?"

"Frank Preston. I need to get a message to my wife in Savannah; I don't know the girl's name who came to get you. But she said there was no paper to write on. So, I gotta tell her I'm alive before they take me to prison. Can they do that?"

"I'm afraid so. But unfortunately, there's nothing I can do about that; it's out of my hands as I will be there with you."

Changing Frank's bandage, the doctor continued talking. "I have a wife, too, and three kids I miss them terribly in Brunswick, Georgia. We're all in this hell together. Someday this war will be over, and God willing, we'll still be alive to talk about it, how men killed each other so the South could remain swollen with pride in our way of life. So why don't I feel proud?" he ended sarcastically.

That was the last time they would have a conversation together. The Doctor wearily picked up his satchel of medical tools and moved to the next soldier in need

They parted, never knowing how their families were connected, an innocent occurrence, all too common in this war. While families took care of each other, waiting for them to return.

Chapter 21

"I've been *in one battle*
and that satisfied me with war and
I would beg to be excused next time."
—Pvt. Haban R. Foster, 34th
Virginia Infantry

Sally walked the dusty main street on this beautiful bright February morning. Spring was coming; she could smell the blossoms beginning to peek out into the nourishing sun. Here in Jacksonville, though, it already felt like the way summer was in Savannah. Warm and comforting.

She had just come from seeing Kent at the hospital. He still had a slight fever, but the doctor felt confident he would be fit to travel by tomorrow or the next day. She was anxious to see if there was any word from Aunt Gertrude or Frank. She missed them both desperately, although she also admonished herself for her growing desire to nurse Kent, even wishing he would throw her an insult now and again, just like he used to. That way, Sally would know for sure he had recovered.

To help reach that goal, she felt the need to visit the magnificent church on Duval and Newnan streets. *It wouldn't hurt that God hears me pray for Frank and Kent in a true church,* she thought.

Although she had been in Jacksonville for three days now, she hadn't noticed until now something different about the Negroes here in Jacksonville. She saw them shopping for their masters as they did back home in Savannah. There were no baskets on their heads filled with all kinds of goods, from fabric for clothes to beautiful pieces of glassware or large bushel bags filled with produce from the markets. Instead, they were walking as though they were socializing, talking, and lounging under trees with each other. Some even smiled at her as she went past, to which Sally returned the kind sentiment.

She did know that President Lincoln had freed the slaves by way of his Emancipation Proclamation. But for the former slaves, nothing much had changed. Within their freedom were laws—Black Codes—meant to keep them close to the white population. For example, it became illegal for any Black person to be unemployed. But, of course, the jobs offered to the Blacks were jobs the white person wanted them to do. Which meant they were still laborers. They couldn't stay out past curfews, own guns, vote, or hold office.

Approaching the dominant church in the city, she also noticed that many of the Negro population were entering and leaving the worship house.

Not having seen a newspaper in weeks, she had no idea what was going on. Then she saw Elinor crossing the street, waving at her.

"Hello, Sally, I was just coming to see how your brother-in-law is doing and help Henry with the children."

"Oh, that's quite all right. I just came from Kent's side; he's improving but still has a long way to go until he's completely healed. I was headed for the church to say a prayer for him."

She hesitated as she looked around at her surroundings. Elinor, noticing, inquired, "Is something wrong?"

"Oh, no. I guess I've been so absorbed in my travels, looking for food and shelter along the way that I'd forgotten about Lincoln freeing the slaves. There are so many here."

"Yes, most of them followed the Yankees here, figuring their army would protect them since they were the ones who wanted them free in the first place."

Sally nodded, indicating that she understood. "I'm glad they're free. Now we don't have to hide our objections to such a horrible way of life for the Negroes. Nobody will be calling us abolitionists anymore."

"Don't kid yourself. There's still plenty of hate out there. These former slaves have nowhere to go once they were set free. Most of them can't even read or write, so I don't know how they're going to live. I should be happy for them, but instead, I feel sorry for them. That church where you're going? That was built only a few months ago for the slaves, or I should say ex-slaves, so I guess that's some progress. Anyway, I'll meet Henry and wait for you to join us. Take your time."

Sally entered the church, and sure enough, she was the only white person in there. Up by the altar was a cluster of women. One had a stick in her hand, motioning to the small gathering, then they burst into song. *They must be rehearsing.* Sally thought.

Then one spotted her sitting in the back of the church. The singing ceased, and they stared at Sally, unsure why a white woman would be in their midst. Was she there to take away the joy they felt when rejoicing in Jesus? Or was she a spy who would report them to the Yankees? They waited for some kind of reaction, a response from Sally. After a few minutes, as Sally had not said or done anything; they resumed their singing and wondered why she was there instead of in the white people's church on the next street.

Sally sat back in her seat, enjoying the gospel songs, which made her think of her childhood slave friends back home. She had not seen the plantation since her parents died and had no desire to return ever again. But that didn't stop her from wondering if Uncle Temple had freed the slaves as he should have. Did they all leave? And where were they now? She especially thought about Dabney, her closest friend, who was a few years younger than herself. As children, they dreamed of running away together when they got older and running a fancy ladies' dressmaking business. Dabney could sew anything. Dabney made all of Sally's and her mother's most beautiful dresses.

Dab, as everyone called her, was always smiling, she preferred to see the world at its best. Sally never asked how she could be so happy being a slave after all the whippings and various punishments she had witnessed. All were ordered by Uncle Temple. One time Dab commented to Sally, "If I think about all the bad that is here, I will cry and never stop." Sally understood and never questioned Dab unless it was about something good; Sally never wanted to see Dab cry. But she wondered, was she crying now?

Chapter 22

"If you want something you have
never had, you must be
willing to do something
you have never done before."
—Thomas Jefferson

K ent's fever had broken during the night. He had been in the hospital for five days, but he was still weak. The doctor told Sally and Henry that Kent could travel, but he would have to be lying down or propped up in a sitting position in the back of the wagon.

Sally turned to Henry and exclaimed, "Isn't this fantastic news? Kent is going to be all right, and we get to leave this place."

Sally and the children were ecstatic to be leaving Jacksonville. Their emotions envisioned Saint Augustine as a better city; first, it was older than Jacksonville, much older, founded in 1565. Consequently, they created in their minds a city of surplus and social engagements that thrilled Sally. It had been so long since she was able to dress up and dance. How she had missed that! But then she sobered on the thought, *what would the city have to celebrate? The South lost the war, thanks to General Sherman.* Sally almost gagged at the idea of his name.

Henry said nothing while the children gleefully jumped up and down, asking Sally numerous questions. "When will we leave?" "Will any of the soldiers try to stop us?" Luke wanted to know if he could ride up front with her and Henry.

When Sally turned to Henry to ask if Luke could ride with him, she saw him scratching the white hairs on the top of his head. She was sure that he had not heard a word of what the children asked.

"Henry? Are you alright?"

Embarrassed by her observation of him, he quickly straightened up with a smile on his face. But then he couldn't hold the smile. It was fake, and he was sure Sally knew it too. She was too smart not to know.

With his head bowed, not able to look at Sally, he shattered her exhilaration. "I'm sorry, Sally. I'm sorry to do this to you. But I won't be going to Saint Augustine with you." His hands were shaking visibly.

"Are you ill? You're trembling."

"No, nothing like that, but I am mad, madly in love with Elinor."

Sally gasped; this was the last thing she had expected. Although she knew they were attracted to each other, she never imagined that their relationship would include marriage in only five days.

"Henry, you can't be serious. You've only known each other for less than a week."

"I know, isn't it amazing? We fit together so well. We have so much in common, and she loves to cook and fuss over me. I haven't had that since my daughter left."

"So why don't you both come with us? Henry, I'll miss you desperately."

"Elinor's life is here; she's never lived anywhere else. I asked her to marry me, and she said yes, but I would love to have you there."

"Marry? When?"

"In a couple of days. Elinor needs time to get a wedding gown or something beautiful to wear. She says that all her dresses have become ragged over the past four years, with little to nothing to bring back the beauty they once had."

"But we were going to leave tomorrow for Saint Augustine. This is too quick! You and Elinor don't know each other, and I need to see if there is any mail from Aunt Gertrude or Frank. I've waited long enough; I don't want to wait any longer."

Henry sympathized with Sally; He gave her a warm smile and looked at the children. Their faces, mired in disappointment, turned now to Sally.

But it was Henry who spoke. "When you're mine and Elinor's age, time is of even more importance. If we wait too long, well, we just don't know how many tomorrows we have, unlike you young'uns." He could feel himself becoming agitated at Sally for not understanding, and she was the last person he would ever want to have a quarrel with.

"Oh, Henry, what are we going to do? Of course, we both want what's best for us, but I don't want to leave you behind either."

Henry took her hand and patted it. "Now don't you worry, Saint Augustine ain't that far away; we'll come to visit."

Sally then took hold of Henry's lower arm, "But we'll miss you; we want you to come."

"Yes," Margaret added as she held her hat in place against the wind, "Miss Elinor could come too, and you can come back here for visits."

"Of course," Sally said, with a bright smile on her face. "Truth is, I don't want to travel alone with just me and the children and Kent laid up in the back. So why don't you and Elinor get married in Saint Augustine, stay for a while, you know, a kind of honeymoon, and then come back here to Jacksonville."

As if she had heard their conversation, along came Elinor before Henry could respond to Sally's proposal.

Putting her arm through Henry's arm, which was at an angle with his hand in his pants pocket, Elinor asked Sally, "Did he tell you the good news?"

"Oh, yes, he did. We were talking about that. What would you say to you and Henry getting married in Saint Augustine? I'll help you find a dress for the occasion, and I'll get to see if there are any letters from my husband." Seeing the blank look on Elinor, Sally felt sure that she would insist on staying in Jacksonville. Then she added, "I so desperately need to know if my husband is still alive."

Without any hesitation, Elinor put her arms around Sally's shoulders, "Of course, we can do that. It's a beautiful idea. But I would insist on one thing."

Fearful of what she might ask, Sally took a step back.

"I want you to be my witness—you know, my maid of honor," Elinor said.

Sally was thrilled.

Chapter 23

"Whenever I hear anyone
arguing for slavery, I
feel a strong impulse to
see it tried on him personally".
—Abraham Lincoln

Kent was still weak and in pain. The bullet had broken two ribs and lodged in the muscle around his lung; miraculously, the doctor was able to remove the shell with no further damage to his lung. The bones would take a while to heal, but the doctor promised Kent he would make a full recovery.

Sally had herself and the children ready first thing in the morning. Suddenly, after all this time getting this far, Sally had an overpowering need to get to Claire's as quickly as possible.

She put on the best dress she had: a blue taffeta with lace around the scooped neckline with more lace and a bow on each of the short sleeves. Her hoop skirt revealed more of the same trim at the bottom. Sally wanted to look presentable when she met her cousin for the first time.

While Henry and Elinor were packing the wagon and setting up a comfortable bed for Kent in the back, Sally and the children went into the hospital to get Kent ready for the trip.

He was sitting up in bed when they arrived with a satisfied smile on his face. She stopped near his bed; she could sense her heart was feeling more than a physical attraction.

She flung her arms around his neck when she saw him, "Oh, Kent, it's just too beautiful to see you looking so much better."

Kent let out an audible moan when Sally nudged him; minor movement could still send waves of agony through his body.

Fearing that she may have done more harm to Kent, she quickly apologized.

"There's no need for an apology; you didn't mean to hurt me, I know that."

Margaret touched his arm lightly. "Are you going to be all right? Cause we couldn't stand to lose you too."

Seeing Amy standing beside Sally, Kent couldn't resist a broad smile; Kent bent from the bed and took hold of Amy's outstretched arms, then lifted her to sit next to him. Without saying anything, she rested her head on his shoulder. A nurse came by at that moment; she whispered in Amy's ear, her sage advice.

"Oh no, honey child, you mustn't make Mr. Kent work so hard."

Sally nodded in agreement, which Kent witnessed.

"Sally, stop being a mother then. We're fine, and I'm ready to go, so let's get out of here."

"Luke, go get Henry to help me get Kent into the wagon."

"Sure enough." Sally didn't have to ask him twice; Luke was eager to leave this town behind them. The desire to finally move out of Jacksonville was not limited to just him. They were all anxious to settle in one place where they could live out this war in a safer haven.

Stepping out into the street where Henry and Miss Elinor were talking to a couple of soldiers made Luke nervous. His first instinct was to run back inside and get Miss Sally. But then he thought about how he was the man now that Kent was laid up. Stepping closer, he wanted to know what was going on.

Henry was shouting at the tall soldier, "You can't hold us up; we're leaving!"

Miss Elinor was trying to calm Henry down with soothing words. "It's all right, sweetie, this officer has us mixed up with somebody else."

"No, ma'am, I don't. I know who you people are; I was here when you arrived. You've broken the law by not signing the voucher in three days as required. Now you can go before the judge."

Luke couldn't believe what he heard, "What difference does it make; we're getting out of here now, so you don't have to worry about us anymore."

The officer didn't even see Luke standing there before he spoke. Instead, he was annoyed to be interrupted by a boy. Then, with a wave of his arm, he motioned Luke to go back to where he came from. As he would a pesty bug of some sort. "Get out of here, kid; this is none of your business!"

"Yes, it is. We all belong together, and we're leaving together."

Henry put his hands on Luke's shoulders. "This here is best left to us adults."

Elinor was getting up in the wagon seat, mumbling, "This is ridiculous." Then, when she sat down, she continued, "Don't you have anything better to do than harass good people?"

As she said it, she saw Sally and the doctor emerge from the hospital with Kent trying to walk with an arm around each of their shoulders.

Henry parted company and helped the doctor get Kent comfortable inside the covered wagon. Then the doctor went to the officer, looked him square in the face, and asked, "Have you no decency at all? Let these people go on their way; there will be no further incidents from them."

"Yes, sir, Colonel." The officer saluted, then walked away.

Sally went to Kent, fussing with his blankets and pillows, "Are you sure you're comfortable? I mean I, hope there is enough cushion for when we come to bumps in the road."

Kent grabbed both of Sally's hands, "Stop it; I'm fine. Although I do love your concern for me, it isn't necessary." His love and admiration for this woman was growing. He knew it but couldn't do a thing to change these feelings. He realized he wouldn't want to, even if he could.

"It's just that I can't help thinking about how you almost died. What would I do without you?"

Neither one of them was thinking of Frank at the moment when Kent replied, "I hope we never have to find out."

Sally surprised herself when she felt the blood rush to her cheeks. She had never felt like that with Frank, not even on their wedding night.

Chapter 24

'The soul that is within me
no man can degrade.'
—Frederick Douglass

Kent survived the trip to Saint Augustine, despite the pain every time they hit a rut in the broad road, or some other obstacle forced a bump to create havoc with Kent's ribs. Sally stayed attentive to Kent; each time she felt a jolt, she would turn around from her front seat next to Henry and check to make sure Kent was not bleeding or in agony. She couldn't help it; her anxiety over Kent even overshadowed her worry for Frank. While they traveled across a wide-open meadow, with an array of wildflowers growing, Sally could see a horizon of buildings in the far distance. It had to be Saint Augustine.

It wasn't that she loved Frank any less; she had realized that she couldn't worry about both brothers at the same time. Her heart just wasn't capable of loving two men at the same time. *Is it me, or are all hearts like mine, unable to choose between two loves?*

She wanted to talk to another woman about her befuddled emotions. But Elinor was driving her four-seated black surrey with fringe around the top and had the children with her. They rode alongside her covered wagon. Sally told herself there would be time enough to talk once they arrived in Saint Augustine.

It was a clear sky that greeted them when they set out in the early morning hours. The air presented a pleasant breeze to prevent the sun from casting heat that would diminish the perfect day for travel, even if the route took only a few hours. Instead, the spring weather made them all exuberant, anticipating a new life for each of them until the war was officially over.

The children talked to Elinor about their father and how they longed to be held again in his arms. They told her they had left a note for him on the front door about where to find them. Mostly they believed he would come home a war hero. Then little Amy broke the spell. "But what if he doesn't come home?"

"Of course, he'll come home!" Luke quickly corrected his sister. "He has to!"

They passed quite a few Yankee soldiers, some moving in their direction, others heading back to where they had come from. They would soon learn that the two cities, Jacksonville and Saint Augustine—seemed almost interchangeable. They arrived only hours later in the afternoon

Sally had tucked the address to Clair's home that Aunt Gertrude had given her into her case with her intimate apparel. As they approached the city, she clutched the paper in her fist, making sure she didn't lose it.

They followed the Saint John River from Jacksonville to Saint Augustine. When the city came into view, they passed through stone towers on either side of the city entrance. More impressive was the Castillo De San Marcos built during the town's Spanish occupation, almost two hundred years earlier. With its cannons pointed toward the river, the fort, frozen in time, was a bold reminder of the city's history

On one side of San Marcus Avenue was the fort; on the other side was the river. A wooden walkway graced the shore, making it possible to admire the coastal water where Yankee ships occupied the territory.

As they came to the intersection of San Marcos Avenue and Cathedral Street, they could see a city bustling with people tending to business, and as Ray had warned them, a large part of the population here was Yankee soldiers. Sally looked again at her cousin's address and asked Henry to slow down. They needed to get their bearings.

"Her address is 210 Saint Francis Street." They're on Saint Marcos Avenue along the river's edge, where homes and shops embraced each other. Some were in better condition than others, depending on the care the residents took of their place. At a short distance farther along, they saw a woman sweeping a doorstep.

"Excuse me, ma'am," Henry said as he tipped his hand to his forehead, "could you tell us where to find Saint Francis Street? We're in search of Miss Claire Holden."

The woman's smile that greeted them suddenly turned into a livid frown. "Why do you want to bother that nice lady? Who are you?" The woman asked without introducing herself or welcoming them.

At that point, Sally took over the inquiry, "She's my cousin, and she's expecting us. It's been a long, challenging journey, so we would appreciate your help. We also have a severely injured man in the back here who needs tending."

The woman's scowl suddenly disappeared, "Oh! You must be the folks she was telling me about only yesterday. She's been awful worried about you, not knowing when you would come. Sorry about being distrustful at first, but she takes care of me, so I take care of her."

"We understand; now, could you please point us in the right direction?"

The woman, who had been leaning on her broom, turned to her right as she pointed down the street. "Make the next right. That's her street. You'll see her house. You can't miss it—the biggest and prettiest one on the street."

Chapter 25

We calculate there are 14,000
wounded in the town.
—Cornelia Hancock,
nurse at Fredericksburg, 1864

The woman was right; as they turned onto Saint Francis Street, they saw on their left a home with large stones encased in the lower half of the house It had a red front door and, on the top level, a wood balcony, which shaded the entrance under it. Though this house was modest in comparison to the plantation house of Sally's youth, it still stood out from the other homes surrounding it. With its window boxes overflowing with an array of flowers in a variety of colors and its white picket fence, it was a home they could hardly miss.

Approaching the door, Sally realized her hands were shaking. She had never met this cousin. Then she started thinking, yes, she had heard of Claire through the years; she was the daughter of Aunt Gertrude's brother, who had passed away years ago. Gertrude was the only sibling still alive, and Claire was ten years older than Sally. *What if we don't like each other?* Sally thought. As eager as she had been to get to Claire's home and meet her, suddenly she felt apprehensive, fearing their encounter would be a dismal failure.

"Well, go ahead and knock," Henry urged Sally. "What are you waiting for?"

Without saying a word, Sally obediently knocked on the bright red door. Listening for footsteps from inside or a lock unlatching, she instead heard a voice from up above her.

Stepping back and looking up, she saw a slim woman with golden-brown hair parted down the center wearing a long brown skirt and a white blouse with a black ribbon tied in a bow at the ruffled neck.

Waving furiously, the woman welcomed them with excitement, almost jumping up and down. Suddenly Sally thought, *oh dear, she was only expecting me and Kent, not all these other people. What will she think of me?*

Then the door burst open; Claire immediately took Sally in her arms, hugging her almost in disbelief. "I was so afraid that something had happened to you! I can't tell you how glad I am to see you safe."

Then Claire stood back to take a good look at Sally, "My, the last time I saw you, you were just an itty-bitty baby." Sally never knew they had once met.

Claire then invited everyone into the house, then turned her head toward the interior to instruct her maid. "Dabney, turn the stove on; we've got a lot of hungry people here to feed."

Sally quickly looked over Claire's shoulders, hoping to see if her Dabney was the same Dabney she had as a childhood playmate. But she couldn't see the maid as Claire ushered them in. Dabney had already slipped into the kitchen.

Henry stopped the introductions by letting Claire know about Kent and his injury in the back of the wagon.

"Yes, of course, I'll get Dreyfuss to help get the man settled in a bed."

When Dreyfuss appeared, Elinor could not stop herself from asking the question with bitterness and sarcasm. "You still have slaves? President Lincoln has set them free."

Claire, stunned by this stranger's inquiry, replied with venom, "Dabney and Dreyfuss are not slaves; I pay them wages, and they live here in my house. If you must know."

Henry was surprised at Elinor's rude manners when entering a host's home. He whispered, "Please behave; we are guests of this woman. How she runs her household is no business of ours.

Henry didn't have to say anything to her about her lack of manners. Elinor was instantly embarrassed when Claire answered her. Extending her hand to Claire, Elinor apologized. "Please forgive me; it's just that I've always been so against slavery that I find I can't keep my mouth shut when I think I see an injustice. I meant no harm to you or your employees."

Claire, a gracious host, let Elinor know she understood. Then to change the subject to a happier topic, Sally told Claire about Elinor and Henry's plan to wed while in town.

"Oh, wonderful! A wedding is always a good distraction from this awful war. We try to have as many parties as we can here. It's the only way to cheer ourselves is with music and dancing," Claire explained to Elinor and Sally.

Sally wasn't paying close attention to what Claire said she was still anxious to find out about her maid.

Elinor could see that Sally's mind was somewhere else. Her eyes darted in all directions as Sally turned her head this way and that. "What are you looking for, Sally?" Claire inquired.

Just then, Dreyfuss appeared, "You called for me, ma'am?

Henry quickly spoke, "Yes, I need help getting an injured man out of the back of the wagon."

Sally ran around the wagon to look at Kent; she felt ashamed that in the shock of hearing a name from the past, she had forgotten to check how Kent was doing.

Returning to the parlor, Sally let Henry and Dreyfuss know that Kent was ready to be moved inside Claire's house. They were standing now in Claire's luxurious parlor. Sally was in awe of the beautiful furnishings. Purple velvet drapes with gold fringe framed the tall windows. Stuffed sofas and chairs in plush blue floral-print fabric offered seating, and walnut and oak tables were shown with polish, while an ornate oil lamp enhanced each table in the room. The walls were painted in a cream color that complimented the purple drapes, while large paintings graced the walls between the windows. A beautiful silver tea service sat on a carved table in the room's center, between two couches.

Sally had thought Aunt Gertrude lived in a grand house, but this was beyond grand; it brought back faded memories of life on her parents' plantation, memories she hadn't thought of until now.

"Please, everyone sit down; I'll get drinks for everyone to have while we wait for dinner."

Just then, Henry and Dreyfuss came in with Kent.

They had his arms around each of their shoulders, "Just sit me down here with everyone. I've been feeling left out back there in that wagon." He then looked at Claire, extending his hand as best he could, introduced himself, and thanked her for her hospitality.

Sally rushed to his side, then sat next to him on the sofa and felt his head for fever. Thankfully, there was none.

"Oh, this is wonderful; you're getting better."

Kent smiled; it felt good to have Sally close to him again.

Claire was asking each one what they would like for refreshments when Kent asked in a desperate plea, "Would it be too much to ask for wine? I haven't had any since we left Savannah two months ago."

"Land sakes, yes! I have some red wine from Paris, just waiting for me to open it."

"How did you get wine from Paris, with the stockades blocking the South from getting any deliveries?"

"I've had this wine in my cellar for years; I only share it with guests like you."

Kent was still curious, "But every plantation that we've seen is in ruins. How is yours spared? Is it because the Union army has settled here for the duration of the war?"

"Partly so. Also, even though this is a large home here in Saint Augustine, a type of plantation that they usually plunder. You have to know that Florida was never essential in this war. Only one major battle was fought here, at Olustee, which wasn't very large compared to other campaigns in this war. The Confederates never defended Jacksonville or here. It was too hard with our extensive shoreline. Early on, Florida was allowed to be part of the Union so that Iowa could become part of the Union too. That's why there isn't as much destruction here and goods are more readily available."

Hesitating, as though thinking through what she was about to confess, Claire proceeded with her story. They would find out about her husband sooner or later, she thought.

"My late husband was a judge and senator. He was also a Northern sympathizer, funding the Southern Unionist Organization out of South Carolina. That's where we lived in sixty-three." There was an audible gasp from those in the room.

"A traitor? Your husband was a traitor?" Kent asked in total disbelief.

Spinning around to face Kent, Claire retorted, "No, he wasn't a traitor, not to his country; he was only trying to help end this war in any way he could, to stop the bloodshed. Please don't hate me. My husband was a good God-fearing man."

"What happened to him?" Elinor inquired.

"General Sheridan's men found my husband and burned our home down with him inside. This home was my family's; we used to come here when the weather got cold farther north. Then, after I lost my husband and home, I moved here permanently."

Elinor persisted in her questions, "But where were you? Why were you spared?"

"I had gone to town to do some shopping. When I came home, all that was left was ashes. So, I went to my sister's house for a while to grieve. I've heard since how Sheridan's men didn't even know my husband had a wife; they only knew his name and where he lived."

Now pacing the floor and twisting a handkerchief between her hands, Claire anticipated their questions before they even asked. "You're still wondering how I can live so peacefully among this Northern occupation. Well, they are aware of what my husband tried to do, so they leave me alone. So, I guess you could say we have a mutual understanding."

At that moment, Claire's maid stepped into the entrance to the parlor and announced dinner was ready. Sally froze. *How could this be? Sally asked herself. Life couldn't be this cruel to expose her to a face she thought she had abandoned, deserted. But never willingly.*

Chapter 26

If I owned Texas and hell,
I would rent out Texas and
live in hell.
—General Philip Henry Sheridan

As Sally stared at the black woman that Claire called Dabney, S couldn't ignore the sense that the maid was staring back at her. Sally studied her face, her eye, those hands, she had to be sure this was her Dabney, the one friend that the war had taken away from her. But there was no sign of recognition From Dabney. Sally still wasn't sure; they were women now, not children any longer. A lot had changed since then. Sally knew she didn't look the same as she had back at Piccadilly; the same must be true for Dabney as well.

Sally rose slowly from her seat, following the others into the dining room. As she brushed past Dabney, she leaned in closer to her ear and whispered, "Piccadilly." Dabney's face made a sharp turn to Sally's face.

Since Sally was the last one to enter the dining room, Dabney grabbed her by the shoulders, exclaiming in great delight, "It is you! I thought my mind was playing tricks on me, making me believe something that couldn't possibly happen after all these years."

Sally wrapped her arms around Dabney's neck and hugged her as she had never hugged her before. "I couldn't believe it, either. How did this happen, you here? How did you get away?" Sally was aware that she was babbling, asking silly questions, but she couldn't help it. There were a thousand things she wanted to know."

Suddenly Dabney's attitude changed abruptly. She snapped Sally's arms from her shoulders. Glaring at her now, she had questions too. "Where have you been? I wrote just the way you taught me. But you never answered." Her voice was harsh, and she had begun to cry. "Why? What did I do that you would forget me?"

Did you never hear of the Emancipation Proclamation? It passed fourteen months ago. Where were you? You could have freed us then." Dabney brushed a tear from her face. The memory of all the times they had lost pierced her heart. She felt like a lover who says goodbye after professing his devotion, creating a lie about everything said in the past.

"No, no, Dabs, it wasn't that way. I never got your letter, and I didn't write to you because I figured Temple would just keep it from you; it would be just like him to do that. Anyway, I didn't want to get you in any trouble."

Sally continued to tell her about her parent's death, moving to the heart of Savannah, and not wanting to return to Piccadilly not as long as Temple was still there. "Didn't Temple release you and the others when he was supposed to?

"Not until some Union soldiers came to the plantation almost a year after the proclamation became law. Then he had no choice but to release us."

Dabney felt ashamed now for thinking the worst of Sally. She resumed questioning her again while asking, "Are you staying or visiting?" Dabney nervously awaited Sally's response, wanting desperately to have her childhood friend back in her life.

"We'll stay as long as Claire allows us," Sally said. Taking Dabney's hands in hers, she continued, "So tell me your story." Before Dabney could begin, Dreyfuss walked in. Bowing his head to Sally, he announced that he had brought in all the baggage and put the horses and wagon into the barn across the street.

"By the way, Miss Sally, this man here, Dreyfuss, is my husband," Dabney explained with a smile on her face that told Sally that Dabney had chosen well.

Looking at her husband, Dabney spoke to him. "Go get Joel; I'd like for Miss Sally to meet him."

"Sure enough. I'll be right back."

"Joel? Who's Joel?"

"He's, our son. A strong, active child with an eye for mischief." Dabney stated with a proud smile. Sally sat on the stool in the kitchen, which Dreyfuss made for Dabney so she could rest for a few minutes in her busy day. Sally now sat comfortably awaiting the arrival of Dabney's baby.

Sally stood when Dreyfuss returned with a wiggling one-year-old in his arms. She took the baby, looking the biggest brown eyes she had ever seen, puffed cheeks, and a tuft of soft black hair on his head."

"Oh my, he's just the cutest babe I've seen, except maybe Amy. God bless him," she said to the baby. Then turning from Dabs to Dreyfuss, she added, "And to you two as well. Which has reminded me, where are my manners gone? We should tell everyone about our long friendship, at supper tonight."

While sitting down again, this time with Joel in her lap, she steered the conversation back to where they were before.

"First of all, stop calling me 'Miss;' we're equals now. Remember that. Now tell me how you got here. Was Temple cruel to you after I left? Did you run away? Or disappear when they freed all the slaves?"

Dabney explained how she had almost died from a whipping Temple gave her when he accused her of stealing a watch from him. Dabney was confident that she wouldn't be alive today if it weren't for the care she got from the other slaves. When Lincoln signed the Emancipation Proclamation in sixty-three, Union soldiers came to the plantation to announce that all slaves were free now, and Temple had to let them all go or pay them as workers. But as soon as the soldiers left, Temple told us that he would shoot any of us that fled, and he did. So, me and a bunch of others waited until night to go when he was sleeping. We didn't know where we were going; we just knew we didn't want to be there anymore.

We were walking along a road, hungry and some didn't even have shoes when we saw many Union soldiers on that same road. We didn't know where they were going either, but we figured we'd be safe with them since they were the ones who fought for our freedom. They were outstanding, gave us some food, and let us sleep by their fire. So Saint Augustine is where they ended up. I met Dreyfuss while I was on the road. Life's been good since then. Miss Claire pays us, and we're saving to buy our own house someday."

Just then, Claire appeared, asking what was keeping them from their dinner. She told Sally that tomorrow, she would take her on a tour of the city. "Oh, and I almost forgot in the excitement of your arrival, there is a letter for you."

Chapter 27

How long will it take the calloused?
hearts of men before the
scars of hatred and cruelty
shall be removed.
—Clarence Darrow

Sally's hands were shaking; finally, she was going to read Frank's words, his thoughts, his devotion to her, and his eternal desire to be home again.

"Dabs, would you be terribly upset if I read these letters alone with Kent? He'll want to know about his brother."

Dabney understood, telling Sally they could go out to the garden in the back, where sweet-smelling azaleas surrounded a bench under a magnolia tree.

Sally took Dabney's advice, went to the garden, and waited for Kent to arrive with Henry's help.

Not knowing which letters were from Frank, she opened the first one Dabney handed to her. It was from Aunt Gertrude.

> My Dearest Niece;
> General Sherman has left Savannah.
>
> He thought it better not to destroy our fair city. Some say he spared us due to a friendship with our mayor. Whatever his reason, I am grateful.
>
> But that doesn't mean we didn't encounter insults and pillaging. On an almost daily basis, soldiers would come into our homes, stealing wood from our fireplaces. When we ran out of wood to burn for heat and cooking, we had to start cutting up furniture or freeze

These vile Union men have attacked women in the streets and their homes. I am all right. One tried to control me, but I chased him out of our family home—what a good laugh I had.

When they finally departed, there was much rejoicing. The far end of the city burned; most of us suspect that Sherman's army did this on their way out to let us know how lucky we were.

Please write to me. I long to hear how you and Claire are getting along. It's been so long since I heard from you. There is no notice of Frank.

Your loving Aunt

"If there is no news of Frank, then this second letter must be from Aunt Gertrude as well," Sally said, looking at Kent, who felt as disheartened as Sally did.

"Go ahead, open the next letter; we won't know anything until we do." Kent encouraged her.

February 18, 1865

Dearest Niece;

I'm terribly worried about you; not hearing of your arrival fills my heart with much pain. Please tell me you and Kent are all right and with your cousin. I pray for your safety every night.

Although the dreaded Union army is gone, we still survive as best we can, despite a shortage of goods available to us.

Now we find out that Sherman ordered all workers at the Roswell Mill arrested for treason and the only people left in the town were women who were marched into Marietta They say that Sherman's excuse was a way to get across the Chattahoochee River. What kind of treason could he be accusing them of? Most of those workers were women with children. They were shipped north, never able to return. Will this madness ever end?

My dear, there is still no word about where Frank is. The paper lists those that are missing in action, whatever that means, but no mention of your husband. I wish I had better news for you.

Please, please write.

Your loving Aunt

Sally and Kent looked at each other perplexed. Then, finally, she expressed what Kent thought, "What in tarnation does "missing in action" mean?"

"I'm not certain, but I believe it means that the person is nowhere to be found, which could mean that they are either dead, deserted, or a prisoner of war."

Sally stood up abruptly while stamping her feet on the ground. "No! He can't be dead! I won't accept that; it's simply not true."

Although Kent felt the same way Sally did, he also knew they had to face the possibility. "The war isn't over yet; there's still a chance that we'll see Frank again, even if it means we have to go looking for him ourselves.

"But, where would we start looking?"

"I don't know; let's wait till this war is over before we go searching for him. Remember, he'll return to Savannah; then, your Aunt aunt will tell him where we are. If we go off searching for him, he could be here in Saint Augustine while we're somewhere else. It seems kind of silly, doesn't it?"

Kent was right; it did sound like a silly notion to go searching before the war ended. Resting her head on his shoulder, she couldn't help but smile at the futility of such an act.

Chapter 28

*I hate newspapermen. They come
into camp and pick up their camp rumors
And print them as facts.
If I killed them all myself, I'm sure we
would be getting reports from hell
before breakfast.*

—William T. Sherman

The next day, Claire was loyal to her word and took the ladies, including little Amy, out for shopping and a town tour. George Street was the busiest with many stores; Elinor was thrilled to find many more goods for the consumer to choose from. They went to a haberdashery and then to a mercantile store, where she could choose from among dozens of fabrics for her wedding dress. She even found gifts for Henry. Sally, Margaret, and Amy were equally delighted at the many beautiful items on display, the likes of which they had not seen since before the war began.

As they walked down the city's main street, they saw a beautiful park where massive sycamore trees with long, wavy, outstretched limbs, created a canopy of shade over the entire grass-filled area between the two roads. They each bought a glass of lemonade from a street vendor, and then they made their way to a park bench under one of those beautiful large trees. The lemonade was refreshing, giving them the energy to discuss what they would do next. Amy quickly sat in Sally's welcoming lap, tired but eager to explore other pretty products they could find.

"What about food for the reception after the wedding?" Elinor asked Claire. Other than the lemonade stands and a few restaurants, they had not come across any place to buy food.

"We'll have to go to the commissary for that. Give me a list of what kind of food you want, and I'll get it for you."

"I'd like to come if you don't mind. It is my wedding, so I want to see what I'm getting and what choices I have." Sally could feel that some tension still existed between the two women. They had pushed each other the wrong way when they first met. It was apparent that it wasn't going to be easy for them to build a friendship. However, they were cordial toward each other.

"Allow me to explain," Claire began. "Nobody is allowed inside the commissary without a card saying that they have signed the Northern pledge. Rules are if you don't sign, you get no food or are forced out of town."

"Not that nonsense again," Sally announced. "We had that threat in Jacksonville. That run-downtown threatened to deport us to some island if we didn't sign. Fortunately, for me, I was already leaving before the Yankees could expel us. So now, what do we do?" Sally inquired.

"We'll have to go to the town hall to sign. That includes your kids, too, and the menfolk."

Suddenly Elinor changed the subject, "Wait, is that a church? Can we look inside? I've always wanted to get married in a church. My first husband and I were married in my mother's house with a justice of the peace. I've always wondered if my husband would still be alive if God blessed our marriage."

Claire explained, "That is the Cathedral Basilica. it was first built by the Spanish when they settled here, more than a hundred years ago. It is a beautiful church considering that it almost burned down once, but the restoration is magnificent."

All the women walked in together, their mouths open in silent awe. The magnificent stained-glass windows cast a glow on the center altar, reflecting silver and gold. A golden statue of God stood between two statues of apostles of God and two apostles on either side of him, all in gold. There was a painting of the first Spanish mass in St Augustine on the ceiling, with a statue of Mary, wearing a large crown and cradling baby Jesus.

Elinor knew instantly that this was where she wanted to marry Henry. Sitting in one of the many pews, she stared at the statue of Mary. Elinor had never been a religious woman, but being here, she knew in her heart that Jesus's mother Mary had made it necessary for her and Henry to come here.

They went to the town hall after leaving the church. The wedding would be in three days. They would buy food the next day for the reception. Claire was busy as soon as they got home, inviting all her friends and important dignitaries of the city to join them for the festivities. Elinor was happy to have her dream wedding, and Claire was delighted to have another excuse for a party during this terrible time.

Chapter 29

*Let me say no danger and no
hardship ever makes me wish to go
back to that college life again.*
—Joshua Chamberlain

As planned, all of them except Claire went to get their passes and sign the pledge the next day. Sally and Kent were not happy about it but went along since they hadn't decided whether they would remain in Saint Augustine or not.

For Sally, her indecision rested on her Aunt Gertrude. She would rather have her aunt here with her. But how could she convince her to move? Savannah had always been her home. Sally thought that, if it weren't for the Yankees' presence, she would be comfortable in this old town. Then, of course, she had to think of Frank. Gertrude couldn't leave Savannah before the war's end so she could wait for Frank to return. There was no rush to make such a decision since the war was not over yet. Kent insisted that the end was very near. But unwilling to believe it, she chose to convince herself that there was still a chance for the South to win. Despite all the suffering the South had faced in the last four years, she firmly believed, like so many, that victory would be theirs.

Kent could see how this war would come to its conclusion. What worried him was how the South would ever retore itself. *Will the end be as bad or worse than the war?"* He wondered. He'd heard stories of multiple marauders, commonly called "Bummers," roaming the Southern states, creating more havoc and terror for its citizens. Another thought entered his mind as he sat outside on Claire's upstairs balcony. *Will we be safer staying here with the Union army present?* When he posed the question to Sally while they discussed the possibility of staying, Sally's quick and determined response was, "No! They better be gone when this is over. I don't want them as neighbors!"

"But as you can see, everybody seems to be living in harmony here. So, I don't think it would be so terrible if the Northern army did stay."

Sally hated that he got her into this conversation. He had spoiled her festive mood. She, Claire, Dabney, and Elinor were decorating Claire's large parlor with flowers and lace. Sally had taken a break to check on Kent when he voiced his thoughts.

"I've got to get back to the decorating; I've had enough of this foolish talk."

Kent could see she meant what she was saying. Nevertheless, it pained him to think about how she would react when his predictions came true.

Meanwhile, Henry and Dreyfuss were setting up the tables and chairs. Kent wanted to help. He had progressed to being able to get around with only a cane. But Henry insisted that he stay off his feet as much as possible.

By the time evening came, the parlor looked and smelled like what would be an angel's dream-like fantasy. Garlands of sweet-smelling hydrangeas, daylilies, and iris draped the walls. The vases on lace-covered tables filled the room with the fragrance of spring's promise. Claire's neighbors had contributed all the lace tablecloths. Each one was anxious to meet their new neighbors.

Sally was exhausted; she collapsed on the bench in the back garden. Dabney and Sally looked at each other, then giggled like schoolgirls, delighted by a well-done job and anxious for the party to begin the next day. No fire would be lit in the parlor tonight so as not to wilt any of Elinor's chosen flowers.

"Now we know what Miss Claire and Elinor are wearing' tomorrow, but what are we wearing? I don't think I have anything fancy enough," Dabney thought out loud to Sally.

"Surely, you must have at least one fancy dress since living here with Claire. She says she has parties all the time, even during this war."

"That's true enough, but even though I live here, and she pays me, I'm still her maid, and the help doesn't go to their boss's parties. You know that, Sally."

"Well, you're going to this one; I'll talk to Claire myself."

"But who will serve the food?"

Sally gave her a satisfied look and smiled, "We both will. You and Dreyfuss must get out there and dance with Kent and me," She was forgetting for the moment that Kent had not completely healed yet. She wasn't even sure why she had said such a thing. *It should be Frank I'm thinking of.*

Sally did speak to Claire about Dabney, telling her the whole history of their friendship. She wanted Claire to understand that this was Elinor's wedding and a celebration for Dabney and Sally. At one time back in Piccadilly, Sally had promised Dabney that they would be friends for life. She told Claire she intended to keep that promise.

Claire didn't hesitate; she was used to defying authority. That was one of the reasons she loved her husband John so much. He took a concept, turned it inside out, then stood by what he believed, not the masses.

"You're right, Sally. Dabney should join in the festivities; you and I and Dabney will take turns serving our guests. It will be fun."

"There's only one problem"; Dabs doesn't have anything fancy enough to wear, and there is no time for her to make a dress. I'll lend her one of my dresses, but if it doesn't fit, they'll have no time to fix it. Would you have something to share?"

"I don't know; I'm a bit larger than Dabney. But if she needs to do some altering, she could stay here and get it done while we're at the church."

"Excellent idea."

Chapter 30

We talked the matter over and could
have settled the war in thirty
minutes had it been left to us."
Unknown Confederate soldier
Defining a meeting he had with a Union
Soldier between the lines.

It was a perfect day for a wedding. The sky was an exquisite shade of blue, and for the first time since leaving Savannah, Sally heard birds singing. Due in large capacity to the fact that where they were now, the echo of distant bombs and gunfire could not be detected. Instead, The sun blessed the day with enough warmth to make each one feel comfortable but not hot.

Elinor had chosen a ready-made purple riding outfit, with no hoop crinoline., It had a soft falling skirt, and a waist-length jacket with black braiding around the skirt's bottom and the jacket's outline. Under the jacket, she wore a white blouse with rows of ruffles exposed under her chin. On her head, Elinor wore a matching miniature western hat with the same braiding around its' base. with a lace bow in the, She looked gorgeous. She didn't want to be in a hoop all day or change her dress before they took off in Claire's carriage for a few days alone.

Sally wore a lavender hooped gown of silk and lace. The neckline stretched across her shoulders to short puff sleeves. She wore flowers in her hair, and Kent couldn't take his eyes off her.

Elinor shed tears of happiness as she took her vows. She and Henry pledged that the rest of their lives would be devoted to each other.

Sally shed some tears, too, thinking of her and Frank's wedding day. It wasn't as elaborate as this one when all the talk around them was about the possibility of war.

People had tried to warn them that this may not be the time to marry. But, scared and very much in love, they plunged forward, thinking if they didn't do it now, the war might stop them from ever being husband and wife. So, as she stood in the church, she said a silent prayer., she turned to the ornate statue of Mary, " God *please Please don't make me a widow, or am I one already?*

Once back at Claire's, Sally was surprised at how many people were coming. She had not thought to ask Claire about who would come since nobody knew the bride or groom.

When she saw Claire moments after her arrival, she questioned how many would be there and how she and Elinor would talk to all these strangers.

Claire assured her that everyone was anxious to meet them. "Consider this your coming out party; you and Elinor are the debutante, so to speak."

Sally laughed at that scenario. "I have to tell Elinor that she's a debutante. At her age, that will surely top her day off." It didn't take long for the parlor to fill up with guests.

Sally was scanning the room for a sight of Kent. She had not spoken to him since their last conversation which she cut short the previous night. It wasn't that she avoided him; she wasn't annoyed, just concerned that he was well enough to come to this reception. She had seen him as she departed the church, but with all the people, she couldn't catch up to him.

Sally couldn't see Kent bending down to talk to Margaret, who sat perched on a step to the parlor, trying to hide, but also at the same time, see all the beautiful gowns and handsome men in uniform.

"Would you like me to get some refreshments," Kent said in his most gentlemanly fashion, to which he received a shy giggle. Then she whispered, "Don't tell anyone I'm here."

Kent smiled, and in mock sarcasm, he responded, "Oh no, I wouldn't think of telling anyone you're here when they can see so plainly for themselves."

Margaret gasped in surprise, then sprinted into the kitchen's sanctuary with Dabney and the rest of the children.

In a few moments, the small band of three began to play, giving everyone in the room an excuse to smile, for a short time, erasing from their minds the terrible carnage that was going on outside their horizons.

To Margaret's delight, Kent came into the kitchen, bowed, and with an outstretched hand he asked her "May I have this dance with you?"

Feeling like she was floating on air, Margaret's dreams were coming true right here and now. She had a crush on Kent from the first time they met. Not only was he handsome, strong, and funny, he was her hero. Taking loving care of her mother's burial, and tenderly took care of her and her brother and sister. Convinced Margaret that she would never marry until she found a man just like Kent.

Kent led Margaret back out to where everyone else was dancing. Swaying to the music, Margaret looked up at Kent's attractive face. "You love Miss Sally, don't you?" Margaret askedKent. Startled by the question, Kent fumbled to find the right words to say.

"What makes you ask such as question?" Kent was amazed that an almost thirteen-year-old girl could be so intuitive.

"I've noticed you and Miss Sally having talks in some corners of the house, I've even seen you two the way you look for each other all the time. I don't mind, I was going to marry you myself when I got bigger, but I guess I should find somebody who's more my age right?"

"Absolutely" Kent agreed. By now the dance had ended and they returned to sitting on the step to the kitchen. Kent still couldn't fathom how Margaret knew of his feelings for Sally when he wasn't sure of his feelings for her himself. Enough talking about Sally, he had to find her, he urgently needed to be with her.

Standing erect now, Kent could see Sally on the other side of the parlor. She was talking to Claire and two other well-dressed men.

Although Kent had abandoned the cane, he discovered that his pain level was the same with or without the apparatus. Strolling was his only option, so his gait looked normal to those who were unaware of his injury. However, he wanted his recovery to be a surprise to Sally.

Coming up quietly behind Sally, he tipped his head to Claire and the two gentlemen. "Excuse me for interrupting, but I was looking for the lovely Miss Sally." Sally immediately turned around to face Kent, standing far enough back for her to see that he didn't have his cane.

"Oh, Kent, this is wonderful. Are you sure you should be walking like this?"

"I'm fine., now introduce me to your friends."

"Oh, excuse me," Putting her gloved hand on Kent's shoulder, she began the introductions. "This gentleman is my brother-in-law, Kent Preston. You all know my cousin Claire. We were just speaking to our Governor John Milton and his Lawyer assistant, Ethan Powers."

Governor Milton outstretched his hand to Kent, "Welcome to our community. I hear you will be our newest resident. I hope you've found it to your liking so far."

"Yes, quite so"; Kent replied. Sally, eager to join in the conversation with such a prestigious man as the mayor, added, "Claire gave us a grand tour the other day." Turning to Ethan, Kent shook his hand as well. Then Ethan went on to explain to Sally why Claire's festivities are always a success.

"Miss Claire surely knows how to entertain in this beautiful home. We try to make it to every one of her parties."

Sally smiled, thinking about how wonderful it was to be among those who can still enjoy life's pleasures. With that thought, another woman joined them.,

"Hello, I'm Mrs. Jensen," said a plump woman wearing a straw hat with flowers around its brim, The hat was wrapped around her head and tied in a bow of shiny blue ribbon to match her dress. Her hair, barely seen from under the hat, was a white-blonde color, indicating she was not as young as she would like people to think.

"Ah, Mrs. Jensen, good to see you," Ethan proclaimed, "Have you met our new neighbors, Sally and Kent?"

"No, I haven't had the pleasure yet.; that's why I came to join you; besides Ethan, I haven't seen you in ages."

Turning to Sally, she continued to dominate the conversation., "Ethan here has been seeing my daughter Emily for some time now, but he seems to have forgotten where we live," She stated as she gently patted Ethan on the cheek. Ethan gave a weak smile but said nothing. It was clear to Sally and Kent that Mrs. Jensen was not the genteel woman she pretended to be; Sally thought, more accurately, that Mrs. Jensen was the demanding type used to getting her own way. Without having met her daughter, Sally felt sorry for Emily.

Ethan recovered his composure quickly; clearing his throat, he asked the ladies if they would like more punch. Claire and Sally confessed they would like to partake, while Kent offered to accompany Ethan to the buffet table.

Mrs. Jensen had said nothing more to Ethan as he left with Kent. Instead, she acknowledged Sally by verbally welcoming her to their town. She thanked Claire for inviting her, and turning to the Governor she said her goodnight, as she extended her hand to him, silently demanding him to bow to kiss her fingers, then she abruptly departed.

"Well, it's nice to see that some people never change, I suppose," Claire said to the Governor and Sally.

"Is she like that all the time?" Sally asked Claire. Before Claire could answer, the men returned with the punch for the ladies. Ethan was relieved that Mrs. Jensen was gone. "Sorry about that I was hoping I could avoid her this evening, but I see I was wrong. She never misses a chance to get her pitchfork out in her pathetic effort to get me to marry her daughter."

"First of all, it's not your fault that she came here, and secondly, is the daughter as bad as the mother?" Kent inquired.

No., Emily is lovely, but would you want to have her mother as an in-law?"

Kent had his hands in his pockets, "Yeah, I know what you mean; I had a woman like that once."

"Like the mother or the daughter?"

Kent let out a grunt, "Exactly like the mother. Scared me off for years."

The Governor governor and Ethan laughed, but Sally felt that to Kent, it was no joke.

Just then, there was a commotion going on at the entrance to the parlor. Dreyfuss entered with three Union officers following behind him. "Sorry, Miss Claire, but they said it was urgent to talk to the Governor."

One of the officers whispered in the governor's ear. Then he instructed one of the men to saddle his horse at once. Then, thanking his hostess and guests, Governor Milton bowed his head, and accompanied by two Confederate soldiers, he bid a hasty departure from Claire's home.

"My word, I wonder what that was all about," Sally said to nobody in particular.

Looking at Ethan, who was as stunned by the Governor's sudden exit, Kent inquired, "What do you suppose could be that urgent at this time of the war?"

"I haven't the faintest idea," Ethan said, looking at the door Milton had just passed through, with a puzzled look on his face. "All I can think of is that our side lost another battle."

Looking at them all now, he explained, "I don't know if you're aware that Governor Milton has always been a strong supporter of state rights; he was active in his efforts to have Florida secede from the Union. He's very proud that Florida has been the leader in providing food and salt to the Confederate army. However, he's been agitated lately due to the defeats of our soldiers; I think one more loss will destroy his spirit."

Chapter 31

*"Yankees have developed a character
so odious that death would
be preferable to a reunion
with them.*
John Milton, Governor of Florida, 1865

Elinor and Henry left the reception in the early sundown hours when the sky was at its peak with oranges, pinks, yellows, and blue remnants. They were so happy and looking forward to a brighter future when the South would return to its former glory of flowers in every yard and frogs, crickets, and birds singing their songs without the sound of guns and men squirming in pain. But most of all, the dead could be buried,

As the guests waved to the departing bride and groom, Kent whispered in Sally's ear, "Meet me in the garden, as soon as you can. I need to talk to you."

When he pulled away, he was smiling, He squeezed her arm, then left. Sally smiled back at him, but Kent didn't see it.

Dabney came beside her, holding Joel in her arms. "It was a perfect day, wasn't it?" She said with a giggle in her voice.

"Yes, it was, but did you see the Governor, how quickly he left the reception? He did not explain his departure nor say when he'd be back. Ethan, his assistant, says that it could be news of another battle somewhere that we lost. Oh, Dabs, I'm so scared I'll never see Frank again."

"What does Kent think about Frank and the governor?"

"I don't know; I haven't spoken to him about it. But, shucks, we hardly had a chance to say more than two words to each other all afternoon. But he wants to talk to me in the garden, so I guess I'll find out then."

Sally ran her finger gently across Joel's chubby little cheeks; he responded with a giggle that produced a big smile on his face. "How are the kids doing? Are they still in the kitchen eating whatever they can steal?"

Dabney laughed.;" Yes;" Yes, they are still in the kitchen, but guess who just walked in to help them?

"Who?"

"Miss Claire! was giving each a piece of chocolate when I left."

"All right then, as long as everyone is happy, I'll go see what Kent wants."

With the sun setting and the glow from lighted lanterns strung on a rope across the width of the garden, a whole new ambiance appeared that didn't exist in the daylight.

Kent sat on the bench, his tie undone, and his shirt's first few buttons opened. Sally thought she had never seen him more handsome; his masculinity called out to her.

Kent had his hand outstretched to her; she put her hand in his and sat beside him.

"We didn't get to talk alone, all day, and I've wanted to discuss something with you."

"Is it about Frank?"

"Yes, umm, sort of, well, maybe… I don't know how to explain this to you."

"Explain what? Have you received a letter from Frank?"

"No, I haven't, and I know you haven't either, which is why we must talk of the possibility of him never coming home."

Sally looked at Kent in horror before she answered. "He's your brother; how can you just dismiss him like that.?"

"I'm not dismissing him. I'm trying to figure out what we'll do if Frank doesn't return. You must accept that, likely, we've already lost him. This whole war and this trip here have changed us all. We've gotten to know each other better, and I must confess, I've grown very fond of you, Sally, and I think you feel the same way about me."

"Kent, what are you saying? You don't know what I'm thinking, not my dreams or anything else. Or has Dabney told you something?"

"Sally, every day when I look at you, I see something new and exciting. You make me laugh and think about things I never imagined. But most of all, I see the compassion in you that I never saw in Savannah—the way you are with the children., I always thought Frank was making a terrible mistake marrying you; I never saw the empathy you have when you are with the children. That spoiled brat I thought my brother had chosen has turned out to be a spirited, beautiful woman.""

She raised her right hand to her chest in amazement at the words Kent had just voiced. She swallowed, not sure what kind of a response she would give. Trying to think fast, she debated within herself, should *I confess that I've been attracted to him also? But would that make him feel less of me, that I'm betraying Frank? Or do I deny my feelings for him, knowing that would injure him? Kent doesn't deserve that.*

Kent was staring at her with anticipation. As he waited for what seemed like an eternity, she finally responded, it seemed like an endless amount of time before she finally replied.

Blurting with an air of exasperation, Sally found her voice. "I don't know how I feel; I'm so confused. I feel attracted to you, also, but I still pray that Frank will return to me. I just don't understand how I can have emotions for both of you at the same time. I wonder if it's possible to be in love with two men at the same time." She tried to control the tears that flooded her eyes while trying to justify her conflicting emotions. She couldn't look at Kent. Finally, when Sally stopped talking, she couldn't avoid his eyes any longer. Kent gently, with one finger, raised her chin to meet his admiring eyes.

"You don't have to choose. We'll both grieve for Frank together., because of our love for him, we can face whatever fate throws at us. It's enough for me to know that you have feelings for me, that I can honestly, even if you can't right now, say I love you."

With no warning to Sally, Kent leaned forward and kissed her with a gentle lingering kiss. Sally thought she should protest. After all, it wasn't proper to kiss any man until you were married and, worse, your brother-in-law. But Sally found it difficult to refuse a kiss like this. It was, tender, and oh, so inviting. Sally thought about how Frank had never kissed her like this.

Maybe it was due to Frank being the first man who had ever kissed her. She had nobody to compare her husband's kisses too. *Yes, that must be it,* Sally thought.

When Kent finished the kiss, Sally's eyes remained closed for a few seconds, so caught up was she in the ecstasy that Kent's lips delivered; she wanted to savor the moment even though Sally knew the guilt she would carry about doing something so scandalous.

Holding Sally at arm's length, Kent suggested that they go on a picnic tomorrow, just the two of them somewhere they could be alone with no interruptions or ears listening.

"But everyone at the reception knows you're my brother-in-law. What if they should see us together?"

Chapter 32

Sunshine let it be or frost,
Storm or calm, as shalt choose;
Choose; though thine every gift were lost,
Were lost, thee Thyself we could not lose.
Lose.
—Mary Elizabeth Coleridge
Poet – "After St. Augustine".

As the weeks went by, Kent, Sally, and Ethan became friends. Often going horseback riding together, or sometimes Kent and Ethan enjoyed a beer at the nearby saloon. None of them had heard anything from the Governor since he had left Henry's wedding almost a month ago. Neither had they heard anything about Frank, or the children's father, Dr. Hicking. Aunt Gertrude continued to send letters to Sally. She was updating her on all that was going on in Savannah but made no mention of the missing men.

Sally tried to avoid Kent as much as possible in Claire's large house. She didn't trust him or herself to keep from jeopardizing their reputations.

Even when in bed, Sally could feel that her physical attraction for Kent had not vanished; she felt her body shiver every time she saw him or thought of him. Trying to ignore those feelings was a futile effort. Kent even haunted her dreams.

She tried talking to Claire and Dabney about her dilemma without mentioning Kent's name. But they weren't much help. Claire thought she should follow her heart if Frank is alive.; after "After four years, he shouldn't be surprised that you have fallen in love with someone else," she said.

Dabney just wanted Sally to be happy, "I know you're talking about Kent; I've seen the way you two look at each other. It's evident that Kent is in love with you. Follow your heart; if it's Frank, you should be with, God will bring him back to you."

"But that's just the problem; I don't know what my heart is saying. How do I know if my feelings for Kent are just physical or if I'm wanting to be faithful to Frank purely out of guilt? I've cried myself to sleep many nights just thinking about both of them. I couldn't stand to lose either of them."

"Well, you're never going to know, Sally, if you keep avoiding him. Talk to him. Talk about each of your plans and what you'll do about it. Will he back away when Frank comes back? Or will he fight his brother for your hand? These are the things you must discuss with him."

"I suppose you're right." Sally acknowledged.

They were in the kitchen, still talking when Ethan and Kent walked in. Ethan spoke first., "We just heard about Governor Milton... Apparently, when he left us, he went to his plantation, Sylvania, in Marianna, Florida. Staff reported that he had killed himself."

Sally gasped, "Oh, my God! Why would he do such a horrible thing?"

Ethan shook his head slowly, "I knew he was in debt, but I imagine it was much worse than I realized."

"We'll get a new governor and hope that he's not as big on spending as Milton was." Kent speculated.

"We already have a new governor, Abraham K. Allison, sworn in the same day Milton's son found his father dead," Ethan related.

"Ethan, please excuse Sally and me; we have plans to go for a walk on this beautiful day."

Sally looked at Kent with surprise and confusion. They had not discussed going for a walk today. But, seeing how he announced it as if so, she had no choice but to go along with his tall tale.

When they were outside, Sally turned to Kent; "What is your problem?"

"My problem is you; I need you to know that I'm serious about my feelings for you, that this isn't a joke or a trick. We can't talk in the house; there are too many people around. Even if they don't know what we're talking about, it will still be an interruption, just like now with Ethan."

Just as they were going out the door, Claire called Sally's name. Turning back,

Sally responded by telling them their location. Claire came holding a letter in her outstretched hand. "This just came for you; I think it's from Gertrude."

Sally immediately sat in a chair, just inside the front door. Kent let out an exasperated sigh, wondering if he would have a chance alone with Sally.

Chapter 33

We'illWe'll fight 'em, sir, till hell
Freezes over, and then, sir, we
We'll fight them on ice.
—Unknown Confederate Soldier

Sally opened the letter; Claire and Kent sat close by her, eager to hear Savannah's news. Sally felt sure that this time Gertrude would tell her that Frank's name was on the list of dead displayed on the courthouse's wall.

March 20, 1865
Dearest Niece,
There is no word about Frank. I continue to ask about him, but nobody knows anything. I'm sorry I haven't better news for you.

I'm so glad to hear that you and Kent are enjoying St.Saint Augustine; I so love hearing from you.

But I have some other possible bad news. I hear that your Uncle Temple seems to have left Savannah, asking where he can find you. A friend has told me that he looks pretty agitated; he claims it's of great importance that he speaks with you. My friend said that she only revealed to him that you left when General Sherman invaded the city. She said she didn't like his disposition, so she didn't tell him where you are. I live out of fear for our safety.

I have heard from several people that he is asking about you. Be warned. you've told me how much you hate him, so be alert and notify friends and neighbors not to reveal your residence. He has never stated why he is looking for you. I do hope that Kent is still with you.
Your loving Aunt Gertrude

"Who is Uncle Temple?" Claire questioned.

"He's my father's younger brother. An awful man, whom my parents tried to have as little to do with as possible."

Kent took the letter from Sally's hand and reread it to himself again. "Your grandparents left the plantation to your father and Temple when he died, correct?"

"Yes, I'm told that when I married your brother, I became half-owner of Piccadilly too."

Suddenly Sally had a terrible thought., "Supposing what he wants is Dabney back?" She was immediately in a panic, "No! I won't let him take her back! She's free now; he can't take her back, right?" looking at both Claire and Kent for assurance.

"Calm down, sweetie," Claire said, resting a supportive hand on her shoulder. Then, turning to Kent, Claire suggested that he see if Ethan was free to come to discuss this situation.

"Where is Dabney? I've got to warn her as well. She needs to know."

Kent was willing to fetch Ethan, but until they knew precisely what Temple wanted, there was nothing Ethan or anybody else could do to help Sally. "Besides," Kent explained to Sally, "Slaves are free now; it's against the law to return slaves to the plantations unless they want to go. But it doesn't apply to those states that didn't accept the Union Government. So, it's got to be something else Temple is after."

Kent left to get Ethan anyway. Then Dabney walked into the room. "What's going on?"

Sally jumped up and ran to Dabs. "I got a letter from my aunt in Savannah; she says that Temple is looking for me. But my aunt doesn't know why."

Dabney, in shock, gasped. "He wouldn't be looking for me. My husband, Joel, and I are free. He has no claim on us!"

"You're right," Claire said, tossing her fist in the air for emphasis. "You all will have nothing to fear; I'll make sure you are protected. I have friends and connections in high places. So don't worry."

Worrying about Frank, along with her feelings for Kent, was taking its toll. Temple's search for her was only adding to her anxieties. Her nerves began to wear on her like barnacles on a pier, stinging when penetrating the skin.

Sally thanked Claire for her support, then announced that she wasn't feeling very well and would go lie down.

"But Ethan may be coming."

"I'll speak to him later," Kent said, "nothing will happen. Not until we know what Temple wants."

When she got upstairs, she found all three children playing with Pickup Sticks with pieces of branches.

As soon as they saw Sally, they came running, "We haven't seen you since breakfast," Margaret stated. Then she asked, "Were you with Kent again?" She said it with a look from the corner of her .eye, teasing Sally and hoping it was true. Margaret had decided a while ago that Sally and Kent would make the perfect couple.

Seeing their smiling faces always cheered Sally; her tensions forever vanished when they were around. For them, she hoped their father would come home, but for her, she wished she could keep them forever. Sally didn't want to think about how to raise these three children alone. She would work that out when the time came. For now, Sally had Dabney, Claire, and Kent to ease the doubts that haunted her daily life. Maybe she would have to go back to Picadilly after all.

Chapter 34

*And I do further proclaim that the
insurrection is at an end and that
peace, order, tranquility, and civil authority now exist in and
throughout the whole of the United States of America.*
—President Andrew Johnson 8/20/1866

St.Saint Augustine was becoming more like home every day. Luke was attending the one-room school in the city, the only one for his age. Margaret stayed home learning sewing and cooking, how to make butter, and other household chores from Claire and Sally. Dabney often let Margaret sit with Joel while she and Dreyfus found time to spend alone.

Amy had stopped asking about her mother and father. But Margaret told Sally how many nights she could hear Amy crying into her pillow, and Margaret was at a loss on how to help her move past the feelings of desertion that her petite body and mind suffered. Although she was now talking, the trauma was not yet gone. Yet in the warm breezes that smelled of fruits and flowers that grew around them, Amy laughed with abandon at the most diminutive natural delights from the earth. She loved the dandelions, with their white-feathered buds that blew in the breeze on Amy's command, or so it seemed to her, and that grew seemingly out of nowhere. She giggled when Kent's beard tickled her cheek when he kissed her good night, but most of all, she cherished the kitten she had found one day on a walk to church with Margaret and Sally. It was a little orange cat with a white belly and the capacity to snuggle as much as Amy wanted him to do. She named him "Snuggles" for that reason. They brought him home and fed him some milk, which he eagerly devoured. Then, like a little mother, Amy made a bed for Snuggles out of hay from the garden and a small blue scarf that Claire gave her to finish the sleeping area to Amy's partiality. In just a few short weeks, they became inseparable. Joel, who was now crawling, was fascinated as well by the tiny ball of orange fur.

Sally was thrilled to see Amy coming alive, out of the tortured shell she had been hiding in ever since they found her and her siblings. Amy had witnessed the horror that captured her soul. Though first there were the whispers of speech Then came some smiles, which grew to laughter, and she seemed content to let life touch her again.

Sally was also a little calmer; days had passed since they received Gertrude's letter warning her about Temple. When Sally had dared to venture outside those first few days after the warning, she was constantly turning her head right, then left, convinced that Temple would show up in St.Saint Augustine at any time. But after almost a week with no sign of him. She was feeling more relaxed.

Kent had gotten a job working at a large stable, grooming and feeding the horses and assisting the blacksmith with making horseshoes. He had never liked being beholden to anybody, especially a woman. Nevertheless, Kent felt the need to contribute to the household hold expenses; after all, they had added five more mouths to feed in the household. Moreover, he enjoyed the work; it cured his boredom in Claire's large home. The only downside Kent could see was not being able to spend more time with Sally.

But ever since that kiss they shared in Claire's garden, Sally had been avoiding him. She was polite but was not saying any more than she was obliged to. Kent was trying to figure out if she was mad or just plain embarrassed. He scratched his head. *Why do women always have to make things so complicated? Nobody saw us, so she has no reason to feel ashamed.*

The problem was she wouldn't even allow him to tell her anything

One day when he returned home from work, Amy and Sally sat on the front stoop, playing with Snuggles. Kent half expected Sally to run back into the house when she saw him coming up the narrow street. But she didn't go to his endless joy.

With one leg bent on the stoop where they sat, careful not to hurt Snuggles, he bent over and kissed Amy's head, then he leaned in close to Sally's ear, "Give me a few minutes to clean up, then you and I will go explore Magnolia Street." His breath in her ear tickled her, and she giggled. Amy looked up, asking what was funny. Kent touched her nose gently, "Why don't you come inside and show me what your brother and sister are up to."

"Margaret is in the kitchen; she promised to make my sugar cookies," Amy excitingly excitedly told him; she was licking her lips at just the thought of them.

"Well then, come on, let's go see how Margaret is doing with those cookies."

Amy jumped up immediately, anxious to get a taste of her sister's baking. But before she left, she admonished Snuggles, "Now you stay here with Miss Sally until I get back." That said, she took Kent's hand and skipped into the house.

Chapter 35

If it is a crime to love the South, its
cause, and its President, then I am a criminal.
I would rather lie down in this prison and die
then leave it owing allegiance to a
government such as yours."
—Belle Boyd, Civil War spy

Sally couldn't ignore the symptoms any longer—the racing of her heart nor the tingling of her nerves whenever Kent was near. The more she tried to avoid him, the more she desired his company. As much as she tried to avoid him, the more intense her memory of Kent and that one magical kiss in the garden became.

Now she pondered what being with him alone would accomplish. Although she had not heard from Frank or found any evidence that her husband could still be alive, she still grieved for him, yet she always felt married. *So why do I desire Kent? Why does the sight of his lean muscular body turn me into mush?* All she knew was that it was time to face the problem.

She had always said, "If you don't meet the dilemma, nothing gets solved." Magnolia Street was a street she had seen before but had never actually walked, or rode down. Her tours of the city with Claire had not given her reason to explore the magnificent canopy walk. It was beautiful, a street full of magnolia and sycamore trees whose branches touched each other, as though they were holding hands with sun rays in magnitudes of color between the long branches, some heavy with moss. Although they were different species of trees, they still longed for each other. It didn't matter what their differences were. Sally looked up to them gazing at what they could manage as an embrace, thinking *"Why can't people be like these trees?"*

Suddenly Kent appeared; he was dressed in a blue plaid shirt and black pants.; he had even shaved his short beard off, leaving a handsome mustache which made him even more appealing.

He carried a blanket over his arm and a basket full of oranges, courtesy of Dabney, bread, and from Claire a bottle of wine, unbeknownst to Sally.

He extended his arm out to Sally, who took it with a shy smile, not knowing what she was getting herself into.

When they got into the wagon, Sally asked what was in the basket. " You'll have to wait until we get to where we're going. It's a beautiful day, and I intend to enjoy my afternoon off."

As they drove on Magnolia Street, it was like driving into another world. She had only driven past it with Claire but had never actually set foot on the street. It was enchanting. Birds were singing, and the air filled with a mixture of sea scents and the fragrance of flowers, which butterflies danced atop.

Finally, they stopped under a sweet-smelling Magnolia magnolia tree. Spreading the blanket on the soft dirt surface, Kent smiled at Sally. "Finally, we can talk about anything we want without spying ears and eyes to question our thoughts and judgments."

"What judgments would we speak of?" Sally asked, confused about his intentions for this afternoon. She needed to know to prepare for one of his usual debates. Unfortunately, they'd had a few too many lately for her liking.

"I don't know., we say something about a person we know, and somebody might tell that person how we feel, which would be most embarrassing."

"Oh, Kent, you do go on so, worrying about the silliest of things. I declare you are the most curious man I've ever met."

Kent laid lay down on the blanket with his arms under his head for a pillow. Then, with a smile, he asked her, "Tell me about the men you knew before my brother."

As much as Sally wanted Kent to think that she was a cultured woman, knowledgeable of the world around her, she also didn't want him to believe she was empty-headed and flighty like many other women back in Savannah. Bowing her head, in an attempt to hide her flushed cheeks and not look directly at Kent, she confessed that there was no other man before Frank. "Oh, there were other men, boys, I should say, they who wanted to call on me, but none of them appealed to me. Not until I met Frank., For me, it was love at first sight. It was the same for him too. That's why we married so quickly." Then becoming forlorn, she added. "Neither of us believed that war would become a reality.

She looked at Kent now, observing his masculinity in a way she had never looked at Frank. Then like a shooting star that appears in the night sky, her mind became aware of why she was so attracted to Kent and what she had missed in Frank. She had never thought of this before. Kent and Frank were opposing personalities. She loved Kent's zest for life, his unpredictable curiosity, and his sense of humor. What Sally loved the most about him was when he was playing ball and pick up sticks Sticks with the children. She thought about how she had looked for him and the children to come home for dinner just yesterday. Instead, she found them by a water fountain in front of a large restaurant. Kent gave Luke a playful push toward the spout when he fell in. Kent laughed with abandon as he held his outstretched hand to Luke, who was laughing too.

Sally spotted a bee buzzing around Kent's head. She leaned forward to swat the insect away. But as she did, Kent, unaware of the bee's presence, leaned forward too, thinking Sally was preparing for a kiss. Instead, when Kent heard the buzzing, Sally raised her arm, moving it to the left. He lowered his head, bent even further toward Sally, and used the moment as an excuse to kiss her again.

This time Kent lingered with the kiss, wrapping his arms around Sally's tiny waist. Sally then gently pushed him away. "I was only swatting a bee away from you.; What gave you the idea I wanted a kiss, Mr. Preston?"

Kent smiled, his blue eyes absorbing the beauty of this woman. "You are the epitome of my dreams. Everything I've always wanted."

His words were affecting Sally, as was his touch. His arms around her now made her feel safe and beautiful.

Kent could not ignore the aching need to be to caress her, make her feel loved and adored as she should be. His kisses were as soft as a puppy's fur and as passionate as she had never experienced before. Not even Frank had ever made her feel like this.

Then he took her in his arms again, saying, "Sally Preston, you are the woman of my dreams." But Sally's response was not what Kent expected or hoped to hear. From the still pulsating rhythm of her body, Sally knew she was in love with her brother-law. *God help me, what am I to do?* Sally prayed silently. One thing she was sure of, she would never tell Kent her true feelings. That would only serve to encourage him. He was leaving her with the fact that she secretly wanted more of what he had to give, while she tangled with the knowledge that she still cared for Frank's safe return to her.

Chapter 36

Sally pushed Kent away, as he kissed her neck. She quickly stood up and faced him, tugging at the blanket they had just laid on. "Excuse me, sir. Get off the blanket!"

"What's your hurry, and why are you calling me 'sir'?"

With a frown on her face, she rolled the blanket into a ball in her arms, marched to the carriage, and ceremoniously deposited it. Then turning back to face Kent, she announced to him, "This never happened. Do you understand me? I never want to speak of it or want anyone else to know of our impropriety."

"Impropriety? Are you kidding me? You wanted it, and I know for sure you enjoyed it a lot! No woman sounds like you just did without feeling a whole load of pleasure."

It was true, but Sally was not about to admit to Kent that she desired him more now than ever. Her feelings of guilt would not allow her. No matter what Kent said, she was still married to his brother, and until she knew for a fact that Frank was dead, they would have to stay away from each other. Regardless of how difficult it was going to be.

"I sure don't understand you, Sally. You're beautiful; I can't resist you."

"You violated me!"

"You think that was a violation? Gee, I never felt any resistance from you. No, what I felt was your arms around my neck, no fighting or the words to stop. Like when Josh tried to rape you, now that was a violation!"

Without saying another word, Sally got into the wagon waiting for Kent to take them home.

When they entered the busy streets, they could see a noticeable difference in citizens' faces and general behavior. People were dancing with each other, twirling a partner in jubilant circles.

"Can you tell me, sir," she asked a gentleman wearing a bowler hat, "what is all the excitement about ?"

"Where have you two been that you haven't heard? The war is over!"

Shocked, Sally and Kent exchanged looks; no words passed between them. Instead, forgetting what was said only a short while ago, they hugged each other.

"We gotta get back to the house and make sure everyone knows."

Sally agreed as Kent snapped the reins to arrive as quickly as they could.

They rushed into the house, almost tripping over Snuggles. Sally picked up Amy, who was sitting on the floor, teasing the kitten with a piece of string."

Sally asked Amy where everyone was; then she heard voices coming from the dining room. Still carrying Amy, Kent and Sally joined Claire, Dabney, Dreyfuss, Margaret, and Luke. They were all talking at one time. But when they saw Sally and Kent, all conversation ceased.

"I guess you heard the news; we heard it just now when we came through town. I don't know what to say. Am I happy or sad?"

Claire spoke first, "I know what you mean; we were just discussing the very same thing. But unfortunately, we've lost the war, so we have no reason to rejoice. We've lost thousands of our men, our homes, and our farms. But we can thank the Lord that we are alive, and there will be no more killing."

"Maybe now, Sally, your husband, will come home, and you children may find your pa again."

Kent took his hat off and scratched his head. Looking at the group as a whole, he asked, "So when did the war actually end? And how?"

"This morning, a telegraph arrived saying that General Lee and General Grant signed a treaty at Appomattox Courthouse on April 9! We're just hearing about it now on the fifteenth!" Claire stated, annoyed, that Saint Augustine still had no newspaper to give them daily news.

Sally hadn't said anything; she was thinking of Frank, her emotions seesawing between anger that he hadn't contacted her in almost six months and fear that he would return a changed man. She had heard of that happening to many men, who without knowledge of the traumas the war delivered to them, and the atrocities they witnessed, the soldiers became a shadow of the men they used to be. Like unwanted spoiled food, they brought home the traumas and fears with them. But now, listening to the conversation, she had another thought. She confided to Kent. "Maybe now the Yankees will get out of here and go back to their filthy home up North."

Kent turned to her, "I don't know Sally; I didn't see any sign that the Union Army was packing up."

Kent's response was not what she wanted to hear. Her heart ached for peace, the south magnificent again, glowing in the beauty of Magnolia and Pecan trees. Instead, Kent's observation of the Northern army only assured Sally that her thoughts were merely fantasies in her mind.

Chapter 37

Massacred at Gettysburg.
—Major General George Pickett

The following day at breakfast, the room was quiet except for the children clapping their hands with glee at the sight of the pancakes with blueberry jam that filled their plates. The adults were still trying to digest the news of the war's end.

In their minds, they were trying to find the appropriate response to a horrific four years, that they would gladly forget. But how do you forget those who died? How do you stop yourself from cheering from the rooftops that you and your loved ones survived? Most of all, how do you return to a healthy life? Did any of them remember what that was?

Kent was determined to find that rainbow at the end of this war; there had to be one, even if he had to create it himself. Looking at Sally, he hoped that she would be his "rainbow."

Finishing her cup of coffee, Claire announced that she was going into town to see a friend of hers. "She lost her son to this war; I've neglected to go to see her these past few weeks; she'll need my company. If anyone else would like to come into town, I can have Dreyfuss drop you off where you want to go."

Sally spoke up, saying she wanted to buy some pecans to make the children's favorite pecan pie.

Kent then spoke up, "I better go with you, just in case Temple has arrived in town."

In her mind, Sally objected to Kent coming with her; she didn't want him to create another situation where they could become close again. Not that she didn't desire an opportunity, but temptation like that she knew could only lead to dire consequences.

At the same time, she didn't want to run into Temple independently. *Yes, it would be good to have Kent by my side,* she thought.

Sally then went to Dabs "Do you mind watching the children while I'm gone? I'd invite you to come along, but then all of us would have to go. Besides, you don't want to be there if we run into Temple, and I don't want the children exposed to him either. It could get ugly."

"Don't you worry, Sally. I love those children; they're so good with Joel. We'll be just fine."

Dreyfuss left Kent and Sally at Saint George Street. It was a sunny day but breezy; the cold air from the river forced Sally to put on her floral knit shawl that Aunt Gertrude had made for her. Seeing that Sally was chilly, Kent put his arm around her to further isolate her from the weather as they walked.

Sally couldn't deny that Kent's attention wasn't heartening. She still hoped to hear from Frank now that the war was over. Sally didn't wish him dead, even though she found his brother more protective and attractive, but mostly she felt secure that Kent would never leave her as Frank did. She only wished that Frank was alive and doing well.

"Shouldn't we be going to the commissary for these pecans?" Kent inquired.

"No, the last time I was here with Claire and Dabs, we found a shop that sells all kinds of nuts. It's here on this street."

Sally had noticed the sullen faces of other patrons she passed. She just figured that they were unsure how to feel about their side losing the war.

This morning though, unlike yesterday, she also noticed remorse on the faces of the Union soldiers. Turning to Kent, she made the observation, "That's odd; why are the Northern soldiers looking so sad? They won!"

"Maybe they are finally feeling empathy for us Southerners."

Sally chuckled, "You aren't serious; they wouldn't know how to be sympathetic."

"Shh, someone may hear you."

The street was busier than usual. Most of the pedestrians were Union soldiers; *Why?* Kent thought.

Saint Augustine at that time had no newspaper of its own. With no publications, any message sent by telegraph was posted outside the telegraph office. Kent usually checked it daily, but he hadn't done so today before Sally headed for the store.

Kent heard his name called; Sally heard it too. They looked around in search of a person that they knew.

Sally saw him first; it was Ethan. "What is it, Ethan?" Kent asked.

"You haven't heard the news, have you? Don't you see twice as many Yankees wandering around?"

"Yes, but why?"

"It's President Lincoln! He's dead!"

Sally felt faint hearing the devasting news and held on to Kent so she wouldn't fall.

"Oh, my God, how? When?"

"All the telegraph said was that he was shot in the head by an actor, John Wilkes Booth. The country is searching for him now; that's why so many soldiers are on the streets."

Sally couldn't believe what she was hearing, "When did this happen? We just heard about the war's end yesterday. A bit late, I should add."

"He was murdered yesterday. I don't suppose there will be much of an Easter celebration today, especially here in the South." Ethan thought out loud.

Sally gasped; turning to Kent, she proclaimed, "They'll blame the South for the president's death!" Fear rose in her. "What will we do?"

Kent patted the hand she had locked around his forearm, "The North can't punish us any more than they have already, and they know it. So don't worry."

Sally then turned her attention to Ethan, "We may not celebrate the way we have in the past, but I still expect you to come tonight for our Easter dinner."

Ethan tipped his hat to Sally, "Oh, yes, Miss Sally, I'm looking forward to it."

Kent gave him more incentive to come by, telling him, "She's making pecan pie."

Chapter 38

Nothing fills me with deeper sadness
to see a Southerner apologizing for
the defense we made of our inheritance.
—Jefferson Davis

Dinner was delicious, especially the pecan pie, which the children devoured in rapid mouthfuls.

Margaret noticed the adults were not as talkative as they usually were during mealtime. "Is everything okay, Miss Sally?" she asked calmly.

"Well, I suppose you should know, and even you, Luke, are old enough to grasp what I'm about to say. Our president, Mr. Abraham Lincoln, was killed yesterday by a dreadful Northern actor."

"But he was a good man; he freed the slaves and—"

"Yes, but there are people in the South who want to keep the slaves as their property. They don't want them free. I guess he was mad at Lincoln; that's why he killed him." Ethan explained. Shaking his head in disbelief that some men and some women are destined to be the town's criers. Filling the minds of ignorant fools who choose to ignore the facts, but hold the negative thoughts as proof of a different scenario.

"Well, I hope they kill that man who killed our President by hanging him," Luke wished out loud as he pushed his chair away from the table. But before he left the dining room, he added, "Why does there have to be so much killing?"

Everyone at the table heard the door slam as Luke went out to the garden. "I should go to him; he's taking this news very hard," Sally said to Claire and Kent.

Kent stood and corrected Sally, "No, let me talk to him, man to man. He'll take it better if I speak to him."

Sally had to agree; it was a better idea.

Kent found Luke curled in a ball on the bench that Sally and kent Kent had often sat on when they wanted to be alone. "Hey, partner, wanna talk about it?" Kent could see the boy was trying hard to hide his tears. He wiped his eyes before turning to Kent. "Why do men say boys never cry?"

Kent shrugged his shoulders, not sure why either. "I suppose it began by a man who thinks that a boy who cries will grow up to be less of a man. But that's not true. I've cried. Would you call me a weakling or something like that?"

"No, never. You're the bravest man I know, besides my pa." Then, lowering his head, speaking in almost a whisper, he asked Kent, "So when did you cry?"

Taking a deep breath and looking Luke in the eye, he explained, "When my ma died. I was a full-grown man, but it didn't matter; when you lose someone you love, you cry regardless of your age."

Luke looked at Kent and gave him a weak smile, letting him know he had made him feel better. Kent then put his arm around the boy's shoulders, giving him a few pats.

"Are we going to Mr. Lincoln's funeral?" Luke asked.

"No, I don't think so, Luke. It will be in Washington. That's too far away. Much more now than we traveled from your house in Brunswick."

Luke seemed satisfied with Kent's words. Then Luke asked another question, "I never did get to eat all my pecan pie. Can we go back in now so I can finish it?"

"Sure, we can, and if there is any left, I think I'll have another slice."

Kent had another motive for wanting to go back inside besides the pie. He wanted to speak to Ethan about something that had been on his mind these last few days.

He hadn't spoken to Sally about it either. That's because they weren't talking that much to each other these days, except for some polite conversation.

Sally was still sitting at the table, chatting to Claire and Ethan. Margaret was playing patty-cake with Amy opposite them.

Kent sat next to Ethan. "I wonder if I could ask a favor of you."

"That depends on what it is. Has this Temple fellow shown up yet? Is he the problem?"

"No, I haven't seen him yet, but then again, I've never met the guy. It's Sally who will have to let us know if he's in town. What I want from you has to do with another friend of mine. His name is Damien. He's a Confederate soldier; we picked him and another soldier up on our way here. When we got to Jacksonville, there was some trouble with some northern soldiers."

"That's when you got shot, right?"

"Yes, but what I forgot to tell you was that Damian killed the soldier who shot me. So they arrested him for murder. I've written to him but have not received a reply. So I'd like to know how he's doing and if you can get the charges dropped."

"What Damian did was self-defense, no law against that."

Sally's ears perked up when she heard Damien's name mentioned. It had been a long time since she had heard that name.

"That's a wonderful idea, Kent. I'm ashamed that I didn't think of checking on his fate sooner. What do you think, Ethan?"

Scratching his head, Ethan thought about his schedule of cases. "Well, I don't have a trial coming up until ten days from now. But, on the other hand, Jacksonville is only a day away, so I suppose if I leave tomorrow, I might have time and be back here for the court date."

Sally leaned across the table and planted a kiss on Ethan's forehead.

"Let's just hope that Temple doesn't show up before I get back."

"That's right; I didn't think about him. I guess Damien can wait ten days."

"No, Temple hasn't shown his face yet. He may never come, so you go to Damien. We'll deal with Temple, Frank, and Dr. Hicking when you get back."

Kent wasn't sure he liked what Sally was saying. As much as he was concerned about Damien, he was more worried about Sally's safety.

Chapter 39

E than stood in front of the Union officer in charge of the jail. He was trying desperately to control the rage that was building inside him. He knew if he wanted to accomplish anything, he had to remain respectful.

Taking a deep, cleansing breath, he forced the words out as calmly as he could. "What do you mean, I can't see the prisoner?"

"That's 'cause he isn't here anymore. He's been tried and sent to Federal prison at Fort Wagner."

Isn't that the Fort that had a mutiny by a Negro troop in sixty-three?"

"Yeah, what of it?"

"As I understand it, those men had no representation, were found guilty, and sentenced to death. Isn't that true?"

It was now impossible for Ethan to remain civil with the prominent, oversized officer and his dictator attitude. Shouting at the officer, Ethan slammed his knapsack down onto the nearby desk. "No man can face a trial without his lawyer present; that's the law!"

"Well, maybe it is where you come from, but not here where us Federals are in charge. We won the war, remember?"

"I demand to see the transcripts from the hearing."

The officer snickered at Ethan, thinking him a fool of a lawyer. "There's no transcript; the trial was by a judge and jury who found him guilty. He's supposed to hang next week."

"Guilty of what?! Defending another man who had been fired upon, since when is that a crime?"

"Look, mister; we're the law now. It's over. Now skedaddle! you're wasting my time!"

Ethan slammed the door behind him as he exited the jail office. He could feel the fury rising in him. He hated the injustices done to men in the name of the law when he knew that ones like this were sheer vengeance. No amount of logic would change the outcome. The North would punish the South any way it could. He took a deep breath into his lungs, though smelling the dusty road mixed with the odors of horse manure and tobacco wasn't as calming as he hoped it would be. He would rather this stench than spend another minute with that pigheaded officer. Ethan knew the only possible way he could free Kent's friend was to get a judge to come with him to Fort Wagner. But where would he find a civil judge in this captured town?

As much as Sally tried, she just couldn't stay mad at Kent. Every time she saw him, she felt the attraction, the yearning to be in his capable arms again. Kent had become the forbidden fruit, and she felt like Eve in the Garden of Eden.

Sally saw him staring at her from across the room many times; his smile when she acknowledged his glance gave her the confidence that he was feeling the same thing also. She appreciated his polite restraint in not approaching her unless she made an effort first.

It was his day off from work, so she knew he would have time to speak with her. Dabney and Claire encouraged her to tell him how she felt. Without saying as much to Sally, the two women felt confident that Frank was never going to return. They hoped that Kent's devotion to Sally would ease the trauma once she faced the fact that she was a widow. Sally had already confessed to them how there was a solid attraction to Kent. Staying away from him was becoming a challenge, which was why she now welcomed having time with him.

Sally found Kent in the stable across the street from Claire's home. He was brushing down the horses; Luke brought more hay into the stall while asking Kent if he had brought enough. Luke was wearing the cowboy hat Kent had bought for him a few days before, and Kent pushed it down over his eyes. "Hey, knucklehead, you know these guys never have enough, so get some more." Luke pushed the hat back up his head, giggled, and took off for another armload of food.

Sally marveled at the interaction between the two of them; she knew she was in love with Luke and his sisters, and now her heart knew that she was in love with Kent.

Sally approached Kent from behind, tapping him softly on his shoulder. He turned around to see her smiling face.

Returning her smile, Kent stated, "Well, will wonders never cease."

"I was wondering if we could talk. Maybe you could take a walk with me?" Sally felt awkward saying the words; society frowned on a woman who would be so forward.

Why was it that the man always had to make the first move? Sally thought it now seemed silly to her.

Bowing slightly to Sally, Kent took her hand as a prince would, saying, "Nothing would please me more, my lady."

Sally was thrilled; without knowing it, he had answered one of the questions she'd had ever since their romp among the magnolia trees. By calling her a "lady," he told her that he did still respect her.

Luke returned with the hay. Kent quickly thought of what to say to the boy. "Hey, partner, Miss Sally needs my help with something. Can you finish brushing Betsy while I get Dreyfuss to help you? I'll see you back at the house. Okay?"

Luke smiled; he loved brushing the horses., "Sure, no problem," he told Kent before he left with Sally.

Chapter 40

"We hold that a soldier's most appropriate
burial place is on the field where
he has fallen.
—Colonel Francis Shaw

Sally and Kent walked toward the brick entrance towers to the city. Without thinking about it, they instinctively searched for each other's hands. Finding them, they latched to each other. Not a word needed to be spoken as contentment flowed through both.

After a few moments, Sally initiated the conversation. "I wanted to talk to you about what we are, I mean…" Sally felt awkward, not sure where or how to begin.

Kent, sensing her thoughts, rescued her. "You want to know where do we go from here? Am I right?"

"Well, yes, and no. I know we can't make any decisions until we know what has happened to Frank. It's been over a week since the war ended, and still, we have no word of him. So, I guess what I'm trying to say is, How long do we wait? There must be someone in this city who can tell us how to find out Frank's fate."

"I've thought the same thing. I've even asked around. I don't know if all these Union men are unconcerned or merely vengeful."

"I know. Even Aunt Gertrude's last letter three weeks ago said she still had not heard anything about Frank."

Sally held back the tears with a sob in her voice as she asked Kent, "When do we declare him dead?"

Kent brushed a tendril from her cheek, "We don't. Not yet. Give Frank more time. I hear there are still soldiers arriving home, walking from God knows where. Hungry, weak, and starved."

Sally bowed her head, ashamed of her loss of faith in Frank and God.

They found a log to sit down on in a forest full of wildflowers and sweet berries. Birds serenaded from the treetops. Sally wanted to discuss something else on her mind.

"Remember the last time we were alone together?"

"I'll never forget it," Kent said with a dreamy smile on his face.

"You asked me about the men in my life before your brother. So, I want to know why a man like you never married and is so desperate that you now chase his sister-in-law."

Kent gave Sally a fake laugh. "So you think I'm desperate, huh?"

Laughing, Sally offered, "I don't know. You tell me."

Nuzzling his nose into her cheek, he explained, "Okay, you want to know why I haven't married. Well, first of all, my brother beat me to you."

"Oh, be serious; you didn't like me back then, nor did I like you." They both laughed, recalling how much they had changed since leaving Savannah almost five months ago.

"So, do you still want to know about my "sordid" past?"

"Yes, why are you making it sound so mysterious? Is it that bad, or maybe I shouldn't want to know?"

Kent patted Sally's hands that she had folded in her lap. "No, it's just that I never thought my past would be of any interest to you. Although I am surprised nobody else has told you about my past already. I mean, most of Savannah knows the story."

Now Sally was intrigued; she became anxious for him to begin this saga.

"One word—*Joan*. That was her name. She took me, heart and soul. I was twenty-one when I met her. I guess you could say it was love at first sight. She was beautiful, a striking redhead with ivory skin and eyes a color of green I'd never seen before. When she walked into the store that first time, I knew I had found the girl I'd been dreaming of all my life.

"She was soft-spoken and polite, and she carried herself with the grace of a princess. The more I watched her move around the store, the more I realized I could see I was only kidding myself. A classy lady like that would have no time for a storekeeper like me.

"She bought a few things, and I helped her carry them out to her buggy. After that, she was all by herself, so I offered to escort her home safely. She accepted.

"She lived in a small house at the edge of town. I was surprised; she looked like someone who lived on a large plantation or a mansion somewhere else in town."

"Anyway, she came into the store a few more times in the following weeks. We'd talk, and she told me that she had moved here from South Carolina; the tiny house was just temporary until she could get a larger home. When I asked her why she left South Carolina and moved here, she said she didn't like the people there anymore. She never elaborated on who those people were, and I didn't ask; I didn't care as long as she continued coming into my store."

"If she was living alone, how did she support herself?" Sally asked.

"She said she had inherited a trust fund from her father. She said that eventually, she would find work.

"Soon I was giving her stuff from the store without asking her to pay for it; I thought I was helping her out. Kent explained while feeling the fool every time he related the story to anyone who asked, Many times, he thought of just ignoring their questions, but he was raised with better manners than that. Kent continued, "Despite feeling the fool that I am, we started seeing each other for dinner and social dances or just spending time together at her place.

"After a while, she would leave town to see some friend or relative, always promising that I would get to meet them one of these times. I didn't think much of it except she wouldn't go for just an afternoon, but for days, sometimes a week. We had admitted our love for each other by then. I trusted her, but I was also suspicious.

"Months went by, and nothing changed. Joan even had my mother and Frank smitten with her charms.

"I was so crazy in love I couldn't see straight. Then the gossip started. When Joan and I were together, I could see the looks people gave us, the fingers pointing our way. I even punched one guy out for calling her a slut. Joan didn't care. She said that she had that effect on people no matter where she went. She said it was because of her bright red hair.

"Then one day, she brought this guy back with her from one of her trips. He looked about ten years older than us, wore a nice suit, and introduced himself to me as her brother. The Funny thing, though, was he didn't have the same color hair as Joan.

"Now I'm genuinely curious. Her brother sticks around for a few days, then Joan says that she was going back to South Carolina with him but promised to return. I kissed her goodbye as usual. But instead of going home, I decide to follow them.

"Well, to make a long story short, it turns out the reason why all the finger-pointing went on, she ran a brothel just over the South Carolina border, and her "brother" turned out to be her husband. They had a racket going. While she was the brothel's madam, they were also spies for the North.

"I was the laughingstock of Savannah. Then to make matters worse, when I got back to the store, I found my money box empty., I went to her little house in a rage and destroyed the furniture; I think I broke a few windows too."

"But why did she have a house in Savannah if they were operating out of the next town?"

"Oh, that house was a cover, so they could claim that they didn't reside in the next town. You know, like a hideout. When they got arrested, I swore off all women; I lost all trust in them. Oh, sure, I flirted with some and even courted a few, but I never committed or stuck with any one of them long. That's why I was never very cordial to you and why I tried to talk Frank out of marrying you. To me, you were like every other woman—just hanging on to a man as a meal ticket."

Sally smiled and shook her head. "Wow, I had no idea. That explains why I didn't like you either. All those women you were courting made you look like a womanizer viper. Frank never told me about your past. You were rude, arrogant, and strutted around like you were waiting for every woman to follow you."

Kent put his arm around Sally; "We've come a long way, haven't we? And not just in miles."

"We sure have, but now we're back to the question of where we go from here."

Looking into her hazel eyes, Kent spoke softly, "All I know is that I'm in love with you, and if the fates allow, I want to spend the rest of my life with you."

They were close to each other now; Sally touched his cheek, "I feel the same way about you. But you're still my brother-in-law."

Chapter 41

"Faithful are the wounds of a friend
while the kisses of an enemy
are deceitful."
—Congressman Thaddeus Stevens,
Northern Republican

Walking back into town, they savored the afterglow of their sensual interlude. Sally gave up trying to deny how she felt about Kent, though she would never admit those feelings to Kent. It would be a betrayal to Frank. She had pushed aside any guilt she felt, convinced that they would never see Frank again. They had done their share of crying on each other's shoulder over Frank, and somehow their shared grief had brought them closer together.

Since the war had ended, the Federalists had raised the prices on many items, but not the costs of Southern farmers' products. Due to the rising cost of goods, there were fewer people on the streets shopping.

"Will the North never stop punishing us?" Sally asked Kent as they walked Charlotte Street.

"The North just wants to make sure that we stay under their control. They won, they have us, and when they see that we'll obey them, then maybe they'll let go a little."

"Umm, well, they better help in fixing all the damage they did to our lands."

Kent chuckled, "Don't count on it. But whatever happens, it's going to take time to get the South back to what it was before."

Sally didn't want to talk about it anymore; she was so happy with Kent that she wanted nothing to ruin the afternoon with talk of defeat.

Suddenly Kent stopped in front of a store. "I almost forgot. I need to go in here to get some fishing lines and hooks. I promised Luke I would take him fishing. I won't be more than a few minutes. Do you want to come in or wait out here where it's cooler?"

"You go ahead in; you're right; it's cooler out here."

Sally didn't mind waiting for Kent; she enjoyed watching other ladies go by, admiring their fashions as they passed. Some wore hats with lace and flowers that coordinated with the dress they wore. Others were not as fashionable, wearing everyday cotton dresses, much as she had worn on the long trip from Savannah. Yet there were others in skirts and pretty lace blouses. For Sally, it was like looking through a dress shop and just as much fun.

She was also admiring the men, although they weren't as impressive as women as clothes go. Nor did Sally think any man was as handsome as Kent.

Then it happened. Looking to the left, through the bobbing heads, Sally saw a familiar face. She wasn't sure at first who it was, but she sensed that she knew him. He was looking from side to side as he walked, not stopping or talking to anyone. The man had a mustache and a short beard, which made identifying him difficult. Then as he came closer, not two feet in front of her, she realized who it was. Quickly she ran into the store; she searched desperately for Kent. Finally, finding him, she grabbed his arm with both hands; she pulled him into a corner. "It's him! He's here; I saw him."

"Calm down. Now tell me who you saw."

Sally kept turning her head to the entrance, afraid that he may have seen her too. "Temple, my Uncle Temple!"

"Are you sure!?"

"Yes, he's looking for me; I saw him turning his head every which way. I can't go back out there."

"All right, we'll think of something."

He turned to the shopkeeper. "Is there a back way out of here?"

"Yeah, go right back there," he said, pointing to the rear of the store.

"Thanks," Kent said, then paid for the hooks and fishing line before he and Sally made their exit.

When they were out in the alley, they looked for any sign of Temple. Seeing none, Kent suggested they go into the church where Henry and Elinor had married. "We'll stay in there for a little while; give Temple time to go somewhere else. Then we'll make it home."

"But he could be anywhere in this city."

"I reckon you're right, but he has to sleep somewhere, so I'm guessing he's staying at the only hotel in town, the Saint Francis Inn on Aviles Street."

"But what if it's already fully occupied? Where will we then look?"

Kent was thinking, only half-listening to Sally, "Yeah, yeah, I know. We'll just have to keep looking, but don't you go searching on your own, promise?"

"Yes, of course. So, what are we going to do now to get back to Claire's?"

"Move straight ahead; we'll stay on Saint George Street until we get to Saint Francis Street to your cousin's. That way, hopefully, he won't see us."

Chapter 42

"Devote your energies to the
restoration of law and order, and
the rebuilding of our cities and dwellings
that have been laid in ashes".
—General Wade Hampton, 1865

K
ent and Sally walked cautiously but with haste, keeping their eyes alert to the sight of Temple. But, of course, Kent, having never met the man, would not recognize him. So all he could do was trust Sally's instincts about approaching Temple if he saw them.

The sun was going down, painting the sky in shades of lavender and bright pink. Kent started thinking about how this could work to their advantage. In the dark, neither Temple nor Sally would be able to identify each other. As they continued to walk, Kent had another thought. *Why are we running from him? We have no idea what he wants, and we'll never find out until we talk to him.* Finally, Kent stopped Sally and told her what he was thinking. "We'll have to face him sooner or later; you know that. For him to come this far looking for us, it must be important. So let's go to the hotel."

"I'm afraid it can't be any good news coming from Temple. He plunges into bad news; it's what makes him happy. But I also know you're right; whatever his motive is for coming here, I'm going to have to deal with it, or I'll never get rid of him."

"Good girl, let's go."

They were almost at the hotel when Sally saw Temple approaching the building. He didn't look happy, but then Sally thought, *When has he ever looked happy?*

They stood where they were, waiting for Temple to see them. He was still looking wildly in all directions; then he spotted Sally.

He walked calmly toward Sally, which surprised her; she expected him to be in a state of fury. But instead, he removed his hat as he came to her. "Hello, my dear niece, it's good to see you."

Sally cleared her throat before she spoke, thankful that her nervous knocking knees were out of view under her hoop skirt. "I heard that you have been looking for me. Oh, and let me introduce my brother-in-law, Kent Preston. So what is it that you want from me?"

"Might I first suggest that we find a café or restaurant where we can sit down and discuss this matter with a beer or any other beverage of your choice?"

Sally looked to Kent for an acceptable solution for resolving any issues Temple had.

Kent nodded his approval to Sally, then responded to Temple. "Yes, I reckon that would be a good idea."

Temple led the way to a small saloon a short distance away. Since it was late afternoon, many of the patrons had started going home for supper, which suited Kent just fine. This way, there was very little noise, and they would be able to concentrate on whatever scheme Temple was creating. This was a good time to be in the Saloon because once the patrons finished eating in their homes, they would be back in the establishment for their after- dinner tipple.

Temple ordered a beer while Sally and Kent ordered coffee. Kent wanted to keep his head clear for Sally's protection.

"So, Uncle Temple, please let me know why you've come here from Piccadilly to find me."

"Right." He reached into his gray cotton shirt pocket and handed a folded document to Sally. "I need you to sign that."

Kent looked over her shoulder as she opened the article. At the top of the page, in bold letters, were the words, "OFFICE OF COUNTY LAND RECORDS." Both he and Sally scanned the entirety of its contents. Then Sally looked around the shabby café, which was just another name for a saloon. Unfortunately, the lighting was not very good, so she wasn't sure if she had read the document correctly. Before she could find another candle or kerosene lamp to put on the table, Kent spoke, "Looks like you want to sell Sally's plantation."

"It's not Sally's!" Temple yelled at Kent. "She hasn't been on that land in more than ten years. I'm the one who has worked that wretched soil. After all the ungrateful slaves ran off, I was left with only a few hands to help me. With the sweat of my brow and fighting off the Northern army, I deserve to sell that plantation for all the money I can get. She doesn't deserve any of it!"

Sally couldn't believe what she was hearing. People were now looking at them after Temple's outburst, but she didn't care. "According to this document, my father willed me half the plantation! Now I may not want to live there because of your ugly face, but half the sale is mine, and there's nothing you can do about it!"

"Oh, no?" Temple was not pretending to be a gentleman anymore; Sally had turned out to be smarter than he thought. He expected her to miss the detail about her half of the plantation. Temple hoped that she would sign without reading the printed words. Now he would have to change his tactics.

"I've heard that your husband is dead or 'missing in action.' Therefore, until he can be proven alive, you have no right to any property as a single woman. So I'll have a claim to all the sale of the plantation." The smirk on his face disgusted both Sally and Kent.

"For you to keep money from the sale of the plantation, you will first have to prove that my husband is no longer alive."

Kent couldn't resist a laugh out loud. With his arm around Sally's shoulders, he said to Temple, "How in tarnation do you expect to sell this plantation? The South is losing the war, and nobody has any money."

"I'll sell it you'll see, as long as you stay out of my business," Temple said with a snarl initiating a threat to Kent.

Sally sat back in her seat, unsure of how to handle this revelation. Taking Kent's hand, she squeezed it, then looked at Temple. "I'll not sign that document. You can't sell without my signing, am I right?"

Temple slammed his fist on the table, demanding, "You will sign, or I'll make your life miserable!"

Kent grabbed Temple by the collar and pulled him across the table, close to his face, close enough to smell the man's putrid breath, "You harm one hair on Sally's head, I'll kill you!"

Kent's attempt to intimidate Temple didn't change the smirk on his face. When Kent released him, Temple had another threat to Kent and Sally. "It's evident that you two have become, shall we say, a couple? All before you, my dear, even know if you are a widow or not. That would make for very juicy gossip indeed. That is, of course, unless you decide to sign. Think about it; I'll give you three days to decide. After all, I am a patient man."

As Temple arose to leave, Kent stopped him with one last question, "Tell me what Sally, your niece, has done to you for her to receive only abhorrence from you?"

Standing with his head held high as though he were the victim, he responded, "She was always a willful child, never adhering to any rules; I see now that nothing has changed."

Now it was Sally who stood up. Pointing a finger at Temple, she charged that he made rules that were cruel and unjustified.

Without responding to her accusation, he merely turned and walked out of the establishment.

Sitting back down next to Kent, she asked him, "What do we do now?"

"Well, we first finish our drinks, then we give Temple plenty of time to get back to his hotel. Then we'll go home and discuss this with Claire.'"

"Why Claire? She has nothing to do with this."

"No, she doesn't, but she'll give an opinion, or maybe she knows a better way of handling this."

Chapter 43

*All the evidence goes to prove that almost
the entire rebel army in Virginia amounting
to less than 120,000 men in the
vicinity of Frederick.*
—General George McClellan, 1862

Ethan stood in General Green's office, waiting for the commander of Fort Wagner to arrive. An enlisted officer stood guard next to the office door.

Ethan looked at his watch; already, fifteen minutes had passed. Then, finally, he turned to the officer guarding the door. "Are you sure that the general knows that I am waiting to speak with him?"

"Yes, sir, I spoke with him myself. He'll be here shortly."

Ethan paced and nervously twisted his riding gloves in his hands, almost wishing he could wring someone's neck instead. He stopped to look out the window, hoping to see the general approaching, but then he heard the door open behind him.

Turning around, he extended his hand. "General Green, I presume."

Ethan was mildly surprised; he had conjured in his head what the general would look like, but his image of the general didn't match what he was seeing in front of him—a short, overweight, balding man who seemed to be about sixty years of age. His speech had a graveled sound as if he was losing his voice. *Does he have a cold, or is this his natural voice?* Ethan wondered.

The general shook Ethan's hand in return, asking, "And you are who again?"

"Ethan Powers, attorney at law from Saint Augustine."

As the general sat down behind his large oak desk and folded his arms across the desktop, he asked Ethan, "What is it I can do for you?"

Ethan explained that he was there to discuss the unlawful incarceration of Damian Aarons.

Immediately the general responded with a vengeance. "The accused has been found guilty by a military tribunal as I understand it."

"Sir, the war is over now, but it wasn't when Damian killed one of your men in self-defense. It would be the same if he were on the battlefield. Bringing a civilian into a military court without due representation is against the law by the constitution of this country."

"So, what would you have me do?"

Ethan knew the General would not simply release Damien without punishment. So thinking as fast as he could, he came up with a reasonable plan.

"You can release him with a dishonorable discharge and a demotion in rank, with no pay." Ethan thought this to be a fair solution.

General Green thought about it for a moment. He rubbed his chin, then got up from his chair and walked to the other side of his office. He had stopped in front of a wood cabinet with a dozen small drawers in it when he spoke again.

"Of course, there is the question of a five-hundred-dollar fine that goes along with the discharge."

"I'll pay that, sir; I don't imagine that Damian has access to that kind of money."

"All right, Mr. Powers. You say that you are from Saint Augustine. Bring him back there, but I warn you if I see or hear anything from him in my territory. I mean, if he so much as rides in front of this fort, I will not hesitate to carry out an execution. Do you understand me? Keep him in Saint Augustine or as far from me as possible."

Ethan agreed, paid Damian's fine, then went to get him.

At first, the guard didn't believe Ethan when he confronted him about Damian's release. "Go ahead, go and ask the General. I just left his office; he should still be there."

Without saying another word, the guard took out his keys. *I guess he's none too bright to believe the truth,* Ethan thought. But then he didn't care; now he would be able to return home, having completed his favor for Kent. It made Ethan feel good. He loved succeeding.

Having never met Damian, he was still shocked at the appearance of the man. He was so thin, filthy dirty, and smelling like a piss pot.

Damian couldn't believe that he was getting out of this jail. "Who are you? And why did you save me? Did you know they were going to hang me in a couple of days?"

Walking out of the cell, Damian took Ethan's hand to shake. Repulsed, Ethan pulled away. "We can shake after you've bathed. When was the last time you ate?"

"I don't know; it was a couple of days ago, I think. It was some kind of hot water, and tasted worse than anything I had in the prisoner of war camp, if you can believe that."

"Okay, I'll get some sandwiches made so we can eat on our way back to Saint Augustine."

"Saint Augustine? Did Sally and Kent get there?"

"Yes, Kent is the one who sent me to get you."

"Well, isn't that a shocker of a surprise?"

Damian smiled to himself. He couldn't remember the last time someone had come to his rescue. He knew he would always be in Kent's debt for his life.

"Let's go to the stables and get my horse and one for you," Ethan suggested.

As they walked across the street, a wagon with a couple in it passed them. Damian was so enthused with the feel of sunshine on his face that he didn't even notice.

A deep male voice called his name. Damian quickly turned toward the sound. Recognizing them immediately, Damian jumped up on the wagon's driver's side, elated to see a friendly face. Smiling and laughing at the same time, Damian greeted them. "Henry! What a sight you are!"

The odor emanating from Damian repulsed Henry, so he leaned back as far as he could. Although thrilled to see him out of prison, Henry shied away from his friend.

Damian tipped his crushed hat to Henry's wife. Feeling embarrassed, Henry introduced the two of them. Damian, in turn, introduced Ethan.

"Will you be staying in Jacksonville now?" Henry asked Damian.

"No, Kent was the one who sent Ethan to plead my case, so I'll be going to Kent and Sally."

"Well, you send our regards to them and tell them we'll be coming to visit soon. Nice meeting you, Mr. Powers." Henry said as he waved goodbye.

Chapter 44

"It was not war; it was murder."
—Daniel Harvey Hill
Confederate General

Arriving back in Saint Augustine, Damian and Ethan felt the same exhilaration as everyone else, including the children. When Damian stood back to look at all their faces, he felt his eyes fill up, then a tear escaped. Brushing it away, he experienced something he had never felt before. A love of life and the warmth of people's acceptance toward him. He had joined the army to fight for Southern rights and had no other reason not to. His life at that time consisted of no direction, nor did he have any connections. He looked up to the sky, to hide the tears that threatened to expose his vulnerability. But most of all, to thank God for sparing his life and for giving him these friends.

He then turned to Kent, knowing he was responsible for getting him out of prison. "I will spend the rest of my life forever in your debt. Any favor you want from me, I'll do, no matter how big or small."

Kent shook his head, "You were the one who saved my life first, so I had to salvage yours in return."

Sally and Claire then directed everyone inside, "Let's give Damian a chance to get cleaned up, then we'll eat; there's lots of food to be had." Claire announced.

They all feasted on chicken, potatoes, yams, string beans, biscuits, and cherry pie. Damian thought, *even heaven couldn't taste this good.* Everyone was talking at once; the thrill of the day filled the room.

Once they had finished the meal, they retired to the front parlor, where Dabney served wine to all the adults and lemonade to the children.

Sally was anxious to bring up the subject of Uncle Temple to Ethan, now that he was back. In the days that had followed their encounter, with Temple, neither Sally nor Kent had seen or heard from him. It was strange since he had said he was giving them three days to make up their minds. It was now four days since they spoke, but it was also a relief not to have heard from him, although it made Sally uncomfortable wondering what he was doing.

"Tell me Ethan what have you discovered about my Uncle Temple."

"Well, he surely hasn't taken care of your Piccadilly Estate. It's in terrible shape, I don't see how he can justify the price he is asking for that place. Nobody in their right mind would pay that much money for a house in that state of ruins. So I would say that our scheme to get back what is yours is the best plan."

Claire was aware of her part in their need to fool Temple. She was in complete agreement that the man was a deranged swindler and tyrant. "The way that man has treated you all your life is a disgrace. I'm glad he's not part of my family."

Unaware to the participants, Dabney stood in the doorway to the parlor, still **holding the tray she served the wine on. Hearing Temple's name she dropped the tray, causing all to turn to Dabney as she muttered nervous apologies. With her eyes filling with tears, she confessed, "I didn't know Temple was here and you've talked to him. Why didn't you tell me?" Looking at Claire she further explained, "He was my slave master at Piccadilly."**

"Yes, Sally why didn't you tell us about this confrontation? We might have been able to help."

"I'm sorry, Dabney and Claire, I didn't want to upset either one of you. You probably wouldn't be hearing about this now if I had thought not to mention it in front of you. But, please, Dabs, I'm telling you the truth; Temple never said your name, so you have nothing to worry about."

"I know, Sally, but I can't help it. Just the mention of Temple's name gets me scared."

Kent put his arm around Dabney's shoulder, and looking into her eyes, he promised, "We'll protect you."

Then pondering how they could remove Temple from their lives, Kent saw Damian walk into the parlor.

"Looks like you're in some powerful deep thought," Damian observed. Dabney and Sally left the men to their conversation.

When they went into the kitchen, Sally could hear Temple's name mentioned by

Kent. Then, pulling at Dabney's arm, she begged Dabs to come back into the parlor. "We've got to listen to what they are planning. You want to know, don't you?"

"No, I don't want to know; the less said about the man, the better it is for me."

"Why?"

"That horrid man raped me. Right out there in the cornfields while you were up there in your ivory tower." All the venom and hatred she held inside her all these years came rushing out like a dam that just burst.

Sally couldn't believe what she was hearing, "Why didn't you ever tell me?"

"For two reasons. He's your uncle, and I wasn't sure how you would react if I told you about Temple's indiscretion. Secondly, what could you have done? Your father was never around to rein him in, so I couldn't even tell your mother. How could she fire her brother-in-law? So, there I was—twelve years old and nobody to turn to."

Sally immediately wrapped her arms around Dabney; through painful tears, she begged for forgiveness. "I'm so sorry for what you went through." Sally's heart was breaking for her childhood friend, whom she had sworn to protect but failed.

Chapter 45

"The flag that was the symbol of slavery
on the high seas for so long a time
was not the Confederate battle flag,
it was sadly the Stars and Stripes."
—Alan Keyes

Sally gave up trying to convince Dabney to come with her to join in the men's conversation. It would only do more damage to Dab's already fragile psyche to force the issue.

Strolling casually into the parlor, Sally asked, "So have you two decided what to do with the problem—Temple? "Yes, Damian has an exciting idea," Kent announced to Sally.

Sitting down, Sally gave them her full attention. "So tell me. I'm anxious to hear this great idea."

Kent permitted Damian to relate what he thought to Sally. "Your uncle doesn't know me; we've never met. So I could be any guy looking to buy property, right?

"Yes, but he still can't sell without my signature." Sally reminded Damian.

Kent then jumped in. "That's the beauty of this plan. You sign the deed. Temple then sells it to Damian, but what Temple doesn't know is that you paid for it, making Piccadilly yours alone. Temple is satisfied, and we get him off our backs."

Sally was a little confused, "But how will I pay for the plantation? He's asking an awful lot for it."

"Ethan will take care of that part of it. Then, he'll get an appraiser to set a price value on the property, which will then get filed in a court of law."

Kent's explanation didn't help Sally's confusion; she frowned, then said, "I still don't have that kind of money."

Holding Sally's shoulders with his hands, he announced, "But Claire does!"

Sally leaped from her seat in the stuffed chair, "No! I will not ask such a huge favor from my cousin, who has been nothing but kind to me."

Kent was laughing now, and Damian was patting her on the back, encouraging her to calm down.

"You don't understand Miss Sally; once you own the plantation, you can sell it and give Claire back her money."

Sally felt a satisfying grin come to her face. "It's all so simple; why didn't I think of it?" she said out loud to no one in particular. "You are all so wonderful to help me like this." Then she proceeded to kiss each of them on the forehead. "If Ethan and Claire were here, I'd kiss them too." Of course, with Kent, she wanted to do more than kiss his head but now was not the time or place. Then she had a second thought, "But Kent, you said it yourself to Temple that nobody has any money these days, so who is going to buy?"

"Probably some big business who might turn it into a store, or something like that." Kent speculated to Sally.

The weight of the entire war lifted from her slender shoulders with the thought that she would no longer have Temple and his disgusting attitude toward her.

Nobody spoke about Temple for the rest of the day. Sally sat outside on the veranda with Amy, reading her a story. But each time she heard a noise, her reading was interrupted. Sally kept expecting Ethan or Damian to tell her that they had begun the plot to deceive Temple. But no word came. At the dinner table that night, silence filled the air with the aroma of burning oak. Then, after the meal, Kent pulled her aside. "Ethan left this afternoon to look at Piccadilly. He should be back in a day or two; then, we can start to implement our plan."

"I wish I could be there to see the expression on his face when he realizes he's been bamboozled," Sally said with a dreamy look on her face.

"Yeah, well, you're going to have to wait for that satisfaction," Kent told her as he wrapped his arms around her slim waist.

"What I would like is a lot more of you available to me at our hideaway," Sally smiled. The hideaway was a small shed they had found one day while strolling in the meadows of Saint Augustine, a short walk from the city limit. Sally had spotted it first, sitting alone, with no road leading to it or any sign of any recent occupation. It was in poor shape, but Sally saw the possibilities.

"Oh, look, Kent, we can clean this up, you know, sweep the floor. Clean sheets on the bed and curtains on the window." Then turning to the left, she saw in the corner a small sink and a brick oven. The entire cabin couldn't be more than ten feet by five feet.

"I see what you're saying, nobody will bother us here."

These last few weeks changed them both once they realized that true love existed between them. Gone were the days of guilt and anxiety about what they were doing. Each glance and every touch of their hands sent signals to Sally and Kent that only proved how much they depended on each other. Destiny had played its hand for each of them.

Every chance they got these days, they spent at their shed. Hidden in a world meant only for them. Sometimes they would lie outside to admire the stars and count their blessings.

It wasn't that they had forgotten entirely about Frank.

For Kent and Sally, Frank was a beloved memory. Never far from their minds, Frank seemed present when something or someone reminded them of him. Like when Kent told Sally how Luke held his fishing pole just as Frank used to do.

Chapter 46

"I should like to lick a hundred
free slaves just once all around. If I didn't
bring 'em to know their places I'd pay ten
dollars apiece for all I failed."
A white South Carolina planter after
the war

Ethan arrived at Piccadilly in Georgetown on the morning of his second day of travel. He was hot, dusty, and hungry. He had hoped that he could travel by train to avoid this arduous journey. But the railroads were not working to Georgetown yet. From what he could see, Piccadilly looked like it could have at one time, rivaled any other plantation in beauty and the land around it.

There were majestic magnolia trees on either side of the drive to the front door. Azaleas and roses encompassed the front of the house. Elegant stones were creating the stairs to the etched-glass double door.

Getting to a closer view of the mansion proved to be a heartbreaker. Shingles were falling off the roof, and the paint in various parts of the home's exterior needed attention.

Opening the door, his eyes and nose were assaulted by a gray mist hanging in the air; spider webs graced every corner of the house. There were a few broken windows. Furniture was in disarray, and the kitchen had some cabinet doors unhinged. There was no way Temple could justify selling Piccadilly for the price he was asking.

Ethan walked out of the house, wondering why the plantation exterior was still pristine while the inside was a total mess. Was it neglect, or did Temple destroy the place himself? Unfortunately, coming up with a plausible answer was a feat Ethan could not conjure in his mind.

He mounted his horse and rode into town to file his report. The rest was up to a judge to decide how much Temple could ask for the place. So far, so good.

Georgetown was not a city like Savannah or Saint Augustine. It was smaller than Ethan had imagined, located on the Alabama/Savannah border. Ethan took in the sights. There were many pine trees and rolling hills, and the University of Georgetown dominated the entire town. Here was a college town with numerous campuses. He saw a jailhouse and a large Baptist church. Then he spotted the courthouse.

After filing the proper papers, he headed back to Saint Augustine. Satisfied He was satisfied that everything had gone as smoothly as it had, and the first step in the hoodwinking Temple was in place.

In the meantime, Sally sat on the balcony above the front door, knitting socks for the children. At the same time, she pondered the presence of all the Yankees still in Saint Augustine. *The war was over on April sixteenth. It was now May 26, and those soldiers have remained here.* She felt gratified and grateful for her life right now. She adored the children, and like Kent, she knew if their father and Frank didn't return, she would raise the children as her own, and Frank would be a cherished memory.

When Kent came home from work, they would disappear to their shed outside of town or Claire's Garden.

Sally dropped a stitch when she heard a wagon approaching. She looked up immediately; it couldn't be Kent; he'd gone to work riding Betsy. The people in the wagon were still too far away for Sally to recognize anyone. All she could tell was that two people occupied the wagon.

Then she thought, *"Oh, silly me, there are many homes and businesses on this street. That wagon may not be coming to our house at all. Picking* up her knitting again, she was determined to ignore the oncoming traffic.

Her curiosity got the better of her; with every few stitches, she couldn't help herself looking at the street again. The wagon was still coming closer to her. Now she could tell the passengers were a man and a woman. However, she couldn't take a good look at their faces. The afternoon sun placed a glare in her path of vision. She put her hand above her brow to block the glare. Seeing more clearly, she saw that the woman reminded her of Aunt Gertrude., *that couldn't be either, she hasn't received a letter from Aunt Gertrude saying that she was coming for a visit., that's something she would never do, arrive at someone's doorstep unannounced,* Sally thought.

Then, as they drew even closer, Sally was confident that the woman was her aunt.

Anticipating a joyous reunion, she put aside her knitting and ran down the stairs to the parlor.

With a smile on her face, she entered the room, anxious to see Aunt Gertrude, but her elation was short-lived. What she couldn't see from the balcony upstairs was now clear. The male driver's face was the face of her husband, Frank.

Chapter 47

*It is called destruction before
reconstruction. People will have to see
the danger of war, the hopelessness
of war, before things can improve.*
—Elizabeth Joyce

Sally couldn't move, not one part of her body even flinched. Somehow, she had become frozen in time, afraid to move or make a sound. Sally felt her heart's rapid pace as though it was trying to coerce her brain to connect with the limbs that refused to cooperate. But all she heard from her mind was, *no, this can't be. I thought my husband, the man I love, was dead. So why can't I bring myself to greet him as any wife would?* Instead, all she felt was anger.

Then Aunt Gertrude's loving arms were around her, "I'm so happy to see you, and look who I brought with me." Gertrude said with a triumphant grin while she turned to point to Frank.

Frank, who had been silent up to this moment, without moving closer to Sally, stretched his arms to her, pleading, "Sally, my love, don't you want to welcome your husband?"

The spell was broken; Sally let her emotions be known. "Don't you dare call me 'your love,'" not one word from you in over a year. I was convinced that you were dead, or you just didn't care anymore! Where have you been that you couldn't send any message to me?"

Kent was astonished at Sally's inappropriate question.

"Sally, there was a war going on, men had a hard time receiving, or getting any mail. How could you ask such a question?"

Frank ignored Kent's comment to Sally, then tried to step closer to her, but Sally backed away, letting Frank know he needed to keep his distance from her.

"No, Sally, it wasn't like that at all; I got wounded on the battlefield, then taken as a prisoner of war. With no paper or a writing pen, I had no way to contact you. Later, when the war ended, we were released, with no horse or any kind of transport. So, I walked to Savannah to find you."

"It's all true, Sally; he was starving, dirty, and smelled awful when he came to my door," Gertrude responded.

Sally listened, but she was still skeptical. Claire and the children had come into the parlor by this time. To see why there was shouting.

At first, Claire had no clue; she had never met Frank, so she wasn't sure who this gentleman was and why he was with Aunt Gertrude, whom she greeted warmly.

"What is the problem in here?" she asked.

Gertrude gave her a short version of Frank's adventure. Upon receiving this knowledge, Claire let out an audible gasp. Gertrude quickly asked Claire what the matter was.

Claire was aware of Sally and Kent's "secret" affair, but she had never admitted any knowledge of the matter to anyone. Claire felt that as they were being two adults, they should be able to decide what was best for themselves.

"Oh, nothing, it's just that all of us in this house thought Frank was not coming home."

Gertrude was mystified, "Well, I must say, I am shocked at how easily you have dismissed Franks' existence."

Sally and Frank were still arguing on the other side of the room. By now, Sally had calmed down some, but all the excitement made Sally feel faint; she sat down on the blue velvet sofa. Frank quickly took the opportunity to sit next to Sally without invitation.

The children had been standing by quietly, unsure what was going on, and didn't like the anger and the resentment that filled the room. Children may not understand all the thoughts and rational of adults, but they do feel the tension even when they don't understand the reasons why.

When Frank sat down beside Sally, and the children, he felt overprotective of them, he went to the sofa and stood behind her.

Frank noticed the children now. He looked at Sally, who kept as much distance from Frank as she could on the sofa. Then he asked, "Who are these children?"

"They are my children," Sally said the words so easily with no hesitation, they had always felt like they were hers, but she had never expressed that emotion out loud before. So it felt good to do so now.

"What do you mean, 'your children'? We don't have any children."

"No, they're not exactly my children; we found them alone and abandoned after some Yankees killed their mother and left them with no food. We couldn't just leave them there, so we brought them with us. That was months ago."

Frank felt empathy for them, having experienced starvation himself. Gently he asked their names. Each one recited their last name as well as their first. The repeated mention of Hicking sparked a hint of recognition in his mind.

"What is it, Frank?" Kent asked. Without turning to look at Sally, Frank continued to observe the children's faces. "I know these faces, but from where I'm not sure."

Then Dabney came in carrying a tray of coffee for the adults, and lemonade for the children, along with sweet molasses cookies; seeing the gold coffee pot triggered his mind. "Is your father a Doctor?" he asked.

Margaret eagerly nodded her head to the affirmative, while Luke asked, "Have you seen our father?" Hoping that he would never have to tell the story, he bowed his head in pity for the children and the man he respected. "Yes, I knew your father. I became wounded during the war. My doctor turned out to be your father. When I had recuperated enough to travel, we got sent to a prisoner of war camp. When the war was over, we both stayed together., he wanted to get to you kids, and I wanted to get to Sally. But as you heard me say before, we had no transport or food. Your daddy just couldn't make it; he collapsed; I couldn't do anything for him because I had nothing. But his dying words were for me to give this to you." Frank reached into his pocket and pulled out a watch. Opening it, he revealed a photo of the children with their mother. "Your father said, "Tell them that I love them very much."

Margaret took the watch, cradling it in her hands while showing it to her brother and sister. "But where am I? asked Amy.

"That's you," Margaret said, pointing to the baby in her mother's arms.

Luke abruptly ran out of the room, again not wanting anyone to see him crying. He ran until he got to the barn, where he almost collided with Dreyfus, who was brushing Betsy.

Seeing Luke's frantic run, Dreyfus stepped in his path, "Whoa, why the rush?"

Luke quickly brushed a tear from his cheek. "My, a man in the house, says, my Dad is dead."

"What, man? Did he give a name?

"He said he was Sally's husband, and he was in a prisoner of war camp with my Papa."

Dreyfus's face turned gray; panic rose inside of him. *What has Sally told him.?* He had to go quickly. He looked down at Luke, "I'm sorry about your father., we'll talk, you and me, man, to man, later." He. "Right now, I think Sally may need help. Find Mr. Kent he'll know how to handle this." Dreyfus hugged the boy again, he knew how much pain Luke was in, he had lost his father at about the same age Luke was.

Chapter 48

In 1865 President Andrew Johnson greeted
Congress with the cheery news that
Reconstruction was over. With the
With the exception of slavery, America would
Be just the same as before the war.
The Freedman's Freed man's Bureau

"So, my long-lost brother finally appears," Frank announced as he stood up from the sofa, where he sat between Sally and Gertrude.

"I could say the same thing about you, brother." Kent reacted to Frank's deliberate words. With his hands in his pockets, he stood defiant, ready to hear a plausible reason for his months of silence. But first, he needed to know, "Are you alright?"

"Yes, thanks to Aunt Gertrude here," Frank confessed as he put his arm around her shoulder, "she fed me and nursed me back to health."

Gertrude patted Frank's arm, "Oh Kent, he was in a bad way when I found him on my doorstep."

Feeling sympathy for his brother while anger wove its way within his compassion-fueled emotions. The war had demolished all forms of communication for the soldiers.

He glanced at Sally; she looked terrified.; she held her hands firmly together in her lap, not daring to move. She didn't want to do anything to escalate this confrontation into a fight she had often seen in her dreams.

Rubbing his chin, Kent dared to ask the question, "So where are you going from here?"

"Sally and I will go back home to Savannah, of course."

Kent wasn't surprised at Frank's response, but it let him know there would be a confrontation between the two of them before they leave left Claire's house.

Kent was only beginning to vent his frustration with the entire situation. Convinced Frank had perished in the war, none of this was supposed to happen. This should be a day of celebration, but instead, they were all afraid of each other's reaction to a possible fury igniting.

Sensing that this was not the reunion Gertrude had seen when she had encouraged' to come with her to Saint Augustine. Frank wanted to go; he wanted Sally to return to him in Savannah.

Gertrude had persuaded Frank that she sent Sally to Saint Augustine when General Sherman's army was coming. "Sally was never running away from you."

Because of Aunt Gertrude's words, Frank had arrived in the city, a confident man coming to get his wife and bring her home where she should have stayed.

Nothing was said between Frank, Sally, Kent, and Aunt Gertrude for a few minutes until Gertrude announced. "Come, Frank, I don't feel welcomed here. We'll find a hotel."

"No, we'll get this settled here and now. I don't wish to linger in this city any longer than necessary. But I'm not leaving here without my wife.

Turning to Sally, he spoke directly to her. "Sally, my dear, you haven't said a word. So what will it be? Do we leave tonight or tomorrow?"

Sally looked up at him, where he was now standing beside an olive-overstuffed chair. *My God,* she thought, *he hasn't even asked if I want to come with him; he merely demands that I come. How dare he?*

Clenching her teeth and forming her hands into tight fists. she picked chose her words carefully. "I don't think so, Frank, this is all so sudden, and I do love living with Claire and the children, and of course, the weather is blissful. So, I'll need some time to think about this."

Kent added to what Sally said as a reminder. "Don't forget, we've got a business matter to take care of."

"Yes, of course; thank you for reminding me." Sally acknowledged.

"What business do you two have?" Antagonism overshadowed Frank's better sense of judgment.; he had to stay calm and not let Sally see the betrayal he felt, or he may never get her back.

Chapter 49

*After the war, many African Americans
Fled north and west to get away
from the south, called Exodusters.*
The Freedmean's Bureau

Realizing that a fight was likely to come, Gertrude wanted to erase the confrontation by encouraging Frank to leave with her again.

No hotel in those days would permit a woman to rent a room on her own.

By this time, Claire had returned to the parlor. She heard Gertrude's wishes to Frank.

Immediately Claire responded, "Nonsense, you're welcome to stay here. Claire's exuberant hospitality was well known in Saint Augustine, but not to Gertrude, who let Claire understand why she could not accept such a gracious offer.

"You're mine and Sally's aunt. Would you turn away a part of your family if they came to visit? Of course not."

Not knowing the animosity, she was forming, Claire assigned Frank to room with Kent, Damian, and Luke. While she had Gertrude sleep in the room with Sally, Margaret, and Amy.

Claire knew exactly what she was doing; wanted Frank and Kent together; that way, they might come to terms with each other.

As for Sally, she hoped that Gertrude could help Sally see which man she belonged to.

Dabney then stepped into the parlor and announced, "Dinner is ready."

They all rose and entered the large dining room. Each person is careful about which chair they chose. Sally invited Gertrude to sit next to her.

Frank immediately sat in the chair on the other side of Sally. too pleased, but an excuse to give Frank why she didn't want him next to her. Then, looking across the table, she saw that Kent had taken the chair directly across her, greatly relieving her anxieties. Margaret sat next to Kent. Sally had noticed that Margaret could quite often be seen wherever ever Kent was. Sally had a strong suspicion that Margaret had a crush on Kent. She smiled at the thought. He was so handsome; Sally couldn't blame her.

There wasn't much conversation at the table that evening. Nobody knew the best way to start a conversation, though they were polite to each other.

At one point, Claire attempted to start a conversation by stating that Dabney was an excellent cook. "Don't you agree?" she asked no one in particular.

"Absolutely. I've never eaten so well until I came here." Kent expressed.

Frank debated Kent's comment, "What a short memory you have. Remember Ma's cooking? Why she was the best in all of Georgia."

Claire, not wanting this dispute to escalate any further, quickly steered it in a different direction. "Oh, you boys forget, in every territory, every town, there is a favorite cook."

Little Amy was the only one to add a final comment, "I like Sally's pies the best." A murmur of giggles went around the table.

After dinner finished, instead of the adults indulging in a glass of wine, as usual, they all retired to their assigned bedrooms.

Once in the bedroom with Sally, Gertrude let Sally know what she was thinking. "What's wrong with Frank? It's clear that he's not a welcome guest." by his brother. Then, getting even more animated than before, she pointed her finger at Sally. "And you haven't shown Frank any wifely affection. So, what's the matter with you?"

Not wanting to divulge her secret to her aunt, Sally merely shrugged, "Nothing is the matter with me. Besides, I don't like his demands; he can't tell me what to do anymore."

Overwhelmed with conflicting emotions, happiness that Frank had survived this horrific war, and knowing that she was going to have to hurt one of the Preston men. Sally couldn't hold back the tears any longer It's just been a shock to see Frank alive; we were all sure he was dead. Through her tears, she begged Gertrude to give her a little bit of time to adjust to the situation."

A thought entered her mind like a flash "Wait a minute. If Frank stays here, how are you getting back home? Surely you can't ride to Savannah by yourself."

"That's why Frank is demanding; you have to come back with us."

"No! That is not the only reason Frank wants me to come back. He wants me to be his wife again. Auntie can't you see? it's been four long years; everything has changed; I've changed. I've seen too much, more than I wanted; it's made me into a different woman. I don't think I can come back as Franks' wife on a small farm; I want more out of life."

Chapter 50

The war is over when they are
Our countrymen again.
Ulysses S. Grant

In the days that followed, Sally, Kent, and Frank avoided each other. Everyone in the house felt the tension, it felt like an imaginary blanket heavy with guilts, and the consequences that the war thrust on them. Even the children knew something was wrong but were afraid to ask. Except for Amy, who looked at Sally one morning and asked, "Is everyone mad?"

How do you answer a child who cannot comprehend the complexities of being an adult? Sally wondered. So instead, she steered her mind to something Amy could understand. "Oh look, there's Snuggles; I bet she's looking for you to feed her."

Placing her chubby hands over her mouth, she, "Oh my, I did forget to feed her." Amy exclaimed as she ran off to get food for her cat.

Sally breathed a sigh of relief; she had dodged another awkward conversation with Amy.

Sally spun around in the dining room, looking for Kent. They had to find a way to talk without Frank being nearby to suspect anything. Frank followed Sally around like a lost puppy; despite the fact they were all trying to avoid each other. it seemed like he wanted to have a private conversation with Sally as much as she wished for one with Kent. Aunt Gertrude was right for wanting to leave that first night here. Having all of them under one roof was too close for comfort.

Then she heard thumping and banging noises upstairs. She started up the stairs, where she met Damian, Aunt Gertrude, and Claire coming down.

"We were coming to get you; it's Kent and Frank; they're having an awful fistfight.

I tried to stop them, but all I got was a bloody nose," Damian explained to Sally while holding a cloth to his bleeding snout.

Clare feeling more than frustrated with the triangle that Sally was responsible for, but not wanting to make it a greater issue by her losing her Temper. She clenched her teeth as she instructed Sally about what she should do. "Maybe they'll listen to you; I suspect the fight is over you anyway. So please get in there before those brothers destroy any of my possessions."

Sally hurried up the stairs. When she opened the door, she confronts Frank's sight, gave Kent a hard blow to the ribs, and immediately went for his face. "Stop it! Right now! Do you hear me?!"

Startled by the sound of her voice, Frank made the mistake of stopping just long enough to turn around and face Sally, while Kent bestowed a blow to his lower back, which crumbles Frank to the floor.

Sally reacts as the only way she knows how which was to tend to the defeated one first. Patting Frank's cheek, she revived him.

Sally suggested to Kent that he help her get Frank on the bed. That's when she noticed Luke sitting on his bed.

"Kent whupped him good, didn't he?"

"You fought your brother in front of Luke? How could you? When did you turn into this Neanderthal?

"Oh, Luke's, alright. Besides, I didn't start the fight. Frank did with his rude comments about you."

Sally knew it was time to send Luke downstairs; this argument would not suit young ears.

After watching Luke leave and close the door, she turned her attention back to Kent. Frank was almost smiling, listening to Sally reprimand Kent. But when Kent mentioned his comments about Sally, he tried to sneak out of bed but was promptly met with Kent's hand on his shoulder, holding him where he lay.

"So, what did my loving husband have to say about me?"

"He says you're not very good in bed, and your cooking is questionable. So, I punched him."

Sally gasped at the revelation. "Frank, how could you say such things? You always praised my cooking."

"I was saying that because he thinks he cares for you." Then, pounding his chest to emphasize his point, "You're my wife, not his, and you never will be his! So, I wanted to discourage him from pursuing you."

Frank tried to get up and go to Sally, but his bruised back forced him down again.

Kent saw his brother struggle and regretted punching him so hard. "Look, I'm sorry I hit you like that. You'll be fine in the morning."

Sally had already left the room without saying a word. Kent left moments later.

Chapter 51

I'm proud to die for my country.
Bullard (Company A 8th
Illinois Regiment)

Sally was so disappointed in Kent and Frank., In her mind, she had imagined that the reunion would be a bit awkward but peaceful when the day came if Frank survived. They would work out their differences maturely, with understanding and empathy for each other and what they had gone through in the past four years.

She wanted nothing more than to get out of the house and think. So, she chose her favorite little shack outside of the city. She had thought about cleaning the place up for a while, but Kent always had other things on his mind to do. Now without him to distract her, was a perfect time. She grabbed some clean sheets, a broom, and some rags from the kitchen. "What are you doing with that stuff? You're not planning on taking part in my job, are you?" Dabney asked when she spied Sally collecting supplies.

"Oh, no, Dabs, I would never do that; I just thought I would do a little cleaning in a shack I found just outside of town. I figure it would be a lovely playhouse for them." Of course, it was a lie, she wanted that shack for her and Kent alone. A place for them to pledge their love for each other, away from any threat by those who might object and turn their love into something scandalous.

"Sally, you wouldn't let those little ones play out there alone?"

"No, no, I would stay with them to make sure they are safe." Sally had to think quickly to answer all of Dabney's questions. Even though she had confessed her feelings for Kent, and Frank to Dabney a few weeks ago, Sally still wasn't ready to confirm just how intimate the affair had become.

As she walked across the crackling dried grass that crunched beneath her feet, she pondered Dabney's questions.

Part of her felt ashamed of what she was doing, while another part of her couldn't ignore the love, she felt each time she looked at Kent. These feelings for him made her luxuriate in the fantasy of happiness for the rest of her life.

The more she thought about it, the more she felt anger at herself. *You're living in a dream world. Nothing is ever perfect; stop fooling yourself. No matter who you choose, someone is going to get hurt.*

Despite the lack of rain, it was still a beautiful day. Not that rain was better than this gorgeous warm sunlight, but for some reason, she always loved going out after a rainfall. Somehow the raindrops that lingered on the leaves gave her the feeling of a fresh, clear day when the flowers sent their beautiful perfume to all for free.

She was still annoyed with the Preston brothers, but the more she thought about it, the more confused she became.

As she approached the shed, she decided to make this little retreat hideout something special for her and Kent.

Opening the door, Sally confronted the one face she never expected to see.; the wrinkled bearded face of Temple whose revolting smile sent terror through her body, one which she had never known before.

"Well, hello, my dear, I've been waiting for you, and I see you've come alone, how delicious," Temple explained with a sinister tone in his voice.

Sally quickly stepped back through the door to get away. But Temple was faster; he reached behind her and slammed the door shut, then grabbed her wrists with his right hand; he then smacked her so hard on her cheek that she fell to the floor. She let out a scream of pain, from the blow he administered to become immediately swollen and bleeding.

"You are a lying little bitch! Do you think Piccadilly is yours now? Well, guess again, little girl. It will never be yours."

Sally looked at Temple with the kind of hate that digs deep into your soul, eating away any source of kindness you once possessed; she screamed at him,

"Why do you care? You got your money!"

"But not nearly as much as I wanted."

"Tell me please; I want to know why you hate me so much. I've never done anything to you." It was a question She had even asked her parents why her Uncle sought her out for punishment for the smallest of fractures.

Her mother advised her to "just ignore him." While her father stated, "I've never been able to figure out the reason for Temple's irritation at everyone around him, it's some kind of disease he has I suppose." Disappointed, by their inability to answer, she never brought up the question again to her parents.

"Oh, you don't think you've done anything to me? I must admit, not in the literal sense, you haven't. But from the day you were born, my brother, your father, ceased to acknowledge me. Everyone in the house worshipped your existence."

Without letting Sally rise off the dirt floor, he knelt to her level, close enough to her to be assaulted by the scent of his putrid breath.

"You got anything your little heart desired while I was ignored and put in charge of those filthy slaves.

Having said that. Temple relaxed his grip on Sally's shoulder. Then he exposed his gun, pointing it at her. Continuing to speak he said "Excuse me; I stand corrected; my presence in the house didn't deteriorate when you arrived. It started with me my; grandfather he stipulated in his will that your father and I would inherit the plantation. Then your stupid father had to go change the document."

Sally ignored the gun Temple held, instead she found the courage to speak, "It's you; you are your own worst enemy.; people don't like you because of how you treat them, if...

He struck Sally again, this time hitting her eye, as he bellowed, "You think I want to hear your fairytales of kindness, just shut up! I need to think."

Chapter 52

*"With one terrible exception, the
Civil War, law and the
Constitution has kept America
Whole and free."*
Anthony Lewis

Back at the house, Kent badgered Dabney for any information she could give him to find Sally.

"She didn't say anything to me about where she was going. But I did notice she had cleaning supplies with her. So, when I asked her where she was going with that stuff, she said she would clean up a little shack that you and her had discovered on one of your walks. She wants to clean it up for the kids to play in."

Kent knew exactly where Sally was, according to Dabney's description. "How long ago did she leave?"

"I don't know, maybe 30 thirty minutes ago." Then, wringing her hands, and close to tears, she asked, "Is she in some kind of trouble?"

Putting his hands on her shoulders he tried to sound optimistic, "I certainly hope not."

Claire and Aunt Gertrude joined Dabney and Kent in the kitchen. Again, making the room seem smaller than it was. "Let's go into the parlor; I'm sure the rest of our entourage will be joining us too."

It was strange to Kent that Frank wasn't anxious about Sally's whereabouts. "Has anybody seen my brother today?"

"He's in his room sleeping." Aunt Gertrude answered.

"Sleeping! Why in the hell is he sleeping? I haven't seen him do much work around here to make him tired."

Claire immediately agreed with Kent then, with no hesitation, she volunteered to "kick him out of bed."

But before she could do it, Frank came stumbling into the parlor, yawning and inquiring, "What's going on? I heard Claire say there was an emergency?"

"Yes, there is Sally left the house hours ago, and we have no idea where she is."

Frank raked his fingers through his brown curls. "So why are all of you just sitting around? We gotta get out there and find her, now!"

Suddenly a thought came to Kent that made him feel like a fool. *Why didn't you think of this before?*

When they were gathering their belongings to set out, there was a knock at the door.

Opening the door, Frank faced two Confederate soldiers., opening the door, worried that they may be here to arrest him for some unknown reason; he breaks out in a cold sweat.

"Is there a Temple Scanlon living here? We've been tracking him for months. We now know that he is somewhere in this city."

Kent had joined Frank when he heard Temple's name mentioned. "What do you want him for? and besides, why are you still wearing that uniform? The war was over a few months ago."

"He's wanted for; treason he supplied the North with vital information, which helped us lose the war."

Aunt Gertrude made an audible gasp as she placed her hand over her mouth. "How could he do that to his countrymen? Treason exactly. worse than that, a coward!"

Frank was more adamant about them, these soldiers could go looking for Temple themselves, we have more important business, finding Sally. Kent, not speaking to anyone in particular stated, "I have a good idea of where she is, follow me." But silently, he chastised himself, *why didn't I think of this before.?*

Chapter 53

"I was always a friend of southern
rights, but an enemy
Of southern wrong.
Benjamin Butler

Sally sat cowering, wedged in the corner of the shed, and afraid to move for fear of riling Temple up again. Her cheek burned with pain inflicted by Temple, and her eye felt swollen; she could barely see out of it.

Temple sat on the bed, his hands on either side of his head; he wasn't saying anything. But it was evident to Sally that he was deep in thought.

Sally started thinking about what she could do to get away. For as long as she could remember, she had always played the delicate southern female. She enjoyed the male species being at her beck and call. But there was nobody around to rescue her this time. The only person she could rely on now was herself. She wasn't sure how she was going to produce the necessary courage, all she knew at this point was that she could no longer be 'the damsel in distress.'

Looking at Temple's face, she was disgusted by his stringy, dirty hair and beard. In addition, he wore a large floppy hat. It looked ridiculous; she had never seen another man with such a strange hat. She hated this man, even more than any man who would do the things to her that Temple did. But most of all she simply hated him because he was her uncle, it hurt more than any pain he caused on her body.

Sally and Temple looked to the door at the same time. There was a noise outside; it sounded like horses and wagons. Temple leaped from the bed to the door. Before opening it, he instructed Sally, "Don't you move until I tell you to." Then he was out the door. "Well, gentlemen, what can I do for you?"

All Sally could hear was someone saying, "Temple Scanlon, you're under arrest."

Then she listened to his laughter, which sounded like a chicken squawking. As she rose from the corner she was in, she headed to the one window in the shed. But from the angle she was, she couldn't see very much. They were too far away; she even found it hard to figure out who was on those horses, with hats on.

Then she spotted it; right by the window was a shovel. A long-handled one. She picked it up to feel the weight. It felt good; she swung it like she would an ax. She was testing it to see how she would use it as a weapon. Then, determined not to be a frail female, shaking, she quietly opened the door. Stepping softly and slowly, she went around the back of Temple, who had his gun pointed at Damian, "And who might you be? Another one of Sally's admirers?" then, turning again to the soldiers, he stated, "You guys are fools. Still wearing that dreadful uniform after you've lost, and you deserve everything you've got. The South deserved to lose."

Everyone had a gun pointed at Temple. But he didn't seem to care. They could see Sally coming with the shovel over her left shoulder to Temple, then one of the soldiers stepped forward to Temple, "Come on, it's time for us to go." As he said that, Sally took as firm a swing as she could, hitting Temple on the back of the head, knocking him to the ground unconscious.

One of the soldiers was awestruck. "Thank you, ma'am., You just made our job a lot easier."

Frank came running to Sally, "Oh my God, look at what he's done to you. I tried to get here sooner, but I couldn't get them moving."

"What are you talking about?" Kent corrected Frank. "You didn't have a clue where she was, and we wouldn't be here now if I hadn't shown you the way."

Sally tried to laugh at the two of them, trying to prove who is more the hero. But smiling hurt too much now.

Chapter 54

With one terrible exception, the
Civil War, law and the
Constitution has kept America
Whole and free.
Anthony Lewis

Sally wanted so much to wrap herself around Kent, but not now, not in front of Frank. So instead, she walked beside him. Then, not wanting to show any favoritism, Sally insisted she walk beside them while they rode the horses.

"If you guys had not come when you did, I'm certain that he would have killed me."

"Why was he there, and how did he find it?" Kent asked Sally.

"He said he knew (whispering now), it was our private place, he said he had followed us one day. He called it our 'love nest.' He figured on one of us sooner or later, appearing.

"Hey, what are you two mumbling about?" Then abruptly, Frank steered his horse so that Sally was now in between them.

The entire situation was getting to be too much for Sally. She had to choose between the brothers; handling their objections to each other was becoming a brutal challenge. But, on the other hand, she saw good in both of them; neither of them was all bad, they were simply two brothers in love with the same woman. A position lots of women would love to be in, that was the root of her dilemma, a challenge, a sort of game, trying to find out where her heart belonged. Maybe those other women who would love the opportunity to choose between two men left Sally feeling like she was lost in a field of corn stalks, with no way of knowing how to get out.

Those who were prone to gossip, spreading false rumors about her and Kent's romance, only confused her even further.

When they got to the house, Sally sat on the front stoop. Allowing Frank and Kent to pass by her. She wanted time to think. She knew only one thing for sure; she loved Saint Augustine, so that was one strike against Frank; she didn't want to return to Savannah. Although Savannah was more modern, and picturesque, her heart, and her lost fear of the Northern army, made her feel safer here, and more comfortable, like when she sits in front of the fire on a cold winter night. Secure in the knowledge that she and Kent would weather this storm of uncertainty.

Suddenly, the door behind her flew open. It was Aunt Gertrude. "Let me look at you"; she took a deep gasp when she saw Sally's eye, and cheek, dried blood on her forehead.

"They tell me that you hit Temple unconscious with a shovel. Good for you! I didn't think you had it in you. "Sally smiled at her dear Aunt "You know, I didn't think I had it in me either."

Rising from the stoop, Aunt Gertrude encouraged Sally to come inside so she could clean her up.

Once seated in the kitchen, it was the children's turn to gulp, viewing her wounds. Sally was thrilled that the children would stay by her no matter what. "Perfect, you're the ones I should be talking with. You do know that I consider you, my children, right?"

The three heads nodded "yes" in unison. "Well then, you may also know that Frank and Kent want me to stay with one of them for life."

"But you're already married." Margaret pointed out to Sally.

Margaret's words made Sally examine her motives, *Yes she was married. She and Frank had exchanged sacred vows in front of friends and family. Do I just throw those promises away like I would a banana peel?*

"Yes, but I can't be married to both of them."

Amy covered her ears as she answered Sally's' question. "Frank yells too much; I don't like it.

Margaret and Luke, who sat quietly nearby, found their voice. "Yeah, we would rather have Kent."

"Okay, I'll go talk to the men now."

Sally wasn't choosing Kent simply because the children voted for him. They had elected the right man, the one she wanted, and the one she would choose over a million other men.

Sally wanted to talk to each one alone, which would be impossible while the two were taking care of the horses. But, as far as Sally was concerned, this was fine she would wait until they returned from the reeking barn. As each of them came through the door, she would talk outside in the garden. So, she settled herself in the parlor, nervous not wanting to hurt either one., she recognized that there was no way to avoid the inevitable

She didn't have long to wait; Frank was back in less than five minutes.

"Frank, will you accompany me to the back garden?" Just as she thought, like a dog in heat, Frank followed without question.

As soon as they entered Claire's beautifully scented patio, Frank took both her hands in his. He started to speak, but Sally put her hand up in front of him. "No, let me talk first because I know what you're going to say." Frank had other thoughts, *why did she have to be so beautiful? Maybe the heartbreak that was about to come would be easier if she were not as gorgeous, with her full perfect size lips, and her luxurious blond hair* Frank surmised.

Not giving Sally a chance to speak, he led her to the garden bench. "I have loved you from the first moment I saw you in the store. Our wedding day and those few short months before the war started was the happiest time of my life. When I was in prison, you were all I could think of; those dreams of you kept me sane."

"Oh, Frank, that's what I wanted to tell you too. Those first three years of the war were agony for me. I would check the mail every day for a letter from you, but when your messages stopped coming, your brother and I mourned for you. It was that shared grief that brought Kent and I closer together. I did love you so much. But four years without seeing you is a long time, and you and Kent are so different. You're a wonderful man, but you've changed, so much I don't recognize you anymore. I've learned that on this journey. I've changed too I'm seeing how this war has affected us all, in so many ways. Plus, I can see how the land and our way of life are never going to be like it was before. She took out her handkerchief, which was tucked inside her yellow bell sleeves. to dab at the tears that trickled down her cheeks.

"I'm the same man you said goodbye to when I left to fight the war. I'm the same man who loved you then as I do now. Don't desert me now when I've suffered so much just to get back to you. …To love you as you should be loved."

Sally felt even more confused now than she was since Frank's return. His words touched her in a way she thought she would never feel again The love she thought was lost in the war by Frank, was still there. She could hear it in his voice, and see it in his eyes. How could she question such devotion?

Frank shrugged, convinced that Sally would reject him while he felt helpless to change the outcome. He could feel the antagonism rising in him, he raised his voice, not yelling, but loud enough to illustrate his frustration in Kent. "I must go see what's left of the store. I didn't check on it when I came home; I was too anxious to see you." Not only was Frank now faced with taking care of the store that Kent would abandon, but it would give him less time to be spent with his farming.

Sally put her hand on Franks's hand which rested in his lap as he listened to the grand clock in the parlor chimes the hour. "Just one more thing—don't hate your brother., my Mama said that not everything that happens in our lives is our fault., it's fate, just what God wants for us."

Frank stood up then, "Aunt Gertrude is getting anxious to get back home, so I guess we'll be leaving in the morning."

It was then at the sound of Frank's words," We'll be leaving in the morning." That sent a wave of regret through Sally. Regret for things she had said and done in the past whether Frank was aware or not. "No, you can't leave without me and those children."

"What are you trying to say, Sally? That you, me, and Kent should share you? That's funny."

"No, wait, Frank, what I mean is that there will be family gatherings, and I don't want to see you and Kent at odds with each other because of me."

"Well, I can't promise that it won't happen, but when it does, it will be on your head."

Sally stepped back from Frank and observed the scowl on his face that wasn't the reaction she expected. She thought to herself,

"Please, Frank, don't be bitter; I'll

"You throw that word *love* around pretty easily when it's the most crucial word in our language. You tell me not to be bitter; well, I'm not; I'm heartbroken. But don't you worry, a part of me is always going to love you too? But here's another thought," he said with a tone of sarcasm, "Did you know that now that the war is over, the Southern legislatures granted an expansion of divorce for both men and women? That should make you happy; life just became more manageable for you."

This time he picked up his hat from the bench and left the garden. Sally watched as he walked away; she was thinking about how he was the same man to who she had pledged her life, only now she had to face the consequences of her actions. Although Frank had taken her announcement rather well, she still felt the pain of guilt. *Maybe in time, I'll feel free enough to enjoy my life with Kent.*

Sally went back into the house, looking for Kent. After searching downstairs with no success, she went upstairs. Passing her room, she saw Aunt Gertrude packing her things. *But, of course, I have to speak to my aunt too. She needs to hear my story from my own lips. Who knows what version Frank will tell her on their journey back to Savannah?*

Sally stepped into the room. "I see you've spoken to Frank already."

"Yes, we've agreed, under the circumstances, we should leave as soon as possible She said as she continued folding clothes into her traveling bag.

Sally leaned towards her and hugged her aunt. "I'll miss you," she whispered in her aunt's ear.

"Honestly? No, I don't think so; you'll be too busy with your new playmate."

Ouch! That hurt. She had to explain to her aunt that Kent was much more than just a passing flirtation. "No Aunt Gertrude, I love him. I realized a while ago that Kent was much better suited to me. He's everything that Frank is not. Compared to Kent, who is exciting, and fun, and he loves those children most of all. We've already talked about how we'll raise them at Piccadilly."

"Which reminds me, you tell me that you had tricked Temple into believing that you now owned the plantation. But it was Claire's money that bought Temple out.? So if you move to the plantation, how will you pay Claire back? You know you must honor your debts."

"I'm well aware of that; I have already talked to Claire about that, and she insists that she can wait for however long it takes us to pay her back. Even if it is years."

"Well, no matter., I disapprove, and quite frankly, I'm surprised and disappointed in you."

Sally realized that she wasn't going to convince her aunt to understand, not now. So she backed out of the room, telling her, "I'll be back later. Don't leave until I can talk to you again."

Sally approached the "Boys" room; as she did, she heard Frank's and Kent's voices behind the door, but she couldn't understand everything they were saying.

Sally started walking away, she thought this was not the time to interrupt them. At least they were talking, not fighting.

She started walking down the hallway with its lush red carpet, silencing her footsteps as she strolled toward the giggles and laughter of her children, who she heard downstairs.

She had not come to the stairs yet when she heard the bedroom door open and shut. Without looking back, it was her name that sent her heart racing and delight her; it was Kent calling to her.

"Sally, wait, let's go someplace where we can be alone; I just spoke to Frank, he thinks that we are going to the water's edge to see if we can catch some fish. So he won't be bothering us. Tweaking her nose, he playfully added, "So I can ravish you."

"No," Sally responded," "I don't ever want to see that little shed ever again." Kent was still smiling at her., "This is no joking matter. We must be responsible adults."

Kent erased the grin from his face. Then, putting his arms around her tiny waist, he declared, "I just can't believe I'm getting the most beautiful belle in the entire South. That's what makes me smile and love you more than I ever thought I could love anyone."

"We'll talk where I talked with your brother in the garden." With that said, she took his hand to lead the way. "I have a few questions for you, mister."

But first, she stopped in the kitchen and poured them each a small glass of brandy. "Just to calm our nerves," Sally explained to Kent as she handed him the glass.

Sitting on the bench next to Kent, she smoothed her simple cotton dress as she asked Kent "So,

"First of all, what was your conversation like with Frank?"

"To ease your mind, we shook hands, and we promised to always be brothers, no matter what."

"Oh my word, that is wonderful to hear! But that's not what Frank said to me. He said that if there is an ill fallout from my decision, then it's on my head."

"What?" He has no business saying that to you."

"Oh, you were just as bad when you told me that whatever happens between you and your brother, it wouldn't be because of you or Frank, but it would be all my fault."

"I never said any such thing to you. I wouldn't be that cruel, not to you ever." Then he took her in his arms.; promising to love her and cherish her for the rest of our lives."

They talked some more before retiring to bed that night. Neither of them could sleep. Their hearts were filled with remorse for any hurt they had caused, while at the same time stimulated by the prospects the future might hold for them.

Morning breakfast was poignant; Sally noticed that Frank and Aunt Gertrude were not there. "Where are Frank and my aunt?" She enquired to nobody in particular.

Luke started to say something; then, he was interrupted by a noise on the stairs.

Baffled by what could be causing all the noise, Sally and Kent got up to investigate. They were met on the foyer's ornate marble floor by Frank and Gertrude.

"We'll be leaving now," Gertrude announced. Frank didn't say much of anything; he picked up as many bags as possible, telling Gertrude, "I'll take these out to the wagon."

"Claire, thank you for your hospitality," Gertrude said, then shook hands with Damian, Dabney, and Dreyfuss. The children, including little Joel, looked lovingly at her as a tear ran down her cheek. "Now, don't forget to tell Sally and Kent to bring you to my home for a visit. Promise?" They all nodded vigorously in agreement. She went to Sally last, "You heard what I said to "your children," so I expect to see you again. By the way, where do you intend to live?"

Suddenly overcome with guilt, Sally burst into emotion, "No! You can't go without me."

Kent stood nearby fear and shock by Sally's declaration dictated his actions. Grabbing her arm, he spun her around to face him. "What are you saying?!

"It's no good Kent, how can we be happy at the expense of Frank's sufferings? I'm his wife, and my place is by his side, don't you see that?"

"But what about all the plans we had, not to mention, our devotion to each other? Doesn't that count for anything?"

"Stop," Sally said as she rubbed her brow as if she could simply erase the bewilderment she was now feeling. "You're confusing me."

"Sally please, don't do this."

Looking at Kent now with loving eyes, she comforted him, "I'll always love you, remember that. A piece of you will always be in my heart. But my place is with my husband."

The children witnessed the whole dilemma with the adults. They had remained quiet the entire time until Sally announced her change of heart when Margaret spoke up. "What about us? Are you leaving us here?"

Amy was crying, Sally's love for the children would never waver. She took Amy in her arms and pledged to her and her siblings. "I would never leave you. I'm taking you with us to Savannah."

"But you asked who we want to live with." Luke reminded Sally.

"Yes I did, but you said it yourself Margret, I can't be married to both. So I must stay with Frank who I am married. So go pack up your things, and then we'll be on our way."

Claire felt proud of what Sally was doing. She was honouring her vows, and teaching the children a valuable lesson at the same time. Shen then invited everyone back into the house for tea while they waited for the packing to be done.

When Sally had finished her packing she found Dabney in the kitchen, "You didn't think I'd leave you without saying goodbye, did you?"

But the words didn't come easy, her tears became a flood of sentiments, "I will miss you the most dear friend, wherever you are, or whatever you need, I'll be there for you. I promise you that."

They both pledged that they would visit each other whenever they could. Before she got into the wagon with Frank and the children, she gave Dryfuss, and Joel a parting hug.

Chapter 55

The ride home was distressing for everyone. With every passing mile, they observed destructive remains of the war, even though it had been over more than seven months ago. Reconstruction of the South was slow and painful.

Although they took a different route than they did arrive in St. Augustine, They still could see more burned and mutilation of homes, dead animals, and the lingering smell of dead flesh, although there was no evidence of human remains. The carnage and the shame felt by Southerners for losing the war was akin to losing a treasured relative.

Crossing a field once lush with green grass and wildflowers now scorched by debris from campfires, and trenches used for battle protection told the story of what went on here.

All were silent, taking in the sights they wished they couldn't see. Sally sat in the front of Aunt Gertrude's surrey with Gertrude, and Frank as they guided the team to Savannah. The children sat in the back, while Damian and Kent rode their horses.

Ahead of them is the deceptive view of the rolling hills of Georgia a forgery of what used to be.

They had traveled for miles with no signs of life besides themselves until a distant vision on the horizon was observed by Frank. "Look." He said pointing to what looked like some kind of wagon being pulled by a large horse, and a lone driver, coming towards them.

Sally wondered out loud, "I wonder who that is out here in the middle of nowhere."

It didn't take long before the stranger came into closer view. He was riding what looked like some kind of small house with the words "Kielty Photos" painted on the side.

"Howdy folks", the stranger greeted them as he approached the entourage. Tipping his faded bowler hat to Sally, he introduced himself. "My name is Orson Kielty photographer. It's sure nice to see some living life around these parts."

The man had a grey beard and wore a leather jacket with one pocket ripped and hanging on the side. His grey pants were dirty, caked with mud in some spots. His tone of voice was disheartening, his horse hung his head as he walked, looking as weary as his master. "You folks from these parts?" He asked nobody in particular.

"No," Aunt Gertrude replied. "We're on our way home to Savannah. What are you doing out here? Don't see anything worth taking a picture of ."

"I've been traveling through the south taking pictures of the effects of the war so that people in other parts of the country can see what went on here."

Sally was almost afraid to ask, but she did anyway, "So how does the rest of the South look?"

"Pretty bad in some parts." He swiped his beard before continuing, "Seems like you folks haven't heard the news."

"What news?" Kent asked as he slid off his horse, and walked closer to Orson, he wanted to be sure that he heard every syllable from Orson.

"It's bad. Real bad." Orson confided.

Frank was getting impatient, to get answers, and move on. "So spit it out, Yankee!"

"I'm not a Yankee! I come from South Carolina! Are you angry?! So am I. It's Richmond. The YANKEES destroyed the city. It's in shambles."

An audible gasp could be heard from the group. "No! Not our Capital. Oh Lordy, how will we ever survive this?" Sally cried out loud.

Aunt Gertrude patted Sally's hand, "Don't you worry, we'll show them Northerners what we're made of when Richmond is restored to its' full glory again."

Orson then waved his hat in the air, apologizing for bringing bad news to the group. "I best be going, but before I leave could I take a picture of you all?

The picture turned out to be one of weary travelers, dirty, and hungry, searching for a return to what life used to be.

As Orson's carriage and fatigued horse faded into the purple horizon, Sally hoped that he would keep his promise to send them a copy of the picture he took of them.

Chapter 56

When they arrived in Savannah, Gertrude turned to Frank, "So where will you be living? With me, or Sally?"

Without hesitating, Frank replied, "With my wife of course."

Sally was surprised her Aunt would ask such a question. She thought she had made it clear to Gertrude that her place was with Frank before they had even left Saint Augustine. Sally felt betrayed, her Aunt didn't believe her. Otherwise, she wouldn't ask that question.

Kent escorted Gertrude to her home on Main Street, while Damian stayed with Frank, and Sally to help open the house again in case there were any squatters. The children were told by Damian to stay in the wagon while the adults check out the house.

When they walked in they could tell that someone had been living there. Dirty dishes were in the sink, some furniture had been moved, and the floor was strewn with garbage. But as they checked each room, it was evident that whoever was there was now long gone.

Sally got to work cleaning the place up while Damian and Frank took care of the wagon and the horses, settling them into the barn

Frank only cared about his garden, ignoring what was going on in the house, he checked what used to be his garden. Most of the crops and flowers were dead. A few sprouts were alive but in sad shape. He immediately called for Luke.

From the day that Frank first met Luke, he took an aversion to the boy. Seeing in him a version of himself before the war, one that Frank loathed. His attitude towards Luke was a testament to his self-hate and the war traumas that haunted his mind every day. These contributed to his lack of any sentiments toward Luke.

Despite Frank's attitude toward him Luke always ran to Frank, afraid if he didn't come quickly enough, Frank would become even more irate.

"Go get a shovel and start digging up all these dead plants. Then we'll replant new ones. Get started now!"

"But…., I have…"

"You don't have to do anything, except what I tell you to do. Do you hear me?!

Frank then left Luke to go back to the barn to see if he could find some other shovel or rake to use in the garden. Even before he entered the barn, he could hear talking and laughter. As he walked in he saw Sally, Kent, and Damian in what seemed like a fun conversation, which infuriated Frank.

"What's going on here?" Frank inquired.

"We were just discussing our school days when we were young," Sally responded.

"I have to get the children settled into school soon. They've missed so much already especially Luke."

Frank shook his head negatively. "No, no, Luke doesn't need no schooling, he'll not need it when he's farming."

Kent was alarmed at Frank's reaction. He thought Frank's attitude would change once they got settled back here in Savannah. Especially here where he supposedly had good memories of him and Sally when they were newlyweds.

"Frank, you're talking crazy, everybody needs an education."

Sally added, "What if he doesn't want to be a farmer? With book learning, he can become anything he wants to be."

Frank looked at Sally with anger in his eyes, "You told me that these kids are ours now, that we'll adopt them, making me their father. So as Luke's Pa, I say what kind of man he'll become. I won't allow him to attend school. The girls? They can do whatever they want, I don't care."

It was true, Frank barely acknowledged the girls ever since they left Saint Augustine. All his adverse attention was given to Luke and nothing to the girls, except when he and Sally were alone in bed at night. That was when Frank would profess all his love to her while begging for her forgiveness for any ill-mannered he may have given her that day. It was like he was two different people, one during the day, and another at night. Sally was becoming more confused each day, not knowing how to handle her marriage, and Frank's animosity toward Luke.

Chapter 57

Life was not easy for any of them. Banks and schools were not operating. With no money available, the southern states suffered economic ruin. Many people were starving or dying if they didn't have land to grow food for themselves. Confederate money was worth only three cents. The Union army had destroyed most of the railroads which disrupted the distribution of much-needed food.

Sally did the best she could to feed the five of them but despite her efforts, they often went to bed hungry. From their five-acre harvest of vegetables, minus what weather, neglect, and Frank's frustrated farming produced, there was very little left for them to consume. In that first spring and summer after their return, they lived on vegetable soup. Fortunately, Claire had the foresight to anticipate that Savannah would not have a surplus of goods as Saint Augustine so she sent them home with sacks of flour and cornmeal. If not for that they would not have survived the winter months.

Reconstructing the South was going to be slow, and hard. President Johnson tried to return Southern states to what they were before the war, but ultimately his plans failed.

Frank's post-war behavior continued his fits of temper that would come without warning kept everyone in the house on edge. Amy had become so scared of him that she would run and hide when he came into the same room she occupied.

Kent had become aware of the situation and would come to the farm to check on the family. He still loved Sally and knew he always would, she and the children's well-being was a constant concern for him. He was also diligent in checking on Aunt Gertrude for Sally. He felt she had enough to deal with.

Every time Sally wanted to go into the city to see how her Aunt was coping, Frank would accuse her of trying to desert him, then he would beg her to not go.

Frank's erratic behavior was taking a toll on Sally. It had only been eight months since they returned to Savannah, in that short time she began to question her self-worth and her marriage. She could also see that Frank's arrogance was affecting the children as well. Each time Amy saw Frank come into the house, she would run and hide in another room. Refusing to come out until Frank was no longer in the house. Meal time became an exercise in tolerance for all of them. Sally insisted on them doing their best to function as a family at the dinner table, she would not abide by any shouting at mealtime.

Then one day Luke came into the house holding his left side, and close to tears. Margaret came to Sally in the kitchen. "Mom, come help, Luke Frank hit him with the troul."

"What set him off this time?" Sally asked Luke as she inspected the bruised side of his waist.

"I don't know, as usual, he was blaming me for the crops not being what he wanted. After he hit me, he started tearing up the plants again, and that's when I ran back here. What's wrong with him? Why does he hate me?" He asked Sally.

Sally threw down the towel she had in her hand when she replied to Luke, "I don't know, but it's going to end now if I can help it." Having said that, she picked up the rifle that stood in the corner next to the fireplace and went to face Frank.

She found him still hacking away at the plants. She came up behind him and yelled, "What are you doing? Stop right now, or I swear I'll shoot. " Frank turned around, and without regard to the rifle pointed at him he stated, "Woman leave me to my business. These are my crops and I'll do what I want with them."

"No, you can't. Those crops are what's keeping us alive. Killing those plants is killing me and the children. Why are you destroying them?"

"Because that fool boy of yours is the one that's killing these plants, not me. So don't be so dramatic."

Still holding the gun to Frank, she demanded, "Stop hating Luke, he's a good boy, you have no reason to hurt him, he's done nothing to you!"

"Put down that fool rifle. I'm no harm to you."

"Yes, you are. You're taking food out of our mouths, and you're hurting Luke. It's going to stop now, do you hear me?"

Frustrated and dilutional Frank threw down the troul. "Fine, I'm done here with you and those brats you call your kids." He turned and with a determined stride, he walked to the barn. Sally watched him go into the barn, then a few minutes later exit on horseback without saying another word to Sally, he took off west.

After three months and Frank had never returned, Sally was grateful to Kent and Damian for their help with the ranch. Kent had never stopped loving Sally, and they were soon back in each other arms again. This time though, there was no guilt involved. Frank had decided to leave with no orders to go from the government, or anybody else.

Sally and Kent had lost all concern for Frank, it was clear that the war had taken its toll on Frank's mind like it had on so many other former soldiers.

When Frank had been gone for 10 months, Sally and Frank decided to move to Piccadilly with the children and Damian. There was nothing to keep in Savannah any longer, Aunt Gertrude had passed away, plus they welcomed the added space the plantation would bring them. Only one thing had to be done before they left, they got married, with only one regret that Gertrude wasn't there to witness the joyous occasion.

The end

Saint Augustine.com/History/Old St. Augustine/ Civil War
By Florida PH

I also included research derived from internet searches, such as on Pinterest, where it was wonderful to see actual pictures.

St. Augustine, Fl. /Old City.com; Colonial Quarter Museum.

I also did a lot of research on the internet. Hours and hours, pages, and pages of vital information I couldn't find anywhere else.

Author's Notes

Writing this book was a total joy for me. I hope it will be for you too. If you're a fan of historical fiction, or you enjoy reading about the Civil War. get engrossed in the lives of Kent, Sally, Frank, and Henry, along with many other characters they encounter on their way. Saint Augustine from Savannah, Georgia.

The irony of me writing this book is that while I was in school, I always hated history. To me, it was too many people, places, and dates to remember. For what reason, I couldn't fathom; all of it had nothing to do with my life in the present.

It wasn't until I met my husband that my thinking changed; his love of history was contagious. Moreover, he made it enjoyable, prompting me to want to learn more.

I'm originally from Staten Island, N.Y., after moving to Orlando, Fl. I discovered my two favorite cities, both rich in history. Savannah and Saint Augustine. So I knew I wanted to set my book in those cities. Thus, "If Tomorrow Could Sing."

This book is not about the battles in the war. We have hundreds of books covering that aspect of the war. Instead, I wanted to delve into the lives of civilians during the war. How did they survive with enemy fire all around them? Children left orphaned, and a woman in love with two brothers. So many questions remain unanswered. But as my title tells you, "If Tomorrow Could Sing,", it would know how to answer those questions.

With the genius guidance of my husband and the encouragement of my children, I hope that I have given you a book about survival, trust, and love.

This book #1 in a series. Next will be "Chasing A Dream".

Enjoy. I look forward to hearing from you; contact me at rosemaryimregi@gmail.com

Printed in the United States
by Baker & Taylor Publisher Services